The Rule of Three

Camille Cabrera

NEWMAN SPRINGS PUBLISHING
320 Broad Street
Red Bank, NJ 07701

First originally published by Newman Springs Publishing 2021

ISBN 978-1-63881-163-3 (Paperback)
ISBN 978-1-63881-164-0 (Digital)

Printed in the United States of America

Chapter 1

Freya attempted to ignore the mounting feeling of tension within her body. Her stifled intuition always knew about a problem before she did. Unfortunately, Freya's senses were unable to warn her against the impending end of her mortal life.

Her intelligent green eyes trailed over the streets below her corner office. She was comfortably situated on the top level of the massive seventy-three-story complex. The building was the tallest in Los Angeles and absolutely impossible to ignore as it reigned supreme over the skyline. *Being the CEO has its perks*, Freya thought proudly to herself.

Eventually her eyes drifted over to the clock on her computer screen. Freya let out a small huff in frustration. It was the third time this month that her assistant was late to work. Although Freya knew that Delilah was a productive and intelligent assistant, she couldn't shake the feeling that something was wrong. She absentmindedly combed a slim hand through her red hair before pulling the long tresses up into a neat high bun. She momentarily wrestled with her waves as the lengthy tendrils argued with her hands about remaining up in a hairstyle. In the end, a few red strands fell away from the smooth bun and framed her heart-shaped face.

A look of calculated dispassion overtook Freya's features as she observed the cars below frantically weaving to dodge jaywalking pedestrians, like ants running back to their hill. She was just about to raise a third cup of tea to her lips when her lacking assistant barreled through the doorway. Instead of verbally acknowledging the slacking behavior, Freya merely arched a perfectly trimmed eyebrow.

Delilah's messy mop of dark hair and slightly ridden up skirt, combined with her suspiciously creased satin blouse, hinted at a very busy afternoon. After taking a casual perusal over her soon-to-be ex-assistant, Freya said, "Please get my agenda for this week and call Mrs. Titan's office to make an appointment for me."

Delilah jutted out her chin, as if in contempt for the menial tasks. She slowly forced out an obviously disingenuous smile, bordering on a sneer, and replied, "Right away."

Freya rolled her shoulders and began to search for a new assistant as soon as Delilah exited her office. Delilah had been a great assistant for the first few months, but recently she'd grown increasingly disinterested in listening to Freya. Obstinate behavior of this type was simply unacceptable at Freya Designs. Freya spent the better part of half an hour e-mailing with HR and providing specific instructions on what she was expecting from an assistant. Near the end of the discussion, Freya realized that her current assistant was still not back with the weekly agenda.

That sneaky woman, Freya thought incredulously. Just as she decided to fetch the documents herself, Delilah finally carelessly strolled into the room with the correct paperwork in tow. Freya nodded her head in dismissal and then scanned over the files. She noticed that the preliminary meeting to attempt to buy out her competitor was scheduled for Friday. A tired sigh passed out of her lips when she realized that after a few more phone calls, she would need to make a trip to the financial department to see their progress with the potential deal. Well, she didn't really need to visit the department, given that her staff was more than capable. Freya knew that most of the files could be sent to her computer, so the majority of the reason to visit the department was to keep them on their toes since micromanaging was in Freya's blood.

"Long day ahead," she mumbled to herself.

The moon was already midway through the sky when Freya finally entered the underground parking lot. Her heels clicked and clacked across the concrete toward a reserved parking spot sporting a silver plaque shining with her name. A satisfied smile played along the edges of her mouth as she read the plaque for at least the thousandth time. All of her hard work and a crazy stroke of luck had paid off. At only thirty years old, she was the CEO of a company that she had built from the ground up. Exactly below her nameplate was her brand-new electric-blue Audi R8. It was an early birthday gift to herself to ring in the big 3-0. Freya opened the car door and slid into the leather driver's seat with ease. She then promptly locked the car. Freya leaned over and placed her purse in the passenger seat and pulled the seat belt over the bag so that it was safely buckled in for the drive home.

The streets of Los Angeles flew by in a flurry of bright lights and scattered cars until she eventually neared the hills. The luxury vehicle ascended the winding roads lined with various trees and shrubs. Freya let out a breath in relief. She reached out a manicured hand and pressed a button to lower the convertible roof so that she could properly feel the evening air on her face. It had been a long day, and this was the first time in over twelve hours that she wasn't breathing in recycled air from the tallest building in Los Angeles. Her lungs hungrily drank in the clean night air with unrestrained greed.

Freya flicked her indicator signal on toward the left and pressed the accelerator a little more than necessary since she was tired and very eager to get to bed. As she rounded a blind curve, a blur of motion shot into the middle of the road. The sudden movement caused her to slam on the breaks and angle her steering wheel toward the hill to avoid veering off the cliff. Luckily the brakes responded right on command, and she barely skidded more than a few inches. The smell of burnt brakes wafted into the cool evening breeze.

"What the hell was that?" The question hung unanswered in the air and drifted out into the road where she was able to see the answer. Freya's heart pounded against her rib cage as she stared at the center of the road and found a very startled mountain lion looking back. Its greenish eyes glittered with the knowledge of something ethereal as it looked toward the car. Freya realized with a shock that the large cat peered past the car lights and right at her slightly shaking form. It was almost as if it was chastising her for driving so quickly in its wooded home. Before she was aware that she had said anything, Freya felt herself apologize to the cat, "I'm sorry, gorgeous."

The mountain lion's body rippled with pounds of underlying muscle as it shook its fur disdainfully. The big cat looked at her one last time before it meandered back up into the hills.

Unconsciously Freya played with the silver necklace that her mother had given to her on her sixteenth birthday. It was an old Irish symbol that looked like a circle with four arrows pointing outward. Freya rarely took off the necklace since it was one of the few items that her mother and father had brought from the old country. She wasn't sure what the symbol meant, but she figured it was similar to a family crest. It gave her a sense of heritage, and it was a great item to play with when she was anxious. Freya absentmindedly kissed the cool metal in a form of thanks to the universe for helping her to stop in time.

She then took her foot off the break and began to drive through the hills once again but, this time, at a much more cautious pace. There was no way that she wanted a repeat of such a strange encounter.

The car engine happily purred as it reached the gated community and waited for the barrier to open. Freya waved to the middle-aged security guard named Jack. She had grown to know him over the years. Sometimes she would get coffee for herself as well as one for him on her way home from the office. The full cups of coffee helped to keep her awake and motivated her to drive perfectly or face the consequences of two spilled cups of joe all over her leather interior. The more she thought about it, the more Freya realized that she wasn't even sure what the morning patrol looked like. She always left the house before they had even started their shifts.

Eventually she arrived at the furthest house from the entrance. It had its own privately gated drive, even within a gated community. Freya instinctively brushed her hands against the programmed remote. She impatiently waited for the final hurdle to her beloved home to open. She wasn't exactly paranoid, but she wasn't overconfident enough to not take the proper precautions when living in Los Angeles as a big-time textile tycoon. Her propensity to avoid problems most definitely extended to her physical home since she lived in a premiere private community at the top of the hills and with additional security measures to boot.

As the gate parted, her two-story brick mansion slowly came into view. Generally Freya shied away from touching antique objects or living in old homes since she hated the aura that some objects emitted. It sometimes felt like homes had a different air to them from their previous inhabitants, which she was sure made her sound crazy. It was almost like the past had a way of getting into the very fibers of an object. Whenever Freya was asked why she liked to buy her clothes and furniture brand-new, she preferred to say things that made her sound extremely pretentious in nature instead of certifiably insane. Generally old objects were not for her if she had no clue where they came from. After Freya watched the recent horror movie *Anabelle*, about the murderous doll, her convictions were only strengthened.

Yet despite all Freya's efforts to avoid old and preowned things, there was just something about this 1920s mansion that drew her in. It was almost as if it held a positive energy around itself from its peaceful time alone on the hill. Rarely certain places had a way of fascinating her, like a moth to a flame. In those moments, even though she didn't fully understand her own fascination, she'd end up visiting the location just to sate the temporary obsession. From the first time Freya set foot into the foyer, she instantly knew that she had reached the end of her house hunt. She felt as if the home was made for her, with all of its elaborate chandeliers, bright windows, and priceless view of the city. It had been three years since Freya had moved into her dream home, and she hadn't looked back since that first tour.

After Freya placed the roof back on her gorgeous car, she hopped out of the driver's side onto her exhausted feet. The trudge from her customized five-car garage to the door felt longer than usual as her heels inched across the smooth stone path. She had meticulously designed the garage to complement the original house and couldn't bear to add an addition, let alone cut a hole in the house to create an attached garage. She had provided exact instructions on its design so that it would blend in with the house she loved so much. In the future, she wanted to raise her family here. To set down roots and finally feel like she belonged in a house that called out her name in such a tone that she had no choice but to answer.

For a fleeting second, Freya entertained the idea of what it would be like in a few years when she finally had two or three smaller redheads racing around the stairs after dinner. She lightly touched her stomach at the thought and let out a snort as she realized that she just wasn't ready. Freya was focused on her career to a fault, but she wondered if she would feel the same way in a handful of years.

Once inside, her exhausted feet promptly stopped by the left stair banister so that she could grab it with one hand and balance as she took off her red-bottomed heels. The sudden change in temperature caused a chill to spread across her body as her toes curled inward upon direct contact with the spotless marble floor. She hastened her pace up the chilly stairs to find her master bedroom in search of a warm shower to thaw her ice-block toes.

Freya could smell his warm and woodsy scent before her eyes were able to find his hulking figure. The room was bathed in bright moonlight, as it was a day away from the full moon. Her eyes settled on Axel's massive build jumbled in a pile of ivory sheets. His blond hair was the only visible part of his hulking body. The rest of him remained a mystery underneath a sea of sheets. Light snoring filled the air as Freya took a moment to truly appreciate her amazing husband. They had been married for a little over two years, and she was sure that her increasingly crazy work hours weren't easy for him to keep up with. Freya wondered if she should take a vacation soon. Not until the purchase of Tina's Textiles was finished, of course. They hadn't had a proper vacation together since their honeymoon, and it wasn't for lack of trying on Axel's part. Freya scrunched up her freckled nose at the realization that it had been a few months since they had even been physically intimate. Once again, not for lack of trying on Axel's part.

After a quick shower, Freya walked over to their oversized bed in one of Axel's enormous shirts. As an ex-professional soccer player turned international model, Axel had an extremely active lifestyle. Freya fleetingly wondered if the ancient Vikings even had a chance at rivaling her statuesque hubby. She tried to slip into bed as quietly as she possibly could, but Axel noticed the dip of the bed even in his sleep and slowly opened his tired gray eyes.

"I missed you. Come here." His voice was still thick with sleep as his arm reached out to her with surprising speed for someone who had been asleep only a few seconds earlier.

Freya let out a playful squeal and allowed Axel to pull her closer into his chest.

She cuddled into his comforting embrace and felt momentarily content.

His perceptive gray eyes almost glowed in the moonlight as he looked deep into Freya's green orbs and asked, "When will you be home before two in the morning? I made dinner for you again, you know." Instead of sounding angry in response to her absence, Axel's voice held a tone of desperation. Pleading.

Even in the tenebrosity of the room, Freya could see the dark circles that clung beneath his eyes and hinted at more than a few sleepless nights. It was the second time this week that she had completely forgotten about Axel making dinner for them, and it was only Tuesday. He had even sent a text message that afternoon as a reminder that Freya only just remembered. For someone so reliable in business, she had become absolutely fickle elsewhere.

She cleared her throat and replied with a tinge of remorse in her voice, "I'm sorry, Axel. It's just been so crazy with this new merger and—"

Axel cut her off with a cold guffaw and quipped, "It's always something, Freya. Last week it was a questionable budget error. The week before that, it was meetings and preparations. Do I need to make an appointment in order to see my own wife? I understand that you have a company, and I want to support its future, but I want to be part of your future too."

Freya felt as if she was punched in the gut. Yes, he was definitely right as things weren't exactly great between them, but she didn't understand why he wasn't excited for the company. They hadn't even really talked in the past few weeks, and Freya wondered what he had been up to while she was gone.

After she released a tired sigh, Freya whispered, "I'll make it up to you." He slowly released her from his grasp and turned around to face the other side of the room.

His large back seemed to mock Freya with a strange sense of failure.

Somehow the weight of Axel's sadness managed to settle within her own chest as she laid a tentative hand on his shoulder. He shifted away from her grasp with one quick jerk.

Axel mumbled, "Don't bother, Freya. You said that about yesterday's dinner… You've made it clear that our future together isn't something that you want to prioritize. I just wish you would have told me before we got married."

"Look, I know that I'm not exactly on the ball, but the company needs me. I need to make sure that every detail is always perfect."

Axel cracked his neck to try and alleviate tension from his stiff body. The gesture looked unnatural from Freya's position behind his massive figure, almost like a nervous tick desperate to break free of the skin. He released his own long sigh that spoke volumes without requiring a word. It was as if he no longer had the energy to try and get through to her.

For a few seconds, Freya sat in the silence of their bedroom as a lone tear trickled down the side of her face. Everything she had spent years working for at her company was finally coming together, just as her marriage felt like it was crumbling through her fingers.

Moonlight that previously illuminated the room was snuffed as quickly as a candle exposed to a windstorm. A cloud had moved to block the comforting rays, even though there hadn't been a cloud in the sky as she had driven home. Freya slowly situated herself farther away from Axel and drew her knees up to her chest. She looked out the large window into the suddenly ominous sky, lamenting the fact that her obsessive behavior was the biggest challenge for their relationship. If only she knew how wrong she was.

Chapter 2

The next day Freya's insides were filled with anxiety, though she couldn't put her finger on exactly why. She hated the feeling and tried to put it aside as she moved from one conference call to another. She remembered that day so vividly. The exact feeling she was now experiencing in her office had sat in her body all morning when she was only six years old. Ms. Harden, her teacher at the time, was lining the children up for a recess snack, but for some reason, Freya could barely sit still. When it was finally Freya's turn to get ice cream from the cafeteria, Ms. Harden had pulled her out of line and escorted her to the principal's office. When Freya was walking to the office, she remembered that she had been so worried. She had thought that she had forgotten to finish all of her homework the night before and was in a ton of trouble. As it turned out, her mother was waiting in the office with tearstained cheeks.

It wasn't until her mother had slowly crouched down to Freya's tiny height and explained that her father had been thrown from his horse that Freya finally understood the feeling in her tummy. After hearing her mother sound so scared, she also began to sob. Her face turned red as she hugged her mother like she was the last person on Earth. Her father had suffered four broken ribs and needed to stay in the hospital overnight. Luckily in the end, he recovered and was able to live a normal life for a few more years. Freya shuddered at the memory and hoped that the feeling within her body, all the way into her bones, was wrong. As the day wore on, Freya felt her unease grow but told herself she just had to finish approving one more document before she could head home. Suddenly Delilah poked her head into Freya's office without even knocking. The expectant look on her greedy face instantly sent waves of distrust washing over Freya's body. Instinctively Freya narrowed her eyes at her assistant.

"Would you like to leave already?" Freya inquired sharply in an effort to dampen the expectant look. If there was one thing that Freya hated more than asking for help, it was feeling pushed around. Delilah's eyes widened in shock at her employer's harsh tone, and she shifted her feet in discomfort.

"Y-yes. It's already six," Delilah mumbled softly.

Freya arched an eyebrow and looked at her phone to see that it was indeed already six at night. She waved Delilah out of the office for the evening with a casual flick of her wrist. As Delilah turned around, Freya wondered why her nerves seemed to spike as she watched the retreating figure slither out of her office.

With her arms stretched toward the ceiling, she finally shut down her computer for the night. The clock on her phone read that it was a little past eight at night. She smiled at herself for leaving before the cleaning crew arrived for once. Freya spent so many nights in the office that she ended up knowing most of them by name. Some nights she would even brew coffee just for them since they were the only ones in the building, besides the building security, at such late hours. At this point, greeting the cleaners tended to be the highlight of her social calendar. Although Freya enjoyed their company during her late nights in the office, she definitely preferred going home a little earlier to surprise Axel.

Unlike the night before, Freya took her time as she drove through the hills, still mindful of her fateful encounter with the mountain lion. In an effort to quell the growing tension in her stomach, she brought a bottle of water to her lips and took a few forced gulps. Her shoulders felt heavy with an anxiety that she couldn't place, and Freya couldn't wait to be wrapped in the comforting embrace of her beloved house. Maybe she'd even accept Axel's advances tonight. It had definitely been awhile. The interest in physical contact was as sharp and fleeting as her last encounter with Delilah.

Finally home, she headed out of the garage and toward her house with an uncharacteristically tense gait. Freya could no longer ignore her gut as she deftly slipped her key into the front door of the ornate house and pushed it open. She felt compelled to enter her bedroom as soon as possible, so for once in her life, she refrained from removing her shoes at the base of the stairs. Her heels clicked and clacked over the marble walkway until she stood outside of her bedroom. Freya's hand hovered over the cool silver handle as she eyed the closed door with bubbling curiosity. She knew that Axel always liked to keep their bedroom door open unless they had visitors.

Axel had struggled with claustrophobia since childhood. He had been locked into his family bathroom for hours when his father had one of his fits of anger. Axel stayed in that bathroom until his mother finally came home from a work trip. He still wasn't sure exactly how long he had stayed crunched up in the tiny half-bathroom. It wasn't long after they met that he had made it clear that small and confined spaces were a definite no. It wasn't in Axel's character to box himself into their ridiculously large bedroom. Regardless of the room's actual size, Axel would not have closed this door without reason.

Freya realized how silly it was to hesitate outside her own bedroom door and pushed it open without further thought. The sight in front of her immediately caused her heart to drop and shatter into a million pieces. Inside her favorite place on Earth, inside her bedroom, and on her bed—Delilah lounged topless. Axel stood a few inches away from the bed, shirtless and with a face full of shame. His electric-gray eyes teemed with regret as they connected with Freya's. Her chest continued to rise and fall. It was the only sign that Freya was still alive. Delilah remained unaffected and continued to leisurely sprawl on the bed.

The lights in the room flickered as Freya's mind became a whirlwind of memories with Axel. Incomprehensible grief erased the color from each memory and left them a dull and lifeless gray. His wedding vows that Freya didn't know she had memorized word for word kept playing on a loop. As the silence in the room continued to fester, so did the erratic lighting. The light bulbs from the large chandelier that hung proudly in the center of the room began to flicker in an unnerving pattern. The erratic electricity slowly infected the other light fixtures throughout the home. Lamps that were previously turned off suddenly came to life and then died just as quickly, as if some invisible hand was forcing the switch on and off.

Delilah jumped out of the bed, and Axel retreated away from her, as if she had the plague, as she attempted to kiss him on the cheek. The brunette had the gall to turn in Freya's direction and sneer. "This has been a long time coming. I can't tell you how long I've wanted to see your stuck-up face streaked in tears."

Freya stood as still as a stone as she simply observed the room. A simmering rage boiled in her body and slowly scalded her shattered heart. There was no way that this woman could be such a vindictive devil, but from what Freya could see with her own eyes, Delilah was, at the very least, a distant cousin to Lucifer.

An unknown energy began to slink through Freya's bones. It was something that Freya had never felt before. A light bulb from the chandelier suddenly exploded into a frenzy of sparks and glass as Delilah let out a startled shriek.

Freya was brought back into the moment as particles of glass landed on the floor. She stared down her assistant as the other woman tried to shoulder past to retrieve her discarded shirt.

"You will leave the shirt. Trash doesn't get to look presentable," Freya said in a voice laced with otherworldly power. It was almost an out of body experience for Freya as she felt like a part of her had died and fractured when she walked into her once-joyful room. Something new prowled through her bones.

It was as if another force was in command of Delilah's body as she changed direction and left her shirt on the white rug. She jerkily hastened out of the room without looking Freya in the eyes. The married couple didn't say a word as the front door slammed and echoed all the way up the two-sided stairway into their bedroom.

Axel remained on the other side of the room with only a bed to separate them, but the distance might as well have been that of the Grand Canyon. It felt like hours, as they remained parallel to each other. Freya stood with her head tilted upward to try and stare Axel down with her green eyes that were now bright and glossy with unshed tears. She allowed the first lone droplet of water to trickle down the side of her face. After that, it was like a dam had burst open as streams of water fell from her eyes and drenched the top of her lace shirt. Freya didn't make a sound as she continued to cry. Eventually she opened her mouth, but no words escaped her, so she closed her mouth for a few more seconds. Finally she managed to spit out. "My assistant? Is this some kind of fucking joke? How long?" The venom in her words hit their target.

Axel shifted his stance and rolled his muscular shoulders back as if to stall. He said in a quiet voice, "A few weeks." Freya took a moment to process the information as a cold liquid slowly spread throughout her body. It felt like every nerve ending she had was electrified tenfold.

Freya whispered in a voice full of contempt, "I can't decide if I want to kill you or myself for not seeing this coming."

Axel stayed where he was for a moment before he slowly crept around from the other side of the bed. "I'd rather you killed me, Freya. I'm sorry. I never wanted to hurt you."

Her eyes appeared almost black as the lights flickered on and off once again. The sudden problem with the electricity only added to the tension in the room. Freya looked the love of her life in his eyes and, in a voice she didn't recognize as her own, declared, "I don't want you to speak to me. Sleep in the guest room until I figure something out." The adrenaline from her encounter with Delilah was still coursing through her body.

Axel lowered his head and slowly walked toward his wife. His entire body was shaking in sadness. His eyes held unshed tears and a strange desperation for someone caught cheating. Axel stood so close to her that Freya could feel him invading all of her senses. He reached out a hand, as if to cup her tear-streaked face, but then thought against it and pulled his arm away.

"Freya, I love you. I was lonely and lost, and I'm so sorry. I don't really know what I was doing. It really just felt like a bad dream."

"Yeah? Well, you just made my worst nightmare come true."

Each word was like a punch to her gut. Freya remained frozen next to Axel. Even after his betrayal, there was still an undeniable pull between them. Freya looked deep into his intelligent gray eyes and didn't know how to put into words the pain within her body.

She wiped her cheek with a shaky hand and thought to herself, *I love you, Axel.* Axel didn't try to embrace her or even offer up a pitiful explanation. His once-impressive form seemed hunched and shattered to Freya in the partial moonlight. It was as if his torn soul was manifesting itself onto his physical features. They simply stood staring at each other, neither daring to lift the immense veil of silence. Freya felt as if her heart had somehow gone through an unspeakable transformation in a span of less than ten minutes. There was no denying that she was somehow a different version of herself than the one who came home.

The air seemed to swirl between them. It felt like an invisible force was reaching toward Freya's neck and increasing the pressure as she continued to look at Axel's once-enthralling gray eyes.

"Go to sleep, Axel," said Freya sternly. "I'll wake you up if I figure anything out." Cold and hollow, her voice seemed to creep around the room like a whisper emitted from a ghost.

Axel nodded slightly and stumbled out the doorway. Freya watched him slowly depart from the room as if she was in a trance. Even after his figure was gone, Freya continued to stare into the darkness. Without really knowing what she was doing, Freya turned toward the bed and carelessly tore the sheets away from her old sanctuary.

The duvet ripped in half from her angry tugs. The sound of tearing linen rang through the air. When there was nothing left to tear apart, Freya furiously pounded the mattress. She let out a screech in sheer frustration.

The large mattress seemed to taunt her with joyful memories—her precious memories with Axel. Vivid images flashed behind her closed eyelids. Freya was brought back to the first time that she and Axel had christened their bedroom. How she had gripped his biceps with such intensity. As if he alone were anchoring her to reality as he whispered sweet nothings into her ear. His warm breath fanned the sanctum of her opened legs and sent shocks throughout her entire body. Freya could smell the moment and remembered, with perfect detail, the feeling of his strong chest warming her chilled body. In that moment, it had felt like their existence had been tied together. It was as if their souls were combined into one. Every thought and passionate feeling had been elevated to the point of nirvana. The way Axel had loved her had felt better than a sinner receiving forgiveness after years of internal strife. The tainted sheets had to go. She wanted to burn them but didn't have the energy to go outside and set a fire.

When they had first met, Freya Designs was still in its inception, and the two of them had practically been inseparable. It got to the point that Freya could sense when Axel was having a bad day at work. Sometimes she would call him when he had just lost a soccer match and realize that he was having a difficult time.

Those memories felt more like tales read from a fairy-tale storybook than a previous time in her life. All the good moments and hilarious warm memories felt corrupted as she viewed them through a now-dirtied lens.

Freya sank down against the bed and continued to stare out of the large bedroom window; she didn't dare sit on the mattress, so she simply leaned against the bed frame from a seated position. Part of her felt like crawling underneath the bed frame itself and crying. She resisted the urge to crawl into a ball and die like a wounded animal. The curtains were slightly parted so that she was able to stare out at the dark night sky. Only a few rays of moonlight entered the room. The ripped duvet and torn silk sheets seemed to taunt her as they sat in a crumpled pile on the other side of the room.

A strong thump continued to invade her senses, and Freya realized that it was the frantic beating of her own heart. Eventually Freya adjusted herself against the side of the bed frame. She sat on the floor and replayed the sight of Delilah with her husband on a warped loop for hours. It was like she was stuck on a strange amusement park ride that was permanently whirling her around at a high speed. Her stomach felt sick, and her limbs now felt weak. Freya adjusted her crumpled form against her once-beloved bed and flinched as memories with her husband came flooding to the front of her mind. Every remembered touch from Axel seemed to burn her skin with a vengeance.

Strong beams of sunlight broke Freya out of her restless stupor. She let out a pitiful groan as her body protested against standing up. Instead of leaning against the mattress for support, Freya crawled away and then stood from her crouched position.

Sluggishly she dragged her sore body out of the bedroom and through the ornate hallways. The biting cold of the marble stairs barely registered against her exposed feet as she mindlessly entered one of several guest rooms.

She found Axel asleep in the smallest room on the second floor. It was odd that he would intentionally cram himself into a room that could barely hold a full-size mattress, but even stranger that it was Freya's first guess. *Maybe he wants to punish himself before I can.* The dry thought invaded her mind as she took measured steps toward his sleeping form. The truth was that revenge had never even crossed her mind. The entire night had been a trail of emotional turmoil that had left her too mentally exhausted to plan something spiteful.

Once Freya was able to look at Axel's face, an urge to caress the stubble on his jaw overtook her. As she leaned over his defenseless form, a few red tendrils of her hair escaped their tucked position behind her ears. The loose strands created a makeshift curtain between them and the outside world. Freya's sole attention was upon Axel's unaffected features. Her small hand cupped the rough stubble over his sharp jawline. Freya gently moved her fingers over his small blond hairs. To her surprise, Axel didn't move a muscle in response to the contact. She found it odd, as he was a notoriously light sleeper. Even when she came home from work in the early hours of the morning and silently tiptoed into their bedroom, she always managed to wake him up.

His response struck her as especially odd as Axel seemed distraught the night before and always had difficulty falling asleep and remaining asleep after a stressful night. Freya couldn't think of a more tense time in her life than last night. She had half expected to stride into the room and see him wide awake with large bags underneath his exhausted gray eyes. It wasn't likely that today of all days, he would sleep like an infant in his mother's arms, but here he was, still unmoving in the tiny bed.

Freya shook his shoulder and realized that Axel seemed less responsive than usual. "Axel, wake up." Her voice was loud and easily filled the miniscule room. A sinking feeling continued to weigh down Freya's stomach as she pulled away to fully look at Axel. In less than a second, her curtain of red hair was drawn back from its position and landed around her shoulders. She climbed onto the bed to try and shake him from a better position.

"Axel, get up." A moment of silence fell across the entire house. The only sounds that reached Freya's ears were her own labored breathing and the few idiot birds outside who continued to happily chirp.

Freya felt as if she could smell the stench of her own fear as she proceeded to climb onto Axel's chest and shake his body from her straddled position.

"Axel!" A high-pitched shriek rang through the air and finally silenced the stupid birds in the yard. Without the pleasant singing of birds, the silence seemed to magnify tenfold.

"Axel, I'm sorry that I ignored you! Get up and I'll stay home from work this week! Get up and we can still have a beach day. One where you splash water at me, and I pretend that I'm mad, but we both know I'm not. Wake up!" Her last sentence ended in a desperate wail. The continued void within her ex-sanctuary shook Freya to her core. In her panic, Freya didn't bother to check for his pulse. Time seemed too precious to waste with her pitiful medical knowledge.

With a growing sense of horror, Freya raced upstairs to grab one of her cell phones. She burst through the entranceway of the master suite and found her phone on the floor. She must have dropped it yesterday and never thought of where it had gone until now. Her hand reached out to grab it with the speed of a striking snake. It took three attempts before her shaky fingers were able to correctly type in her password.

As she was frantically pressing in the numbers of the emergency response line, she slipped down the flight of stairs. Freya tumbled down the polished marble staircase, and from somewhere in her mind, all she could see was Axel. Freya landed sprawled across the ground of the second floor landing with her left leg bent at an unnatural angle. In her panic, she didn't even bother to check herself for injuries. Freya grabbed her phone that had landed a few feet away. It now had a partially shattered screen and bits of the screen protector angrily jutted outward.

Freya ran back into the guest room with the delusional hope that Axel was awake. She desperately wished that the entire debacle was just a sick joke or an extremely twisted dream. Instead the harsh reality of the situation shook her just as intensely as she had rattled Axel only moments before.

One thought swirled around her mind as she frantically talked to a dispatch officer. *Axel wasn't there anymore.*

Chapter 3

One month. Thirty-one days. Seven hundred forty-four hours since Freya's world imploded like a dying star. The warm California summer turned increasingly unbearable as if it had decided to give one last hurrah before losing the battle to fall. In Los Angeles, it was common to have a warm August and an even warmer September. But Freya wasn't sure if this year was living up to its predecessors since she was no longer permanently located in the City of Angels and had moved to a small town just a few hours away from her permanent address. She still wasn't sure how she had settled upon the anonymous town. It was as if it had called out to her when she had searched online. She had typed "wish" into the search engine, and the computer had autopopulated the rest. Freya recalled the recent events in a blur as she sat on the kitchen chair of her new home in Wishburn.

Her breathtaking home in Los Angeles was still as neat and tidy as ever, although the estate was now devoid of its inhabitants and had only the infrequent visitor for maintenance. Freya watched the workers come and go through the security feeds in order to pass the time in her new abode.

Time became an estranged concept to Freya. One month ago, every second that she had spent trying to resuscitate Axel had felt like a lifetime. It was as though each second she had waited for the ambulance to arrive had aged her body a year. Now every day felt like the mere blink of an eye. Days felt fleeting and overwhelmingly meaningless in the grand scheme of life.

Once she left the city, there was very little that truly tethered Freya to her old reality. Nothing seemed to sparkle or shine the same, and things that were once dull and uninteresting now effectively captured her attention.

Freya remembered how she had called her mother in tears for guidance. That first night in the hospital, it was as if she had regressed into a little girl all over again rather than an intelligent and powerful CEO. Her mother had flown out immediately from San Francisco to console her eldest and only daughter. Freya had shown her mom to one of the many other guest rooms in her home. She and her mother had both stayed in one of the various guest rooms that week for different reasons. Freya hadn't been able to bring herself to pick up the ruined silk sheets in the master bedroom. Her mother, whom Freya often referred to as her first name, Joan, had made herself useful and given Freya's staff temporary leave. There was no reason for everyone to watch Freya mourn. Joan had figured that the best way her daughter could pick up the pieces of her broken life was with her dignity and privacy intact. Joan hadn't breathed a word of Axel's marital indiscretion to anyone, mainly because Freya hadn't told her. Freya loved her mother but knew fidelity was definitely a touchy subject with her. Although Freya had never openly broached the topic with Joan, she had a sneaking suspicion that it was part of the reason that her mom never mentioned him.

When they were both still in Los Angeles, Joan had slowly entered the room where Freya was curled up on a lounge chair with an untouched cup of cold coffee beside her. Freya's foot had been wrapped since she sprained it falling down the marble stairs in her rush to assist Axel. A fresh pot of coffee and two large mugs were precariously balanced in her mother's arms as she sat down beside her daughter. Joan had fine wrinkle lines between her eyebrows from constant frowning that had only increased since the loss of Freya's father. For once, the frown on her face, as she had entered her daughter's living room, appeared to stem more from concern than from disapproval. Joan took a few seconds to hand Freya a new cup of black coffee and then suggested Freya leave the city or at least her home for a little bit. It was too much of a reminder, and after all, places had a way of remembering events.

Joan had reminded her daughter that the company could survive without her hawkish observation skills. It also didn't hurt that Freya could still hold weekly video conference calls to make sure everything was still running correctly. For a few days, Freya had mulled the idea of leaving Los Angeles over with a bitter taste on the back of her tongue. Freya had invested countless hours into innovating the best environmentally sustainable textiles that were now used by international designer brands. She had successfully nurtured her small company until it grew to worldwide notoriety but had effectively starved her marriage until it wasted away. She was never home, and every time Axel had tried to express how he felt, Freya had barely listened to him. The guilt was eating her alive.

Two days later, Joan had spoken a second time to Freya about leaving Los Angeles and also expressed concern about her daughter who was noticeably in a free fall with her weight. Freya had always had a natural hourglass figure, but the pain of Axel weighed heavily against her increasingly frail shoulders. If it wasn't for the daily alarm she had set on her phone to eat lunch that first week, she probably wouldn't have eaten at all. Nothing appealed to her. Joan always brought back delicious foods that were usually her favorites and even went so far to bring back the finest Michelin star meals in Los Angeles on several occasions. Each time, Freya said thank you but proceeded to only nibble and get a few large bites in at best. Group settings felt too intense for some reason, and on the one occasion that she agreed to go with her mother to the grocery store, it felt like the people were pressing into her with their presence. Freya couldn't explain it, but the amount of people had just felt too much. She had stopped halfway into the outing and went to sit inside the car until Joan was finished.

The second conversation with Joan was much more productive since even though Freya was heartbroken, she was still extremely logical. Joan had reminded her that Freya's brother, Aidan, could look over the company for a little; after all, he was the vice president of finance for Freya Designs.

After making a few arrangements to ensure that everything would be fine in her absence, there was nothing left to do but to make a fresh start.

Memories from the last month continued to wash over her as Freya now stood in her new kitchen and stared out the window of her rented home in a quiet little town of just over five thousand people. Freya gripped the countertop and tried her best to ignore the rest of the room that was overflowing with symbolic pleasantries. Scores of condolence cards and flowers littered the white countertops with stale words of encouragement. Freya was most grateful that her mom had dropped her life to come and help her adjust. Joan had just returned to San Francisco two days ago, but to Freya, it only felt like a few minutes. She had nothing to effectively fill her time except attempt to heal. But from what? Technically no one had died, and marriages fell apart every day. There had been no physical violence or mark on her body that she could point to and claim that once it was healed, everything would get better. Freya felt like the pain she was experiencing somehow made her a fraud.

A small sigh escaped her parted lips as she put down her warm cup of coffee and decided to face her inevitable visit of the day. Freya took unhurried steps through the much-smaller rural home. It was designed similar to a log cabin and was just shy of two thousand square feet. It was newly constructed, and Freya was eager to be its first renter, even though it wasn't exactly her favorite style of architecture. There was no way that she wanted to live in someone else's home with a vivid past and history clinging onto every doorknob and banister. In some odd way, it just felt too personal to step into a home used by another person. Freya figured that she just wanted a symbolic fresh start, and so leasing a literally new home was the perfect way to realize that goal.

She had picked up and moved a few hundred miles away from her friends and brother to get a little perspective with only a gut feeling to go on. Maybe she really had given herself severe brain damage when she had tumbled down the stairs. That would explain such an erratic choice.

It was a small town where all the locals seemed to want to genuinely hear about your day and where even ordering a black coffee took a few pleasantries and multiple minutes. Freya didn't mind, though. The change of pace was slower, and the forest surrounding the little town made it feel as if it was out of a storybook. It was a sleepy town where anything could happen, in Freya's mind. Where maybe she would be able to get a better grasp on life in a place where the air smelled fresh and sharp with greenery. The plants looked more vibrant and healthy and the townspeople more rustic and rooted in their ways.

Sooner than Freya wanted, she found herself outside the freshly painted guest room door. It was on the bottom level of the two-story pseudocabin. The birds outside continued to chirp and twitter as Freya opened the door and walked over the plush cream carpet with her fluffy pink slippers. She scanned over the room with a bright and hopeful gaze that quickly dulled. After a seemingly infinite moment of silence, Freya drew out a sigh and said in resignation, "Good morning, Axel."

Chapter 4

Freya looked toward the center of the room with a sinking heart. Except for the steady beeping of the heart monitor, it was almost as if she were alone. The sight of multiple tubes that extended from Axel's immobile body twisted her stomach. He no longer looked like her strong husband. Instead his nearly lifeless form reminded her of some sick and cheap science fiction movie where the cyborg was just charging up enough battery to destroy all of humanity. The dramatic image caused Freya to roll her shoulders in an attempt to ease some of the tension.

"You're being ridiculous, Freya. Get it together. He's too blond to be the Terminator anyway."

Axel still hadn't awoken since that fateful morning when Freya had called 911. After three experts had seen him, they all came to the same conclusion. Axel was in an indefinite coma, and none of them could tell Freya why. Not a single medical professional could even put their finger on why it had happened. By all accounts, Axel was so strong that he might as well be the first person to live to be two hundred years old—on paper, at least. As Freya continued to stare at him, she could see the subtle signs of his body getting softer from lack of use. He remained in the same position, except for the times when the nurse Freya had hired or herself would move him around in bed in order to prevent bedsores. His face was still the same, and it was most definitely Axel, but somehow he seemed smaller. Or maybe it was just in Freya's eyes that he somehow looked less like the man she loved.

After another moment of silence, Freya let out a subdued sniffle that she told herself was from allergies. She leisurely walked toward the right corner of the room closest to where Axel's bed was positioned. Freya had placed his bed right next to the window so that he could have the warm sunrays and occasional fresh breeze touch his face when she opened the window. The light-blue drapes were a cheerful touch to the otherwise dreary scene. Although Freya usually hated drapes, this room seemed like the exception to her rule. Freya quickly reached the right corner of the room and saw the light-blue accent chair that perfectly matched the color of the drapes. A small wooden bookshelf was placed beside the chair, almost like a nightstand for Axel. The bookshelf was relatively sparse in reading materials with more open space than books.

When Freya was in the hospital with Axel, she was told that the voices of loved ones were supposed to help people who were comatose. Meg, the nurse that Freya had hired to take care of Axel, had offered to talk to him like an old friend if it was too much for her. Freya had politely declined the offer. That asshole was still her husband, and she planned to talk to him whether he liked it or not. Instead Freya encouraged Meg to speak with Axel and talk him through the procedures that she was doing for at least the first time or so. Freya had cringed slightly at her own odd request, but Meg, who was well into her fifties, didn't even bat an eye. It gave Freya a strange sense of comfort to know her request wasn't absolutely loony.

There were only three books on the small bookshelf so far, and Freya was almost finished with the third. She made a mental note to hunt down the best bookstore in Wishburn. Since arriving, Freya could practically count the number of times that she had actually left the house on a single hand. Between unpacking, checking in with Freya Designs, and panicking that Axel needed saving from an imaginary machine malfunction, it was safe to say that Freya was busy trying to keep herself preoccupied with mundane tasks and worry.

However, something about the pleasant morning weather had sparked a little hope in her. Today felt like a good day to explore at least the main street of town. After all, from a logical perspective, Freya knew that she was only avoiding the inevitable. It was better to try to socialize for herself as well as to salvage her reputation with her curious neighbors.

A ring of the doorbell tinkled through the air and gave Freya pause. She reached for her phone and saw that it was already two minutes to noon. She had read aloud continuously, for almost half an hour, to Axel without noticing the time. An image appeared in her head of a sweet but strong woman in her late fifties from Haiti with gorgeous curly dark hair. She had a sharp mind that was matched only by her witty and cutting tongue. Freya wouldn't openly say it, but she adored Axel's nurse.

With a little elbow grease, Freya eased open the heavy wooden door. Meg entered with her bag wearing a pair of blue jeans and a blue scrubs shirt that read "Meg" in black embroidery. Meg's eyes scanned over Freya's appearance in an almost-clinical manner. She arched an eyebrow in inquiry at Freya's nicer-than-usual attire. Instead of sweatpants and a messy bun, Freya had on a pair of black jeans and a thin long sleeve to fend off the start of fall.

"Good afternoon, Freya. Are you leaving the house today?" The question was spoken more as an observation.

Freya let out an embarrassed chuckle. She had always been outgoing and thrived on interacting with people. It was strange that in less than a month, she had earned herself the reputation of a shut-in. *Well, that's going to change,* Freya thought to herself. "Yes, I was thinking of venturing out to explore a bit. Don't worry, I'll be back before you leave. If you need anything, like a glass of water or cup of coffee, feel free to grab it yourself when I'm out."

It appeared Meg wasn't having any of Freya's procrastination tactics as the old woman practically tossed her out of her own front door. She hollered from the doorway, "You're procrastinating! Go make friends!"

A bubble of laughter escaped Freya's mouth at the absurdity of the situation. She absentmindedly rearranged her long red mane as she strolled along her driveway. Freya's gaze traveled upward to admire the massive tree in the middle of her front yard. The pine needles on the impressive Sequoia were still as green as they were in spring, but the same could not be said for the other trees on the block. Fall was slowly approaching as the last warm tendrils of summer hung in the air. A few odd leaves were already turning a golden brown, as though in a race to see which leaf would be the very first to fall and welcome the new season.

In Los Angeles, it was rare to truly experience seasons unless you happened to drive by a park. There was very little variation in weather between the warm summer months and mild November chill. Freya grew excited at the idea of getting to watch the changing of the seasons from the comfort of her mini log cabin. Her backyard was extremely vast and touched the edge of a forest that went on for miles. She would watch the birds and the occasional raccoon dawdle around the yard in the early morning and twilight hours. Freya fleetingly wondered if she would be lucky enough to see deer if she started to walk to town earlier in the morning.

The walk to town was a little over fifteen minutes, and Freya was eager to stretch her legs. After a month of being a glorified couch potato, the idea of a stroll through the sleepy streets felt like the perfect precursor to a day of socializing. In Los Angeles, the last few weeks before she left to Wishburn had been quite overwhelming. It was almost like walking around a dark room your entire life but only finding out after someone turns on the light switch. There were just too many people that Freya was suddenly too aware of.

Each home on the cul-de-sac was properly spaced so that every front yard had an ample amount of room. Upon further inspection, Freya counted only four homes on the generously divided lots. The other three homes were created in almost-identical American Craftsman designs. Freya realized that the entire cul-de-sac at one point was a track home project. Most likely the home previous to the little log cabin fit into the design scheme of the tiny street. Freya realized the irony that just like her new home, Freya was also the outsider to the block. A smile graced her slightly chapped lips at the realization that she had the newest and oddest home.

As she continued to stroll toward Main Street, the houses seemed quaint and friendly. There were tiny bicycles strewn across lawns and swing sets or tire swings tied onto mammoth tree branches. In the span of ten minutes, Freya had waved to two different mothers tending to their little broods. The sight was bittersweet as Freya couldn't help but wonder what her own children with Axel would have looked like. The only thing that Freya passionately wanted more than the success of Freya Designs now seemed less achievable than the odds of people waking up from unexplained comas. A leaf landed on Freya's head and caused her to momentarily stop walking in confusion. She reached upward with slight trepidation and then let out a chuckle as the leaf floated toward the ground. *That definitely beat reaching up and feeling bird poop.*

From a distance, the main street seemed more like a fictional village plucked from a Hallmark film than a town with actual residents. The buildings were one and two-story complexes nestled together in a relatively straight line. Hues of brown, blue, and white covered the wooden buildings and added to the cheery atmosphere. Upon further inspection, Freya saw that there were a few townspeople bustling from shop to shop. The air was crisp and clean to the point that taking a deep breath in the middle of a park in the city didn't even come close.

A white-painted wooden sign hung proudly above the entrance of one of the buildings. The word *Market* was painted in neat cursive in bright-barn-house-red paint. The vibrant color immediately caught Freya's attention and drew her closer. It was a quaint two-story building that clearly had been around awhile but was still properly looked after and loved. Freya walked up the two front steps that creaked in protest at the added weight. Even from the outside, Freya could tell that the market was one of the older and larger buildings. A screen door with an open sign helped to obscure most of what was inside. Curiosity got the better of Freya, and she reached out an excited hand to open the door.

The light tinkling of bells welcomed her into the store as the door hit the bottom of a wind chime shaped like the American flag. As Freya turned her attention outward, the rows upon rows of items for purchase struck her as impressive. She wasn't exactly sure what she had expected to find in the market, but a store with such a wide variety of products definitely wasn't it. Freya walked across the weathered wooden floorboards to the produce section. Heavy footsteps from the other side of the room caused Freya to look upward in search of the owner—or owners.

Two separate pairs of eyes stared intently at the town newcomer. Presently the two strangers emerged from what Freya could only guess was the stockroom. A tall blond man with a small layer of stubble across his cheeks promptly walked over to Freya. His impressive build hinted to her that he was, at one point in his life, extremely athletic. *Maybe he played a sport in his college days?* The question passed through her head with a healthy combination of curiosity and speculation. A bright smile filled the unfamiliar man's face as he said, "Welcome to Wishburn. A few of the townspeople were taking bets on when you were planning on saying hello."

A sharp guffaw escaped Freya's mouth at the new information. Although it wasn't exactly a total surprise since Freya figured her reluctance to meet the locals was definitely fuel to the gossip mill fire.

"My name's Freya. Nice to meet you. Unpacking and getting everything sorted ended up taking more time than I thought," Freya smoothly explained away her lack of socialization and kept a practiced cool smile upon her lips.

"My name's Scott, and this here is my store." Scott moved slightly out of the way in order to give Freya a better view of a woman who was around Freya's age with a mocha-colored complexion and intricate hair braids. As Freya looked over the woman, the strong feeling that the market clerk wanted nothing to do with her was almost overwhelming. She peered warily at Freya with large brown eyes, as if Freya were a poisonous snake that could strike her at any moment.

Scott seemed completely unaware of the interaction as he gestured toward the woman who looked as nervous as a rabbit in a snake hole. Scott spoke casually, "This is Tanya. She has been kind enough to help out around here since we graduated high school together."

He made a show of cupping a hand over his mouth teasingly but spoke loudly enough for Tanya to hear. "Don't worry, if Tanya here likes you, the rest of the town will be soon to follow." As Scott turned toward Tanya for confirmation, Freya noticed how Tanya tried to compose her face into a mask of casual approval.

Less than five minutes into officially meeting Tanya and the woman was already acting like Freya had tried to merge onto her car on the 405 freeway at rush hour. Freya decided that it definitely wasn't anything she had said or done to the other woman and concluded that Tanya must simply be wary of strangers. Freya waved politely at Tanya, who awkwardly reciprocated the gesture.

Freya turned her attention back to Scott, whose friendly demeanor put her at ease. He seemed to radiate a warmth that was rare to find in the world. His blue eyes were shining with kindness and apparent curiosity at the newcomer. Scott casually brushed his blond locks away from his face and asked, "Do you need help finding anything in the store?"

Her eyes widened in recollection at his gentle prompt. Scott had unintentionally helped her to remember her dwindling book supply. Her mind suddenly uncovered memories of Axel when they were back in Los Angeles a few years ago and shopping at a much-larger supermarket. At the time, Freya had just popped her kneecap playing a game of pickup soccer and wasn't able to stand, let alone comfortably shop for groceries. Axel had picked her up and effortlessly placed her inside the shopping cart. She had spent the afternoon laughing so much that her stomach had hurt. They had gone down every food aisle, and Axel's wonder at her knowledge of shopping deals was almost the same as how she imagined people reacted to seeing fire for the first time. A combination of awe and admiration had graced Axel's face as they stole kisses in between the expansive aisles. Freya placed a stray piece of her red hair behind her ear that was falling into her face. She smiled politely in an effort to hide the tidal wave of emotions that threatened to drown her at the memory.

She responded, "Actually, Scott, do you have any books or does Wishburn have a bookstore? I'm trying to make it a point to read more now that I'm here."

Scott let out a chuckle. "Yes, we have a few book options in this store, but you should really visit Aimée's Bookstore if you're itching for a better selection."

He started walking toward the back of the store. After passing a few aisles, he stopped walking and turned to face Freya. He made a sweeping motion with his hand similar to the one that the iconic Vana White did on television. A snort escaped Freya's nose at the cheesy gesture that brought an easy smile to her face. Freya couldn't remember the last time that she had really smiled and decided to bask in the rare moment.

Scott's smile was infectious, and Freya listened with rapt attention as Scott pointed out, "There should be about five or six different options. I try to change them up every month or so in order to have a little variety. You might want to head over to Aimée's if you're an avid reader. But I do have her beat in the vegetable and canned food departments." Scott crossed his well-defined arms over his chest in an exaggerated show of pride.

His smile and lame jokes led Freya to let out a stream of girlish giggles. She wasn't sure if he was flirting with her or just being friendly, but in the moment, she couldn't be bothered. It had been ages since Freya had had a normal conversation where friends and relatives weren't tiptoeing around her like a priceless vase that could topple over and shatter at any moment. Scott had no idea about Freya's situation. To him, she was only a young woman new to town, and Freya loved the newfound anonymity. She laughed so hard that she had tears of joy threatening to escape the corner of her eyes. She could feel the slick moisture as her vision became slightly blurry. Freya hastily wiped the back of her hand against her eyes in order to stop any water droplets from falling. Her face was flush, and her breathing was rapid as she tried to collect herself.

Freya felt that her heart was noticeably lighter as she responded, "Thank you. I will have to come to your store on the regular. Could you point me in the direction of your canned goods?" A quick perusal of the titles told Freya that they were all classics written by the literary genius William Shakespeare. She fleetingly wondered if that was Scott's simple theme of the month—Shakespeare. She had already read the five available novels on the bottom shelf but didn't feel the need to tell Scott.

She was brought out of her internal musing as Scott indicated with his right hand that the canned foods were on the other side of the shelf. Scott opened his mouth to say something, but the tinkling of bells flitted through the air as the front door opened to reveal a relatively mousy woman. She looked as if the doorway was threatening to eat her alive. That is if the green turtleneck sweater didn't swallow the skinny woman up first. Her messy brown hair looked stringy, as if it wasn't properly managed, even from where Freya was standing. She looked as if she had been a gorgeous woman at one time, but her confidence and fight had left her years ago. Freya slightly narrowed her eyes at the other woman as if that would help to see more of her. Although the aisle was blocking the view of the bottom half of her outfit, Freya figured that the bottom would most likely match the disheveled appearance of the top.

Scott turned his head in the direction of the door and Freya saw the casual joy melt from his eyes and be replaced with something similar to concern. He turned toward Freya and said, "I'm going to go speak with Sally. Let me know if you need any help finding anything." He walked at a leisurely pace out of the aisle and toward the lady in green.

"Good to see you, Sally. Please come in. Is there anything that I can help you with today?"

Freya made an effort to ignore their conversation as best as she could. She didn't want to intrude on personal matters, or worse, get caught trying to eavesdrop. The last thing that she wanted to gain was the reputation of a nosy neighbor the very first day walking around in the town. Freya picked up a few cans of vegetable soup and then moved around the edges of the store in order to get her staple items like bread and lettuce. Freya was mindful not to get too much as she would still have to carry them back to her house. After Freya had enough items for lunch and to last a few odd meals, she walked over to the front of the tiny store to check out. There were a few pens and pencil packets near the cash register. Freya assumed they were the remains of a temporary back-to-school section. As Freya reached the register and looked around for Tanya or Scott to help her, she realized that Tanya had disappeared for almost twenty minutes. It seemed that Tanya had slunk into the back of the store for some reason or another.

As if reading her mind, Scott poked his head over one of the aisles and called out, "Tanya?"

There was a moment of silence in answer to his question. Scott furrowed his eyebrows slightly but walked over to the cash register. He quickly moved around to the other side of the counter as he ran his long fingers through his blond hair and looked around the store once again, most likely for any sign of Tanya.

"Thank you for helping me, Scott."

He quickly waved away the thanks as he replied, "My pleasure. Welcome to Wishburn."

The wooden floorboards barely creaked as someone walked toward the checkout area. Freya turned around and saw that it was the woman that Scott had called Sally. Freya looked at her for a moment and realized now that she was closer to her in age than she had originally guessed. Her face would look young except for a handful of lightly etched worry lines. Freya smiled at the brunette. "Hi, I'm Freya, and I'm new to Wishburn."

With one hand, she desperately pretended to dig inside of her jacket pocket for her wallet, offering the other woman an escape from the obligatory handshake. Somehow Freya knew that the gesture would be a little too forward for the skittish-looking woman and didn't want to put her through an uncomfortable situation. Freya dug her hands into her other jacket pockets as she patiently awaited a reply.

The brunette consciously pulled her hair behind her ears, as if to make herself more presentable. She licked her lips and unsteadily replied, "I'm S-Sally. You m-moved across the cul-de-sac from me."

Finally I'm meeting my neighbors. I shouldn't have been so nervous and put this off for so long. It was foolish to think that meeting them should make my situation any more real. As if meeting them would somehow solidify Axel's coma. Freya allowed her internal monologue to ramble as she finally pulled her black Prada designer wallet out of her bottom jacket pocket.

Sally was holding a carton of eggs, a packet of ground beef, and a copy of *Macbeth*. As soon as Freya saw the book, she immediately remembered to ask about Aimée's Bookstore and how to get there. She angled her body so that she could include both Scott and Sally in her question. Before asking for help, Freya made a note to compliment Sally. "I love that play, Sally. A great choice. Would either of you be able to tell me how to get to Aimée's Bookstore from here? Is it within walking distance?'

Scott discretely nodded his head toward Sally who was practically glowing since she was so eager to share what she knew with Freya. Sally's brown eyes lit up as if she hadn't been complimented in a while. She stuttered out a shy but eager, "Just head out to the right, and Aimée's is four stores over. You can't miss it. It's the best place in town." As if suddenly remembering where she was, Sally suddenly blurted out, "Sorry, Scott! The grocery store is a really nice part of town too." Her cheeks held a tinge of embarrassment at her offhand remark.

Scott let out a booming laugh at Sally's extreme thoughtfulness. It was obvious that Sally meant no harm in the remark and was only explaining her love for the bookstore.

He sent a smile Sally's way to assure her that there were no hard feelings.

Freya turned to the still-abashed brunette and asked, "Would you like to come with me to Aimée's? I'm going over there as soon as I check out. I can wait for you, and we can walk over together. It would be great to explore the town with a new neighbor."

Freya was surprised at her own extremely approachable behavior. She rarely was so open or outgoing with people in the city. Something inside of her took an instant liking to Sally in a strangely maternal way, even though they were roughly the same age, from what Freya could tell. As Freya watched the other woman's slightly freckled face, she saw an array of emotions across her delicate features. Her face showed surprise, elation, and, for some reason, disappointment.

"Th-thank you for inviting me, but I can't come. I'm sorry. I have to get home right after I leave Scott's, but I'm sorry." Sally wrinkled her forehead with her response, and Freya wasn't able to tell if that was from disappointment at not being able to come along or fear of letting Freya down.

The response seemed odd to Freya, but she didn't want to pry any further. Scott finished packing her groceries into a brown paper bag and handed it over along with the change to her twenty-dollar bill.

"Maybe another time, Sally. Oh, thank you, Scott." Freya checked the weight of the bag to make sure that the handles wouldn't break. Upon closer inspection, Freya realized that Scott was already ahead of her and had double-bagged her groceries just in case.

As Freya was about to open the door to leave, a strong voice called out, "Wait! Take a flyer for the Autumn Festival." Scott was holding out an orange piece of paper sporting a pumpkin graphic and details for the event written in bold font.

Freya walked back to take the flyer and looked it over before folding it and putting it inside of the bag of groceries.

"Thanks, Scott. This sounds like fun. I'll hopefully see you both around town before the festival."

Sally gave a small wave goodbye and then whispered, "Yes, hope to see you around town."

Freya waved at the two as she closed the door and was once again welcomed by the nice weather and warm sun on her pale face. Freya adjusted the bag of groceries so that it was resting on her hip as she ventured toward Aimée's. People walked on the generous sidewalk and peered into shop windows. Freya thought it was odd that so few people were on the streets, until she realized that it was Monday afternoon, and most people were still at work. It also didn't help that she had no clue what a small-town population looked like on an average day. After years of working, even on the weekend, a strange thrill went through her at the realization that she was the one out of the office on a weekday. She felt a rush similar to that one time she had played hooky during her senior year of high school. The day was an unofficial senior ditch day since it was the day of prom, and it was customary that the entire senior class skip school to get ready. Since it was such a prestigious and niche school, the professors and principal unofficially sanctioned it. Even the one time Freya had ditched her responsibilities in her entire life, it was expected and encouraged.

It took less than five minutes before Freya came to a two-story brick building with the words "Aimée's Bookstore" painted in large white cursive across the red bricks. The outside looked cared after, and Freya could already tell that Aimée was just like Scott and took great pride in her business. Flowers that had yet to bloom were planted in a neat row outside of the little shop. The windows on the first floor were full of new books and exclusive editions. It was a tantalizing display for any bibliophile and instantly caught Freya's interest. However, the second-story window looked like a living room. Aimée most likely owned or rented the entire building so that she could live and work all in one place.

Freya approached the front door, and as she was about to grab hold of the doorknob, she noticed a symbol similar to the one on her necklace etched into the center of the handle. A circle with four arrows pointing outward was just vaguely visible after years of use. Freya knew very little about her Irish heritage and wasn't sure what the symbol meant, but she had a strong feeling that the symbols were of the same origin.

The metal was cool to the touch as she wrapped her slim fingers around it and pushed the door open. Books lined the walls and covered at least four massive rows of bookcases. A fluffy stuffed cat immediately caught her eye. The cat looked like the epitome of a cat-show-winning Russian ragdoll with its long and shiny black fur. Freya jumped backward and almost dropped her groceries when the cat leisurely blinked its large green eyes at her and then gracefully leapt from the wood counter onto the concrete floor. The animal let out a sharp meow, as if in greeting, and sauntered over to Freya with the usual grace and temperament of a domestic feline.

Freya placed her bag of groceries on the floor and bent down to welcome the little creature. It leaned its fluffy body into Freya's shin in greeting and flicked its tail upward. She slowly placed her hand outward and allowed the cat a chance to smell her. To Freya's shock, the black cat began to purr as it rubbed itself around her body. "Hello, pretty lady. Do you have a name?" The question was supposed to be rhetorical, but to Freya's surprise, a smooth voice from behind her back provided an answer.

"Her name is Amethyst. She doesn't have a collar or a chip because she's obviously more than my pet."

Freya craned her neck around to find an extremely tall blond woman lounging in the doorway of a back room. She was wearing a white spaghetti-strap maxi dress and her straight straw-colored locks were partially pulled away from her face in a half-up-half-down hairstyle. Upon closer inspection, Freya noticed that the woman had her arms folded over her chest in a vaguely defensive position. She immediately guessed what had upset the woman.

Freya let out an embarrassed cough and replied in a casual manner, "You're right. Amethyst is part of your family and not just a pet." In Los Angeles, it was more common than not to call pets family members and to treat them more like kids than anything else. Freya assumed that she had accidentally insulted the woman by referring to her cat as a pet.

Freya's reply seemed to mildly confuse the statuesque blond as a quick frown crossed her nearly flawless face. She ran her fingers through the cat's perfectly maintained black fur once more before she placed her hands on her knees for support as she stood upward. "My name is Aimée, and this is my store. You passed the threshold without any trouble. Why are you here?"

Now it was Freya's turn to arch her eyebrow in response. The woman was definitely eccentric in Freya's mind for such strange phrases. The door was heavy but not anything out of the ordinary. Freya jokingly thought to herself, *Please tell me that I'm talking to a woman who was once the president of her high school drama club.* It was the only sensible explanation for Aimée's dramatic sentence structures. The woman did have an expansive collection and a bookstore in a remote town, so the dramatics had to come from somewhere.

Freya walked over to Aimée and realized that she definitely could be a model with her tall figure, high cheekbones, and unblemished skin. Looking at the other woman's skin was like glancing over fresh snow after a snowstorm. In order to shake Aimée's hand, she had to angle her hand slightly upward given their height difference. "It's nice to officially meet you, Aimée. My name is Freya, and I was told about your bookstore. Only good things, I promise."

A beat of silence passed between them until Aimée reluctantly reached out her hand. The entire time, she looked as if she was trying to solve a complicated puzzle as her eyes slightly narrowed in concentration. *What a dramatic woman*, Freya thought to herself. Aimée stepped away from shaking hands and then bent down to pick Amethyst up from the ground. The little creature mewled in discontent at the movement, but then found a comfortable place to rest in Aimée's arms after it squirmed around. The cat seemed to be sizing Freya up with its deep green stare. Freya decided that she needed to explore the book section before she ended up in a staring battle with a cat.

"You have a lovely store. I'm going to look around for a bit."

Freya couldn't disappear into the bookstacks fast enough as she felt Aimée's intense gaze as it burned the back of her neck. She noticed a sign and realized, much to her dismay, that she had ended up in the cookbook section. *Maybe if I start reading recipes to Axel, he will wake up from his coma just to tell me to be quiet*, Freya thought drily. Although the concept was humorous, it was totally untrue. Axel was the one who was an amazing cook between the two of them, so it was fair to say that he would probably wipe the floor with any generic cooking recipe instead of resorting to following it. His mother had been a Michelin star chef and had made sure to teach Axel before she eventually passed.

Freya wandered aimlessly around the quaint store until she found a section packed with classic American literature. She had always been a fan of great fictional classics and decided to see what was available. The majority, Freya had already read as a young teen and didn't care to revisit. Her eyes scanned over the various spines until they landed on one of her personal favorites. *The Great Gatsby* by F. Scott Fitzgerald called out to her, just as it had the first time she read it. She loved the expert depiction of 1920s opulence and heartache. It comforted her as a child, and she wondered if the pages still held the same magic. Freya realized that her old copy was most likely still in a box stowed away in her mother's attic in San Francisco. There was no point in calling Joan to spend multiple hours rifling through her old things and then paying to ship it to the tiny town of Wishburn. She picked up a copy and walked to the counter where Amethyst had gracefully leapt earlier in her bookstore visit. The counter was partially made from a glass case that was built for protecting valuable books. Freya peered inside the glass case and felt her eyebrows gradually rise in amazement. In the center of the case an early edition of the King James Bible rested on a soft white pillow. Freya wasn't a huge book connoisseur, but she knew enough to get by in most conversations.

Aimée noticed that Freya was finished looking and walked around the cash register to ring her up. Aimée picked up the book and mumbled, "A classic heartbreak." She handed the change back with the paperback novel and, with little fanfare, offered a half-hearted wave goodbye.

Freya placed her new book on the top of her groceries and began to walk back toward her home. There was something strangely exciting about her newfound anonymity. People along the streets casually glanced at her retreating figure. She noted that they continued to stare until she was out of view of the main part of town. Freya let out a sigh that she didn't know was within her body. Apparently it was something that she was prone to doing when tired. Even a quick buzz into town seemed to drain her energy as she rubbed her tired eyes with the back of her left palm. Recently it felt as if social interactions were draining her emotional and physical batteries at double speed.

Before she knew it, Freya was already turning onto her street. The stroll was much easier than she remembered when heading to town, and Freya decided that was partly due to the anticipation she had felt the entire walk. The fallen leaves from the large trees crunched beneath her boots. Her pace increased slightly at the thought of getting into the kitchen and preparing a grilled cheese sandwich and tomato soup for lunch.

It had been awhile since Freya had prepared lunch or any real meal for herself. As if on autopilot, she ended up making two grilled cheese sandwiches and an entire can of tomato soup. Freya put both servings on the dining room table that she still had yet to properly use.

Freya saw that Meg was just putting away her supplies into her bag as she entered Axel's room. Freya knocked on the archway of the room to alert the older woman of her presence. Freya casually leaned against the doorframe and asked, "Do you have time for lunch? I made too much. Old habit, I guess." Freya looked over to Axel; she was speaking to Meg.

She noticed that Axel had new clothes and that he had been repositioned. Although Axel didn't need assistance breathing and was luckily tube-free in that regard, he still needed help in every other aspect. The tidy bundle of wires behind his bed was a visual reminder of his current state, and it made Freya's stomach turn at the sight. She was beyond happy that Axel was properly taken care of and that there was still hope that he would wake up. Yet an equally large part of Freya was absolutely crushed at the sight of him looking so vulnerable and wondered if this was the new normal. The past month had felt like she was trying to drive a car, but she wasn't allowed to put the car in drive or reverse. Simply stuck in neutral.

Meg zipped up her bag and then looked kindly at Freya with an unrehearsed ease.

"Yes, lunch sounds good. You can tell me all about the town as we eat."

A small smile pushed against the edges of Freya's lips as she moved away from the doorway. "I would like that, Meg."

The two women chatted down the hallway and entered the open kitchen. As they sat down to eat together, the room somehow seemed brighter. Neither one of them noticed that the flowers around the kitchen had a little more life in their petals than they had before.

Chapter 5

The ground was littered with varying hues of bright orange, yellow, and gold. Leaves steadily fell in the sleepy town of Wishburn. It was a little over a week since Freya had first ventured into the town. Most of the trees on the cul-de-sac seemed to have shed a majority of their leaves, except for the one in Freya's front yard. It remained untouched by the changing of the seasons, as if it were growing completely unaware of any rules of nature outside of itself. Its large branches stretched outward, and its green leaves collected sunlight.

Freya pondered the strange concept as she eyed the tree through her bedroom window. She had taken a break from wrestling with her thick hair to answer a few texts from Aidan about Freya Designs. The questions were relatively simple, but Freya appreciated her brother running the changes by her, even though he was temporarily in charge. Aidan was a wonderful brother to Freya and had been more than willing to temporarily give up his position of VP to help her and the company. Freya felt that Aidan's eagerness to step in stemmed partially from a soft spot that he had for Axel. The two were thick as thieves and were often found scheming at work and family events. When Freya's company had just started, Axel had loved pulling pranks on Freya. Aidan was only too happy to assist his brother-in-law. Neither Aidan nor Axel had brothers of their own, so the pair had instantly taken a familial shine to each other.

A cursory glance at her phone screen reminded Freya that she needed to finish taming her hair and throw on some clothes. She settled on a minimal makeup look and hair that was left down and pinned back by two bobby pins on the right side. She didn't want to get unreasonably dressy for the Autumn Festival. The flyer advertised a pumpkin-carving competition, a haunted hayride, and festive fair food. It didn't seem like an event that called for an elaborate red carpet look, and for that, Freya was grateful. Her metallic-toed booties echoed throughout the house as she walked toward the front door. She absentmindedly pulled at her white turtleneck and made sure it was properly centered. Freya was traditionally curvy in the sense that she had an hourglass figure. Her ample chest and bottom caused many items to feel a little snug. It was always a pain for her to find clothing since she often ran the risk of looking too risqué or tacky in outfits that other women looked perfectly cute in. Over the years, Freya had learned how to properly showcase her body in a way that was sophisticated and alluring. The skin-tight white cable-knit turtleneck and black flare jeans with booties were a perfect encapsulation of her refined style.

Freya opened the door to her newly leased Jeep Grand Cherokee and drove toward the festival. The car was a more practical choice for a town densely surrounded by woods, and Freya didn't want to have any headaches about unforeseen ice. If there was one thing Freya couldn't stand, it was a headache from being unprepared.

Her seat heater kept her comfortable on the colder-than-usual Saturday morning. A thin layer of ice had accumulated on the roads and driveways the night before. The drive took a little over ten minutes before Freya finally spotted the edge of the lake. It was supposedly a major geographic focal point for the town, and both the Autumn Festival and Summer Festival were held at the edge of the lake every year. The two festivals were the largest fundraisers for public projects. This year the goal was to help renovate the middle school.

Freya pulled off the main paved road and drove into a patchy field of grass that was the makeshift parking lot. The car handled the uneven terrain with ease. Freya heard the rocks and gravel crunching under her tires as she carefully steered toward the other cars. Children zipped around the parked cars with unconfined glee as parents desperately tried to herd them to the rows of tents.

Childish shrieks of joy filled the air, and the smell of popcorn and cotton candy danced through the chilly breeze as Freya parked and emerged from her car. Suddenly a small girl, with locks the color of sunbeams, barreled into Freya's legs. The little girl was clearly on a mission to beat two nearby giggling boys to the fair. Freya looked more closely at the little girl, whose extremely blond hair was pulled high into two pigtails. Tiny fingers grappled with Freya's dark jeans for traction, and Freya instinctively steadied the small child. Her tiny blue overalls and pink tennis shoes were already covered in either grass stains or dirt. It was hard to tell exactly which organic matter was the culprit as the spunky kid buzzed toward her friends. The little girl reminded Freya of someone, but the resemblance was too vague for her to place. A high-pitched "Excuse me! Sorry, miss" was all that was left in the little patch of settling dust.

Freya chuckled at the lively behavior and walked to the festival at a much more controlled pace than her spritely counterpart. She observed all of the townsfolk around her as they talked and laughed in little groups. A large sign over a wooden stage proudly proclaimed the pumpkin-pie-eating contest at noon. Directly to the right of the stage, the pumpkin-carving contest was already well underway. People from about the ages of eight to eighty-eight huddled together in teams of two and created spooky masterpieces. Freya wondered if the competition was for bragging rights or an actual prize. As Freya continued to leisurely survey the contestants, she spotted a familiar face. Tanya from the supermarket was chatting excitedly with another young woman, who looked to be around the same age, with light-brown locks and stunning blue eyes. The two were engaged in lively conversation as Tanya gestured emphatically with a spatula full of seeds. A tap on Freya's shoulder caused her to turn around and see Scott's welcoming megawatt smile.

"Hi, Scott! It's so good to see a familiar face in the crowd."

Scott nodded his head and said, "I'm glad you came. If you ever plan to become a true citizen of Wishburn, then you definitely have to start here. Almost half a year's worth of gossip and drama is always cultivated at this event. It's also a custom, and maybe even a law, that every person in Wishburn simply *has* to try out the hot apple cider and fresh cinnamon rolls from Mrs. Tellian's food booth."

A hot apple cider sounded absolutely delicious to Freya. She couldn't even remember the last time that she had warm apple cider.

"Well, lead the way, Scott. I'm on a mission to live like a local, but I have one question for you first."

Scott's eyebrows slightly furrowed in apprehension, but he shrugged his shoulders and replied, "Shoot."

"Are the cinnamon rolls better than the ones that you can get at the mall with the blue logo? Those things were like my kryptonite when I was a kid."

"Well, then prepare to die, Superman. Mrs. Tellian's baking skills are completely unmatched." Scott wiggled his eyebrows to add emphasis, but only succeeded in looking absolutely ridiculous.

Freya couldn't hold in the snort that erupted from the back of her nose as she laughed.

Upon hearing her strange laugh, Scott burst out into his own fit of bellied laughter The duo walked toward an area where the tents were arranged in a semicircle to resemble a pop-up food court. Each tent proudly displayed a sign with their individual menus and pictures of their confectionary delights. Some of the items mentioned were typical festival foods like kettle corn and hot dogs, but others were more elaborate and piqued Freya's interest, such as the chicken and waffle sandwich. Freya nodded her head at the food choices and followed Scott's athletic figure toward a tent that already had a few people waiting in line. The sight struck Freya as especially impressive since the fair had only officially started twenty minutes ago and planned to stretch into sundown. The line of eager customers moved at a steady pace as Freya and Scott discussed the different places that she had yet to see in Wishburn.

A sense of foolishness wrestled around in her stomach with the knowledge that she had spent over a month in the town and had yet to learn where the public library or even the hospital were located. The line moved quickly, and it was their turn to order their treats in no time. The cinnamon rolls smelled delicious and were coated in a generous helping of fluffy frosting. Scott asked for two hot apple ciders and two cinnamon rolls. The elderly woman was somewhere in her sixties and looked as though she knew how to eat her way around a kitchen. The old lady smiled kindly and winked as she went to get the goodies. Scott was about to pay for both of their snacks when Freya realized that she had to step in and put the record straight.

"Thank you, Scott. Please let me pay for mine. Also I have to tell you that I'm married, Scott. It's…complicated, but I am married. Besides the tour guide never pays for the guest."

She was hoping that the extremely lame tourism joke would help soften the blow and hopefully offer an avenue for conversation. Her face held a look of tentative apprehension as she waited for his reply. Even though Freya figured that Scott wasn't vengeful or easily self-conscious, she knew it was still too early for her to assume his reaction to the possibly uncomfortable information. It was only their second time really talking to each other, after all.

Freya felt bad for not telling Scott when she was in the grocery store, but she had just wanted to feel like her life wasn't in shambles for at least a few minutes. She realized that it also didn't help Scott's impression of her that she had taken off both her wedding and engagement rings and started to wear them on a necklace. Freya wasn't exactly sure where she wanted to stand with Axel and had decided to keep the rings on a necklace while she pondered what to do.

Scott retracted his hand from the inside of his pocket and, with some effort, casually shrugged. His consistently easygoing behavior made it simple for Freya to slip into a contented smile. As if to signal not to thank him yet, Scott held up his palm and teasingly suggested, "Actually how about this round is on you since this tour guide will work for free and is trying to salvage his pride."

"That's a done deal." Freya plucked her Prada wallet out from the top of her purse and took out a crisp twenty-dollar bill. Freya held out enough money for her portion and his.

She handed it over to the kind elderly woman who she assumed was Mrs. Tellian. Freya's eyes widened in surprise at the two monster-sized cinnamon rolls that the salt-and-pepper-haired woman painstakingly handed over. The frosting was dripping onto the paper plate, and it looked as if the rolls had just been made that morning and then doused again with another generous helping of delicious gooey goodness. Freya heard her stomach grumble in approval of the sweet sight and handed Scott his own. Another woman who looked like a much younger version of the mastermind baker handed Freya and Scott their hot apple ciders. They thanked the busy little family and strolled toward a few picnic benches that were placed in the center of the food tents on a generous carpet of hay. There were four wooden picnic tables and a few black-and-white-checkered picnic blankets sprawled around the area. Freya watched as a couple around their age sat alone together on a blanket and huddled into each other for warmth. The man gently placed the palm of his hand on the woman's swollen stomach as he affectionately rubbed his manicured beard against her neck. Freya looked away from the personal moment that was on full display at a public event. It instigated a feeling of loss.

Scott directed Freya to a table as they sat down on one of the scarce seating arrangements. Two boys, who were around high school age, were already comfortably seated at the table, but when the youngsters looked over to see who was joining them and noticed Scott, the boys smiled and then quickly tried to contain their enthusiasm. Instead they offered extremely solemn head nods to the newcomers in an effort to look cool and collected beyond their fourteen or fifteen years.

Freya playfully nudged Scott in the shoulder with her own after watching the interaction with interest. She leaned closer in order to avoid any prying ears and asked, "They seem like an adoring fan club. Is this just part of the small-town charm?"

Scott barked out a throaty chuckle and shook his head so that his blond mane momentarily flew in the crisp afternoon wind. He self-consciously rubbed the back of his neck and replied, "I guess my football records at the high school are still posted. Back then, I was on a path to play for U of T on a full ride and eventually get out and play pro. That was until my body started to fall apart. My knee blew out the last game of my senior year, and that was it for football. I'm now the proud owner of Scott's Supermarket and the biggest provider of canned goods in Wishburn."

The pained look as Scott stared aimlessly past her head struck a chord within Freya. He too was yearning for a version of his life that at one point had felt like his to claim. The ghostly fingers of the past were still firmly grasping his heart and tearing it out as he continued to stare into a world that Freya could not see. Scott slowly brought his gaze back towards Freya's face as he let out a weak smile and then took a gulp of his apple cider in an effort to temper his emotions.

Freya could practically taste the bitterness of his pain that time had failed to dilute. She reached forward to grab his large hand within her much-smaller fingers and gave them a comforting squeeze. They sat in silence for a few moments as the children continued to chatter, and the playlist of old songs from the 1990s cheerfully blasted through several standing speakers at an excessive volume.

A feeling of dread suddenly blossomed within Freya's stomach. It hit seemingly out of nowhere but struck her senses like a freight train at full speed. If she hadn't already been seated, she was sure that the intense feeling would have brought her to the ground in a second. Her heartbeat thrummed in her ears, and her vision momentarily blurred.

Something was wrong.

Freya removed her hand from Scott's and brought it toward her chest. She could feel her heart frantically pounding against her hand, as though she was running a marathon instead of sitting idly at a picnic table.

Scott turned to Freya in confusion at her sudden action. "Are you okay, Freya?" The question was so simple, but she honestly had no idea how to answer. She stood from the table without even bothering to throw away her apple cider or the cinnamon roll. The two treats were still largely untouched as she had only taken three bites at most.

With a magnificent amount of effort, Freya walked away and sputtered out, "I'm sorry. I have to go."

She wasn't sure exactly what was happening, but she desperately needed to get away from the fairground. The Ferris wheel and townspeople surged past her in an indiscernible blur. Freya's feet momentarily stumbled over a bundle of extension cords from one of the food booths. Luckily she regained her footing just in time and continued in the direction of the lake. Most of the festivities were centered about a half-mile away from the frigid banks, so after a few minutes of walking, Freya found herself alone. The piercing call of a lone bird echoed ominously around the shore as she desperately searched around for some type of sign. Her sharp green eyes darted in every direction, only to find wisps of branches in lieu of full bushes and blooming flowers. Each barren tree branch seemed to point toward whatever was just around the bend in the dense remnants of foliage.

High-pitched voices were squealing in excitement just beyond her line of sight. Like a moth drawn to the dangerous flicker of a flame, Freya flitted toward the noise. Once again, she placed a hand to her chest and faltered in unexplained agony. Each breath was a struggle to draw into her body. A painful burning sensation that she had never known before crept around her limbs as she desperately forced herself toward the noise.

The slick sheen over the rocks warned her of ice as she treaded cautiously without proper traction. It was difficult enough to walk on rocky terrain in heeled boots in general, and a Herculean task to walk on ice-covered rocky terrain with lungs that felt like they were about to burst.

Kids. A young boy with a tree branch was leaning over a rock over-hang toward the frozen lake below. His limbs desperately stretched out in vain as the stick wasn't long enough to even brush the surface of the frozen lake. A little boy in a puffy white jacket saw Freya emerge from the trees and toddled over to her. His tiny body was wracked by sobs, and his face had large tears pouring down onto the cold ground.

The small freckled face managed to huff out in panic, "Help! I'm sorry, everything fell in. Help!"

The young boy collided into her knee at full speed. Freya instinctively scooped him up into her arms, jacket and all. The thin ice of the lake had a hole right where the elder boy was avidly reaching. He was close to throwing himself into the frigid water with his dedicated but fruitless efforts. Freya sharply called out, "Get away from there! You're going to fall in!"

To her shock, he frantically looked Freya in the eyes and screamed, "No! She fell in!" The air instantly rushed out of Freya, and the hairs on the back of her neck stood to attention with the new information. She clutched the boy closer to her chest as she looked more closely at the surface of the lake. Just when Freya was about to have a strong word with these kids, she saw movement a few feet away from the hole underneath the ice. Freya could make out the strikingly small childlike figure. Immediately Freya placed the little boy on his feet and rushed toward the edge of the lake. "Both of you, go get help at the fair! Tell them someone fell in the lake! Go straight to the fair!"

The boy, who was still leaning precariously over the edge of the water, at last retreated from his perch and quickly scampered down the rock. He dutifully grabbed the younger child's hand, and the two ran off in the direction of safety.

Freya catapulted in the direction of the lake without a moment of hesitation. "Please don't let me be too late. Please don't let me be too late."

The desperate plea reverberated from her anxious lips like a broken record. She paused only for a moment in order to yank off her shoes. In her haste, Freya managed to pull the zipper right off her left bootie as she tossed them both aside. She snatched up the discarded stick that the little boy had used earlier and lowered herself onto the ice. A shiver immediately flooded through her body as her knit turtleneck came into contact with the thin layer of ice. In the back of her mind, Freya knew that the wrong move could spell disaster for herself. Although Freya had grown up near the sandy shores, she had watched enough movies where people fell through the ice to understand the gravity of the situation. Random images and snippets of informational dialogue whirled around her mind thanks to her propensity for watching survival documentaries and television shows when she couldn't sleep. For a moment, Freya was glad that she suffered from random spells of insomnia.

Another much-larger shiver rattled her body as she tried to reposition her body to distribute her weight more evenly on the precarious ice. People with years of experience around icy lakes and ponds drowned every year. Freya was hoping against hope that the understanding of ice that she learned from television shows was enough to keep her from falling into a watery grave.

With every inch that Freya cautiously moved, the wind seemed to increase its velocity, as if to mirror her anxiety. Freya was finally at the edge of the hole in the ice and realized that she was over two meters from shore. At the very corner of the hole, she could see bright-blond hair bobbing in the water.

Freya shakily brought her arms forward and tried to inch the body into the open by pressing it between the sheet of ice and the stick, and then pulling it toward her. A sharp snap invaded the air as the stick split down the middle. In a spiral of fury directed at her failure for wasting precious time, Freya screeched, "Damn caution! Stupid ass stick!"

She inched herself to the edge of the hole, letting out a hiss in the process. Her shirt had ridden upward, and the ice was now burning her exposed stomach. *So much for survival videos,* Freya thought to herself as she dove headfirst into the water. The freezing water immediately stole her breath from her body. It was so cold that for a second, all she could think about was the extreme temperature as she started to sink to the bottom of the lake. For a moment, her body went into shock, and Freya forgot how to swim until she caught sight of blond hair reflecting in the sunlight above her face. She started to swim toward the hair like her life depended on it. Freya thrashed out blindly and managed to grab hold of a strip of the child's clothing. She desperately began to strike her free arm upward in order to relocate the break in the ice. Her lungs felt like they would explode at any second as Freya fought to hold her breath and not open her mouth. It was as if her mind was fighting every natural instinct in her body as she continued to keep her mouth firmly shut.

Freya's fist continued to smash upward, and her punches were met with resistance at every attempt. Black spots began to dance at the corners of her vision when suddenly her hand was free. She thrust upward again and realized that there was a break in the ice. With a profound amount of effort, Freya kicked herself and the child that she was still dragging to the surface. She sputtered and shook as freezing droplets streamed down her face from her soaking hair. *How did Bear Grylls do this again?* The thought was jumbled as even her mind was impacted by the cold. She looked toward the edge of the ice that Freya knew she needed to climb onto. Freya crept closer to the edge and kept treading water in order to keep them both afloat as all of her limbs began to burn with exhaustion. She had been exposed to the water for less than two minutes, but her body was already drained of all of its energy.

With more will power and energy than Freya thought she had left, she sporadically treaded water as she rolled the little girl onto the ice. A loud cry of exertion left her blue lips when the little girl was finally spread out on the ice and no longer in the water. Freya then moved to the other side of the hole and spread her arms out so that it looked as if she was giving a wide hug to the ice. Her legs slowly began to butterfly kick as she kept her arms wide open. The constant splashing of the water was the only sound that she could really hear as Freya listened with heightened anxiety for any indication that the ice was cracking. With one final kick, Freya heaved herself out of the lake and began to painstakingly inch her way toward the unmoving child. Freya didn't dare stand up on the ice to walk; instead she grabbed the tiny foot that was closest to her as she continued to crawl, spread out on her tummy. She pulled the little girl behind her to shore and prayed that the ice would be able to hold them.

Finally Freya reached the edge where she figured it was safer to stand and break the ice and fall into maybe three or four inches of water instead of continuing to crawl. She comprehended that she needed to try and get out of the water as soon as possible in order to try and start getting the little girl to breathe. Every muscle in her body was shaking as she finally reached the shore and began chest compressions. Freya realized with a shock that she actually recognized the little girl from the parking lot as the one that tumbled into her legs not more than two hours ago. The last time that Freya had seen her, she was practically giddy with excitement.

Her porcelain skin was as pale as the ice that Freya had dragged her from, and her lips were a dark blue, like the color of a dirty icicle before it finally fell off a roof.

At first, Freya wasn't exactly sure what to do. It was such a catastrophe that knowing where to start in any shape or form felt like a disaster in itself. She gently placed her palm on the pale cheek, still full with the baby fat of youth, and collected herself. Freya mumbled, "I risked my life for you, the least you can do is breathe."

Freya began weak chest compressions to the chorus of "Stayin' Alive" and began to repeat the words aloud through her chattering teeth. In the distance, she grew vaguely aware of people yelling and the thunder of pounding feet. She wasn't exactly sure when help finally arrived as she couldn't tear her gaze away from the little girl who somehow reminded her so much of Axel. Silently but desperately, she willed the child to spit out the water and take a deep breath.

A woman with slightly graying hair suddenly came into Freya's eyesight as she kneeled next to Freya and said, "I'm the town doctor. Let me take over."

Freya's movements were almost robotic as she mechanically moved away to watch from a distance. It was a strange out-of-body experience, as she could see and hear everything that was happening around her, but it felt as though she was merely watching from above—a passive onlooker. Freya couldn't tear her eyes away from the motionless child, even as others from the town arrived to help.

Aimée suddenly burst around the corner as if the devil himself was on her heels. She began to shriek, "Layla!"

She tumbled down the embankment and landed a foot away from the doctor and impromptu patient. A man with a striking resemblance to the little girl soon joined Aimée's anguished form. The man grabbed Aimée by her waist and pulled her closer, as if the gesture could protect her and take away his own pain at the same time. Freya was only vaguely aware of her surroundings as she continued to watch the little girl. *Breathe, come on, Layla.*

A splutter of water followed by a sharp cry of joy from Aimée was all it took for Freya to crumble backward. She sat facing the little family and the doctor as her soaked jeans rubbed against the jagged rocks. Her body had fallen so that her legs were sprawled outward and her shoulders were slumped forward in sheer exhaustion.

As if sensing Freya's intense stare, Aimée looked upward and spotted Freya. Aimée's eyes were bloodshot as she tightly grabbed the dark-haired man's hand wrapped around her stomach. A look that Freya couldn't really understand passed across the blond's face before she nodded her head and mouthed *thank you* toward Freya. In response, Freya only gave a shaky nod.

Scott's tousled hair interrupted Freya's view of the family. His mouth was moving, but all she could hear for a few seconds was an extremely high-pitched buzzing noise. Freya squinted her eyes and tried to focus on Scott's voice. Freya felt as if she was mentally switching channels on a radio in order to find the right frequency. The longer that Freya remained silent and unresponsive to his comments, the more anxious Scott's expressions and movements became. He turned to the doctor who was still hovering from a distance over Layla. The child, whom Freya presumed was Aimée's daughter, now had two blankets around her body as her father gingerly picked her up in his arms.

Aimée's eyes shot toward Freya, who was now staring at nothing in particular and unable to hear anything around her. Freya felt like her entire body was made from stone.

The tall blond walked over toward Freya's obviously exhausted and shaking form.

Aimée crouched down and grasped Freya's freezing right hand with her own.

Immediately an electric current shot through Freya's body, and her hearing was restored.

Still hazy, Freya was reminded of the time she had sat in the back of her mother's station wagon in a mall parking lot. Her mother had accidentally left the car lights turned on, and when they had returned from shopping, the car battery had died. A young couple had been kind enough to help jump-start their car. They had hooked up their jumper cables to connect the couple's car and Freya's mother's station wagon. To Freya's shock, her mother's car was not broken like she had thought but only needed a little jumpstart from a different source of energy to start again. The memory vividly flashed behind her eyes as she held hands with Aimée.

The statuesque blond clutched Freya's hand until she opened her eyes with a gasp. Her hearing had returned with a vengeance. The drastic contrast between pure silence and noisy chaos had given her a jolt. Although Freya couldn't put her finger on it, she felt somehow more alive than she did a few minutes ago. Her body was still cold, and she was shaking to the core, but somehow everything was just a little more bearable. Aimée leaned close to Freya's ear and whispered in a conspiratorial manner, "Thank you, Freya. You saved my daughter. How exactly did you know?"

Freya smiled and met Aimée's grateful blue orbs. "Of course, Aimée. Is she okay? I don't know. It was just a gut feeling."

Aimée stayed quiet for a moment, as though she were slowly putting the last piece of a complicated puzzle into place. Her face held a look of pure shock as she stared at Freya. "Freya, why don't you come over to my place sometime next week so that I can make you a thank-you meal. Please don't say no. It's the least that I can do."

Freya let out a throaty chuckle as Scott placed a blanket over her still-shaking shoulders. "I would love to go to your home for a meal. Thank you." Her heart felt lighter with the knowledge that she was able to at least save someone. From the other side of the lake, it felt like someone or something was watching her, but Freya figured everyone was looking at the crazy woman who had jumped into the frozen lake. She thought hopefully to herself, *Maybe it's downhill from here.* If only she had known that nearly drowning in a lake was only the start to her ill-fated adventures in Wishburn.

Chapter 6

A faint sneeze echoed through the paneled bedroom, followed by a sigh of resignation. It had been four long days since Freya's dip in the lake, and the incident had successfully given her a cold. The warm bowl of chicken soup felt comforting in her aching palms. Usually Freya refused to eat in bed as she found it extremely unsanitary, but the sniffles and stiff joints seemed sufficient to justify an exception to the rule. Luckily her cold appeared to be short-lived and was already breaking, as evidenced by the copious amount of tissues tossed in the general direction of the trash can. After another round of sniffles, Freya plucked yet another tissue from the box that was placed dutifully by her side like a loyal lapdog.

Freya looked at her phone as tears threatened to spill onto the cotton sheets. Scott had been to the house twice since her unplanned dip into the lake. He had been extremely helpful when Freya had lost every fragment of dignity and needed to be carried from the lake and back to the festival grounds. Although her energy had returned, her limbs didn't want to cooperate. The doctor wasn't confident how Freya had managed to get herself out of the lake, let alone Layla who had been in the water for at least a few minutes.

Even though Freya had talked with Scott at the Autumn Festival about her marriage, the reality of her situation was finally setting in. Axel wasn't waking up anytime soon. Freya opened her contacts and stared at Scott's information. It would be so easy to type out a message and press send. Less than three seconds, and Freya could take Scott up on his offer for a first date. Freya continued to stare at her phone as her thumb hovered over the reply arrow.

Another sneeze ripped through the room, and Freya let out a frustrated groan. She testily rubbed her nose with a reused tissue. Scott's name seemed to grow as if the font itself was amplifying in size just to mock her.

Freya allowed a furious hiss to rip through her mouth and tossed her phone across the room. She bitterly mumbled, "Can't send a text if I don't have a phone. Axel is my husband. I love him."

"You look amazing, sunshine." Meg stood in the middle of the doorway with a teasing smile on her lips and a bright-red energy drink in her right hand.

Freya let out a stuffy snort and joked, "Thanks. I'm competing in the Ms. America pageant next week."

The older woman shook her shoulders with a jangle of laughter and walked forward to give the bottle to Freya. "I finished cleaning Axel. Would you like me to read to him today?" The question was casually asked from a place of kindness and compassion for Freya's mostly bedridden state, but it still tugged at her heart.

"No, thank you, Meg. I plan to start reading *The Great Gatsby* to Axel either today or tomorrow. It really depends on how quickly I read the last two chapters of *Middlemarch*. Between you and me, I think that I'm more excited than Axel to start one of my favorite books."

Meg didn't even bat an eyelash at Freya's dark sense of humor. Instead she rearranged her dark hair as it was coming undone in some places from her tight bun and mumbled, "*Middlemarch* would put me into a coma."

The two women shared a similar taste in what they considered quality comedy, and that just happened to include extremely biting banter. They already shared a fair amount of sharp jokes that tended to make light of dark situations. "Don't let me keep you two. That's a sad book if there ever was one, child. Reading one slow book just to replace it with an American tragedy." She sent Freya a wink and walked out of the room.

After another two days spent cooped up in her room, Freya was finally feeling well enough to get out of the house—and not a second too soon. Freya could easily video chat Aidan and look over charts from the comfort of her bed, but the errands that had been delayed for nearly a week were less flexible. She desperately needed to run to the supermarket now that her appetite had returned full force, and the idea of eating another can of soup made her want to cry.

Freya put her car keys in her silver chevron puffer jacket and closed the front door. She had decided that driving would be the best option so that she could bring back a proper amount of groceries. She was just about to unlock her car when movement from across the street caught her eye. Sally's unmistakably frumpy attire slowly came into view. Her long green skirt billowed around her waif-like frame in the light breeze, and the fabric dragged along the ground as she meandered down the sidewalk. Her arms were already rubbing up and down in order to try and retain some semblance of warmth.

Without thinking much of it, Freya started her car and drove over toward Sally. At the noise of the engine, the tiny woman instantly looked up from her feet. When she realized who was behind the steering wheel of the Jeep, she offered a large wave and a somewhat deflated smile. Freya rolled down her window, then put her car in park as she leaned out the window. "Need a lift? I'm going into town to get some groceries and would love some company."

In true Sally fashion, the small woman seemed hesitant to accept the invitation, as though it might be a trick or a fake offer of kindness.

Freya hollered, "I could really use a town buddy. Staying at home alone really tends to get lonely."

After a few more seconds of feet shuffling and deliberation, Sally scampered around the large SUV and hopped into the passenger seat. The temperature outside was well into the forties, and upon closer inspection of her passenger, Freya realized that she was lightly shivering in her threadbare green dress and hoodie.

Freya was about to turn up the heat, but something around Sally's neck gave her pause. Under poorly matched drugstore makeup were two massive bruises in the shape of handprints peeking above the neck of her hoodie. They were fresh, from what Freya could see through the mess of light-orange foundation.

As casually as possible, Freya turned up the heat as she put the car in drive and then lowered the radio to the perfect background noise for a conversation. This wasn't the first time, unfortunately, that Freya had seen the signs of abuse. In fact, a few of her employees had struggled with instances of domestic abuse, and those were just the ones that she and her company were made aware of. Freya had hired a domestic abuse specialist to work with her HR team because so often, survivors felt trapped in a vicious cycle and were rightfully scared for their lives and the lives of their loved ones.

Freya wasn't sure if this was the first time in Sally's particular situation that she had been physically hurt. Suddenly Sally's timid and skittish nature made so much sense to Freya that she had to bite her bottom lip to keep from saying anything hasty. She took another sidelong glance at Sally and noticed the bags underneath her eyes and how puffy her face was in general—doubtless from crying last night or earlier this morning. Freya tightened her hand on the steering wheel as if mentally grabbing hold of her conviction to help Sally. She only knew one thing for sure, and that was turning a blind eye to Sally's situation was just as bad as holding Sally still for another beating. Freya let out a shaky breath that was luckily covered by the music from the radio.

"Sally, you have a very nicely sized house. Do you live with anyone?"

The question seemed to take her by surprise, but Freya kept her eyes on the road, as if it was the most casual question in the world.

Sally hesitated for a minute before she clasped her hands within her lap and stuttered, "Y-yes, my husband, Tom. We've been together since I was in high school."

Freya nodded her head in encouragement. She didn't want to cut Sally off, in case she wanted to say more or wanted to get something off of her chest. The car was silent for a beat before Sally sniffled out. "I-I was young. I-I—we aren't the same people now."

The weight of her last sentence settled into Freya's stomach like rocks sinking to the bottom of a lake. *If I ever meet this bastard, I'll do my damnedest to take care of him,* Freya thought to herself miserably. She didn't know what to do since everything she did had the strong possibility to make things much worse for Sally. If Freya was honest with herself, it felt like she didn't know what she was doing. In the past, it always felt like she was at the top of her game, but now she wasn't even sure what she was playing. She had gone from knowing everything to knowing nothing, and now she had no choice but to take each day as it came.

Freya decided to volunteer a little information about herself so that the conversation felt less one-sided. "I'm married too, but it's complicated. We are definitely not who we were when we met. Mostly because I wasn't able to be honest with myself about where we were heading. I didn't take charge of my life." The statement was a bit of a fib, but it felt like Sally might need to hear the statement out loud. Freya quickly added, "Look, I know it's silly, but I haven't had a girl's night in forever. Let me know if you ever want to come over to my place. We can have a sleepover and just watch movies and talk. My house gets lonely… It's a little too big just for me, so you'd really be doing me a favor, Sally."

"Slide Away" by Miley Cyrus floated through the car speakers as Sally silently mulled over Freya's offer. From the corner of her eyes, Freya could see Sally absentmindedly picking at the loose threads on her gray sweater. As the CEO of a textile company, Freya had to bite her tongue to refrain from making an offhand remark about the importance of not picking at a fraying garment. At this point, the frivolous comment would probably make Sally cry, which was the exact opposite of what Freya was trying to accomplish. Freya once again sucked her bottom lip into her mouth as she busied herself by clicking the left hand turn signal.

A tiny voice whisked through the car and softly replied, "I would love to have a girl's night. It's been a while for me too since I don't really have many friends anymore. I would really like that, especially if the house is too big for you…"

Freya instantly chimed in. "It's *way* too big. I'm not used to all of this space, and it gets creepy at night. Walk across the street whenever and as frequently as you want to. Heck, if you don't want to live across the street, I have a spare room. A housemate would definitely help with the loneliness." Freya was mindful not to mention splitting the cost of housing like in a typical roommate situation. In domestic abuse situations, it was common that those facing abuse were also suffering from some form of financial abuse. Meaning they had no money or property to their name and therefore had nowhere to go if they left the situation. Freya hoped that the statement would at least entice Sally into coming over for tea or a chat more often. Even if the chances of Sally agreeing to move in were negligible, Freya just wanted to plant that seed. Freya wanted to drive home how welcome Sally was to come over whenever she needed.

Main Street had a few parking spots in the front of the various stores, and Freya was slightly grateful that they were standard parking spots as opposed to parallel parking options. Parallel parking in a tall SUV without scratching the rims always felt like an Olympic sport to Freya. Even though the car was on a lease and technically not hers, that didn't mean that she was going to treat it with any less respect. Luckily the street was wide enough to accommodate comfortable parking and passing traffic.

She was just about to turn into a spot when she let out a surprised, "Oh!" With a tinge of embarrassment, Freya turned to Sally and asked, "So sorry, Sally. Where are you going so I can drop you? I was so caught up in driving that I didn't ask earlier."

Sally looked up at Freya with doe eyes and replied, "D-don't worry. I was only headed to Scott's to pick up more beer. It's the only place I'm allo—I go."

Freya caught the mistake that Sally so hastily tried to cover up, but only nodded her head in acknowledgment. Freya's blood was boiling, and she was 90 percent sure that anything she had to ask Sally in regard to that statement would come out more like a furious hiss.

Instead Freya proceeded to park her car, grabbed her recyclable bag, and hopped out of the driver's side. The two walked into Scott's Supermarket, and the bell above the door rang out in greeting. Tanya was sitting behind the cash register and looked up to see the newcomers. To Freya's surprise, Tanya sent her a friendly wave instead of scampering into the back of the store like she had the last time. Freya called out hello in greeting and then picked up a shopping basket so that she could grab a generous amount of groceries.

Freya had successfully filled up the hand basket halfway with vegetables and tofu before a strong voice gave her pause. "Hi, Sally and Freya! Sally, if you're ready to pay, then I'm sure Tanya can help you."

Scott was wearing a smart blue button-up shirt and tan slacks as he smiled kindly in Sally's direction.

"Oh, Sally, I'll unlock the car so that you can put the beer in the trunk while I check out. I'll only be a few more minutes."

A small nod of her head was the only form of indication that she heard both Scott and Freya as she tentatively crept over to Tanya with two twelve-packs of beer. Freya pressed the unlock button and heard the evident beep in confirmation as Tanya then helped Sally to carry the beer to the Jeep.

Once the two were outside, Freya turned to chat with Scott. She casually tossed a can of chili and two cartons of eggs into her basket for good measure and then decided to call it a day.

Scott looked toward Freya and said, "I'm glad that you're feeling better. That was very brave, what you did for Layla. Crazy, but still very brave." His eyes held a newfound respect and admiration, and Freya felt compelled to look away in part because she felt Scott's feelings were wrong.

Freya turned back toward Scott as he continued, "I know that you said it's complicated with your husband, and you obviously aren't wearing your rings for whatever reason... I would love to take you out for a proper bite to eat." His eyes held such vulnerability, and his jaw slightly clenched and unclenched in anticipation of her response.

A tiny voice in the back of her mind whispered, *You should enjoy yourself with Scott...go out to dinner and see where it leads... Axel cheated on you, so you don't owe him your loyalty.* It felt as if she was at war within herself, as part of her wanted to accept Scott's invitation, move on, and feel better. However, a larger part of herself thundered that she owed it to herself to be loyal. That just because Axel had hurt her, it didn't mean she needed to go out of her way to give herself a free pass. Besides; she only wanted to use Scott as a distraction from her tangled emotions.

"Thank you, Scott. I doubt anything will change, but if it does, then you'll be the first to know." Freya held his gaze for a moment and then slowly walked over to the cash register to check out. Scott followed behind and placed her groceries inside of her reusable bag. "Scott, do you happen to know anything about a Tom? Sally mentioned that she's married to him, but I haven't seen him around and if I have seen him, I didn't know."

The question was meant to sound like a casual question and change of subject, but it was apparent that it struck a nerve. Scott's blue eyes clouded over slightly as he gripped the can of chili that he was bagging a little tighter than necessary. "Yeah, I know Tom. He was second-string quarterback when we were in high school together."

"Oh, really? Do you have any photos playing together? Then I can say hi if I see him around town."

It didn't escape Freya how Scott seemed to now visibly bristle. "Look, Freya, I'll show you a photo of us together, but he doesn't exactly look the same. The guy is bad news. Sally and I were sweet on each other before he stole her away. It's best you don't mention me if you ever have to talk to him."

Scott was always so playful and warm that it was so strange to see him turn so serious and concerned. The information shocked Freya since Sally seemed aged in ways that Scott was not.

She nodded her head. "Okay, how about a photo so I know who to avoid then? If my Wishburn tour guide advises against something, then it must not be a sight to see."

The forced injection of levity worked, and Scott allowed a tight smile to escape his lips. He finished bagging Freya's groceries and placed the remaining groceries that didn't fit in her reusable one into a paper bag. Then he reached behind him and plucked a framed photo off the back wall. "This was from when we were seniors. Tom is in the back." Scott pointed to a slightly scowling figure with a buzz cut and dark, almost black, eyes.

Even from the photo, the man looked somewhat imposing.

Another cursory glance over the photograph, and Freya let out. "Oh, look at you. Front and center for this photo shoot." Scott was kneeling and held the football in one hand as some of his teammates were smiling and patting him on his shoulder. It didn't take a genius to look at the photo and see the obviously brotherly love among at least most of the teammates. "Thank you for showing me. It's a great photo, and you've barely aged a bit." Although Scott had more smile lines around his eyes and a more defined masculine figure, he had somewhat remained the same.

"Thanks for the kind fib, Freya. I'll hopefully see you around town soon." Scott was chuckling, and his eyes were slightly squinted in glee as he handed Freya her two bags of groceries. Freya figured that Sally was probably already sitting in the car and wondering what was taking so long.

"See you around, Scott!" Freya hustled out the door as it jingled with her exit and found Tanya and Sally both chattering away by the open trunk. Tanya noticed her presence first and gave a small smile in her direction in greeting. If Freya didn't know better, she'd have sworn the woman had been abducted and replaced by aliens. Her reactions were absolutely night and day from the last time they had interacted. But Freya wasn't really one to poke a bear by asking for an explanation about the other woman's behavior. Sally finally turned around to see Freya, and her eyes were filled with a light that they generally didn't have.

"Tanya, it was so nice talking to you, and it really made my day." Sally seemed genuinely thrilled to have had a chance to speak with Tanya, and she walked forward to help take one of the grocery bags from Freya's arms and put it in the trunk.

"Thanks, Sally. It was good to see you again, Tanya. Did you win the pumpkin-carving competition?" The other woman widened her honey-brown eyes slightly at the question, but then showcased an award-winning smile.

"Yes, my girlfriend and I won. It's our third Autumn Festival in a row that we've won. It takes us weeks to plan our designs, but we always want to top the one from the year before."

Freya smiled as she placed the final bag of groceries in the trunk and then reached upward on her tiptoes to press the close button. "Congratulations, Tanya! That sounds amazing. Do you have any photos of it?"

Tanya reached into her back pocket and pulled out a white iPhone. Her fingers quickly glided over the password screen in a flurry and then flitted through her photos until she finally found one and turned her phone around toward the group. The pumpkin was carved to represent an elaborate scene of the main street of Wishburn. Each distinctive building was accounted for, and the light from the candle illuminated the image like a morning sunrise over the little town.

"It's genius, Tanya. You both should be very proud."

Tanya let out a megawatt smile and preened. "Thanks, Freya. It was my idea, but Alysheigh really put it together. She has an art degree from Otis." She tilted the phone back toward herself so that she could admire it once again.

"V-very pretty, Tanya. I didn't go to the Autumn Festival, but now it feels like I did." Sally nervously wrung her tiny hands in front of her body as she continued to stare longingly at the photo. Freya looked sideways at her new little friend and felt that her lack of attendance might not have been of her own volition. *Tom, you bastard.* Tanya allowed a dulled smile to grace her lips as she turned to the other woman. "Don't worry, Sally. There's always next year. We're kind of just soaking in the win, but we will be back to designing our pumpkin for next year in no time." Freya didn't doubt her for a minute. Tanya definitely seemed to have a competitive flare.

Freya rolled down her window and shouted to Tanya, "Keep me in the loop! I love creative projects and pumpkin guts."

The athletic woman threw back her long braided hair and laughed in glee as she waved goodbye. Main Street passed by at a gradual pace as Freya stopped frequently for kids running after lost soccer balls and young couples with overly excited puppies. It brought a smile to her face to witness the joyful vitality of the tiny community. She glanced Sally's way and couldn't ignore the fact that her driving companion seemed to feel the same way. Her slim chin rested precariously on the palm of her right hand as she gazed wistfully out the front window. Freya reached toward the center console and increased the volume of the radio ever so slightly as the two relaxed into a comfortable moment of silence.

Chapter 7

Freya wanted a new book to read in private. The irony of that conviction didn't escape her, but Axel wasn't exactly an active participant in their recent reading sessions. She wanted to find a thought-provoking book and privately bask in its beauty and intelligence. Freya wanted to feel like the only sunbather on a bright Florida beach. She craved to establish a sense of separation from Axel. It felt strange, but she wanted a book that she didn't have to share with Axel. After several phone calls with Aidan, she decided to visit Aimèe's bookstore and pick out a book that she could really dig into without having to read every word aloud.

The idea was enough to entice her to leave the house and brave the increasingly freezing weather. Scott had mentioned to her that it occasionally snowed in Wishburn near the middle of November, and after she heard that, all she could think about was buying winter tires and finding two sets of chains for her four-wheel-drive car. A small smile graced her face as she thought about how exciting it would be to be able to try her new car in snowy terrain. The weather definitely seemed to support the theory of eventual snow, but there was still a little over two months before the arrival of snow season.

With that thought on her mind, Freya quickly threw on her ankle-length puffer jacket and zipped up a pair of black metallic-tipped booties in order to add an ounce of fashionable flair to her oversized attire. She looked at herself in the rearview mirror and arched her eyebrow upward in approval of the new look. Freya thought to herself, *You can take the girl out of LA, but you can't take the LA out of the girl.* It had never occurred to her that she would end up living somewhere with cold weather, but the idea excited her and gave her the perfect excuse to buy a warmer wardrobe. From the comfort of her bed, thanks to online shopping, of course.

Tires squeaked in protest at the sharp turn, but in Freya's defense, there was only one half-visible sign from the main road. She let out a pleased hum from the back of her throat as lower-than-normal gas prices greeted her. Meg had been right about the unassuming station after all.

Gas wafted through the air as the pump steadily whirred to life. A beep joined the chorus of station noises as Freya locked the car and headed inside to place a few dollars on her pump. As she opened the door, a large figure brushed beside her. There were two sets of doors, so the attempted squeeze by a stranger was more than unnecessary. Freya held her ground, and instead of getting smaller, she widened her shoulders and muscled into the gas station first.

A teen sat behind the desk, and Freya smiled a polite greeting as she walked over to the counter with her necessary change in tow. To her surprise, the figure that had assaulted her peripheral vision loomed closer than necessary.

"How are you today, miss?"

The unintended slight caused Freya to wince as she replied, "Good. Can I please have $30 on pump number 4?"

Her hackles rose as the person behind her loomed closer into her personal space.

That's it, buddy.

Freya whipped around and stared down the man behind her who had managed to creep less than two feet away from her back. The space could comfortably fit around six people in line, and they were the only two in line.

"I'm almost finished. If you can just back up, then it will be your turn sooner." Freya sent a sugary smile in the gawker's direction. Her request obviously startled him as his large belly shook with every inch he retreated.

Apparently he was unused to being reprimanded. He wore thick sunglasses and a hat, but there was a slight tinge to his cheeks, as if he was embarrassed.

Freya returned her attention to the youthful attendant and made an effort to articulate a thank you. A small receipt landed in her palm. She then briskly walked out the doors and filled up her tank. It didn't escape her that the grimy stranger left seconds after her and sprinted back to his vehicle without bothering to fill his tank. The large black truck sped off into the distance and turned the curve in the road so abruptly that it looked more like a toy car prepared to fly off the track.

A quick glance at the clock on the Jeep's dashboard told her that it was a little bit past noon. In less than ten minutes, Freya had parked her car and was walking along Main Street. The wind had a sharp sting to it as she breathed deeply and felt the cold air circulate inside of her lungs. The chilly air swirled within her chest and caused her to wrinkle her nose in dissatisfaction. A nearly imperceptible shiver tickled her body as she tried to zip her jacket upward to cover her exposed neck. Although it was still early October, the changing temperature was a vastly different experience.

Freya wrestled with the zipper as a man across the street caught her attention. For some reason, she could swear that he looked vaguely familiar. He was walking in the direction of Paddy's Pub that was on the furthest end of Main Street. Freya narrowed her eyes in concentration as she watched the obviously oversized and out-of-shape man as he hobbled along. His hairline had mostly receded, but he seemed committed to the illusion of hair as he combed it over to one side. Freya was able to notice this fact from across the street as a large gust of wind whirled through the street and picked up the man's hair. It stood upward and exposed his shining scalp and then landed in a messy attempt at a comb-over.

Freya squinted her eyes and unintentionally held her breath, as if that would help her to gain a better view. When the lumbering man moved in a way that made his profile more visible, Freya was able to get a better glance at his rough features. That was absolutely Tom from the photo in Scott's store—the same man who had threatened her at the gas station. A generous amount of weight and several anger issues later, but that was most definitely Tom, as he licked his lower lip and leered at a fit young mother cradling her small child. His beady eyes seemed to follow the youthful woman as she walked obliviously down the street and cooed at her toddler. *Sally is batting way below her league with this creep.*

Freya's lips turned downward in disgust as if she had tasted something repulsive at the sight. The scene reminded her of a hungry fox prowling for its next meal outside of a rabbit's den. But at least in nature, predators hunted for survival and not for selfish sport. No, Tom was more of a rabid dog than an instinctive animal. The strange glint in his eyes only bolstered Freya's presumption. It was most likely a result of the sun reflecting on the windows and shining directly into his eyes, but Freya decided to accept the visual as a representation of Tom's character.

The air just above his head seemed to vibrate as if there was more information about him just out of Freya's reach. The sensation wasn't completely unfamiliar; Freya often felt as if there were glimpses of something meaningful hovering just above certain individuals. Freya mumbled to herself, "I really need to get my eyes checked. Guess it's time for reading glasses from all of these contracts."

Before Freya could be bothered to think about the repercussions, she quickly crossed the street and followed him from a distance. She swiftly weaved around other pedestrians as her mind came up with several worst-case scenarios all at once. None of them ended well for Sally, but Freya wasn't even sure how much time Sally had left if she stayed with Tom. There was no guarantee that Tom's next fit of rage wouldn't be Sally's last squabble. The thought of Sally possibly dying helped to temper Freya's nerves.

If there was one thing that Freya wanted, it was a sense of control. Sitting helpless for hours next to Axel as he remained silent was slowly eating her alive. After years of always knowing what to do, she suddenly felt powerless and at the complete mercy of the universe. She sped up and decided to make herself known to Tom about two doors away from the bar. The street passed in a blur of puffy jackets and business signs, but her sights were solely locked on a stout lumbering figure. A mental image of a bridge troll popped into her head, and Freya snorted out a breath of crisp air at the nearly uncanny resemblance. If Wishburn was a fairy-tale town, then Tom was the resident villain. Freya moved her slim legs twice as fast as normal in order to cover the gap. Once she was near him, she immediately detected the pungent scent of beer as it wafted off his clothes. Whether it was from day-old spilled beer on an unchanged shirt or from an early morning indulgence, Freya wasn't sure.

"Hi, my name is Freya, and I'm new in town. We met earlier at the gas station. You're Sally's husband, right?" The simple question seemed to spark a nearly imperceptible change in Tom's features as he rounded his girth in the direction of Freya's cheery greeting.

"Welcome to the town, sweetheart." The first half of his greeting was abruptly coated with sugar once Tom recognized Freya's face. The glint in Tom's eyes made her want to crawl into a ball and hide. Freya felt like he was mentally undressing her, despite the fact that she had mentioned his wife, Sally, not ten seconds ago.

"Tom, can we talk alone for a minute? I know just the place for us." It took every fiber in Freya's body to act as if she were interested in such a piece of scum. Freya used her most placating voice. It was the same one she liked to use with difficult business partners at the start of a meeting in order to describe the situation and regain control. She tried to keep her voice low and fleetingly wondered if the mandatory drama class that she had taken in high school might actually prove useful.

To her utter amazement, it seemed more than enough to convince Tom as he eagerly inched his potbelly closer into her personal space. Tom pushed his combed-over hair further to the side and let out a crooked bright-yellow smile.

"Lead the way, doll." He lurched along as Freya reminded herself that she had to walk and not run to Aimeé's Bookstore. *Genius half-cooked plan, Freya. Lead Tom into the bookstore and pray confronting him will scare him into leaving Sally alone. What could possibly go wrong?*

It wasn't a great idea by far, but it was the only one that she had. She tried to tell herself that one idea, even if it was bad, was still better than none. Freya couldn't silently observe Sally's abuse or allow Tom to victimize other women at random public locations. If Freya had the chance to help fix a terrible situation, then she would take it. She didn't want to acknowledge that her desperation to help Sally was deeply rooted in a need to reach a warped sense of repentance. It was as if a part of her thought, in the deepest parts of her mind, that if she completed enough good deeds, that maybe Axel would wake up. Talking to Tom was her attempt at making amends with the universe and gaining a sense of control that Freya had lost the day that Axel had fallen into a coma.

After a few seconds, the oddly matched duo finally reached the shop door. It seemed that they both read the handwritten sign at the same time as Tom's wolfish grin spanned across both sides of his face like some knockoff Joker. Freya's features grew stony from trepidation. The sign read in large cursive letters, "Enter at will. Grabbing some nutrients and will return momentarily." The sign absolutely screamed Aimeé from the eccentric wording to the extremely dramatic handwriting.

Freya mentally gave herself a pep talk that if Sally was brave enough to face this man in her house every day, then Freya could face him in a public place for a few minutes. She reached forward and pulled open the door to signal Tom inside first. She didn't want to make the situation anymore awkward by turning her back to him and giving him the opportunity to feel her up or ogle her backside. He immediately obliged and moved over the threshold with an unusual amount of effort for such a menial task.

"This will probably shock you, but this is my first time in this type of store. A man of my caliber, you know, can only get information from the finest places like television."

A strong emotion that was nearly the same as revulsion began to bubble upward within Freya's stomach. Tom was so confident in his own physical and mental prowess that it was nearly sickening. From his confident blemished grin to his wide hovering stance, she wanted to punch him at least once for all of it. Freya clenched her palms so tightly that she could feel her nails gradually cut into the soft flesh of her palm. The chaos of her furious emotions remained well hidden beneath a perfectly practiced calm veneer.

Her languid smile remained flawlessly in place.

Freya decided it was now or never to confront Tom as he slowly crept forward and closed the distance between their bodies.

"Tom, I saw the handprints around Sally's neck. Even though there is no excuse for what you have done, I want to know why."

"Listen, doll. I came into this store of books for a good time, not to be accused of things that I haven't done like some damn witch hunt. Sally and I had some good times. I really loved her when she was with Scott. She was pretty and hot and always listened to what Scott had to say. Nothing was the same once I convinced her to date me. She became awful."

The irony of his words didn't escape Freya as she looked at his stormy and foreboding demeanor. A witch hunt was a claim that couldn't be further from Tom's situation. In the old days, both extremely powerful and vulnerable women were persecuted for their oddity and power. A white male claiming that he was being persecuted—especially as an abuser of women himself—was infuriating. "So you found a way to get Sally because you were never able to measure up to Scott?"

"No! Sally was the best-looking girl in school. Of course she had to date me. But the bitch has a mouth on her. Sally just got worse after I married her, and her parents' house became mine."

It felt as if Freya's eyes were about to permanently cross from confusion. If Freya's anger was at the top of the chart before, then this new information placed her off the scale. Freya was pretty sure that Tom had threatened Sally to date him. It was as if he never truly saw Sally as anything but a way to compete with Scott.

Freya narrowed her eyes in disgust. "I'm going to give you two options, Tom. Either you leave town forever, or I make your life hell and make sure that you end up in jail, penniless, and miserable for the rest of your pathetic life." Freya held her head up high to emphasize the sincerity in her words.

"Listen here, you little bitch. I don't know who you think you are, but if anyone should be scared or leave town, it's you! You don't want to be the reason that Sally's life suddenly becomes complicated, do you? We can have fun, and I'll forget about this little talk."

"Leave Sally out of this, you coward!"

"She's the disobedient one. I can tell why you bitches are friends. She's probably told you everything, and that's why you're here to extort me. She just has to keep her mouth shut and do what I tell her to do. But she loves to get me mad. Don't worry, I'll deal with her once and for all after I take care of you."

Tom reached forward and roughly grabbed Freya's forearm. His sweaty palm encircled her slim wrist like a vice as he pulled her further into the store and in between two bookshelves. Freya let out a furious yelp as she tried desperately to pull his fingers off her already-bruised skin.

"Sally isn't your property! Let go of me, you chicken! If you let me go now, then no one has to know who you are."

Suddenly the air was swiftly knocked from her lungs. It took her a moment to process that Tom had backhanded her face so hard that she had stumbled into the corner of a massive hardcover book. The air was pushed out of her body so quickly that it felt similar to when she had nearly drowned. The sharp corner dug into the flesh between her ribs and nestled deeply toward her organs. It happened in less than a second, but the sensation left her wheezing. Freya felt her cheeks redden to a color several shades darker than her sunset-colored hair.

Instead of experiencing a more logical response like fear, Freya felt pure rage flood through her bloodstream. "Leave Sally and get out of this town, you coward. You think beating women will make you a man? Do you think that keeping her down and afraid is the work of a real man? Let's see what you're made of."

Freya's mind worked on overdrive to find a way around Tom and escape. Although Freya was smart, she was humble enough to realize that his brawn might be the end of her if she really ended up in a fight with him. Freya figured her best option was to stall until he moved enough so that there was an opening and she could escape. Hopefully a random passerby would enter the store, but Freya knew such luck was slim at best.

None of those options proved possible as Tom released a furious howl and launched himself at Freya. She blindly grabbed a thick book from behind her and hurled it with a vengeance. The book connected with Tom's nose and a sickening crack resounded through the air. A sharp scream thundered around the room as he scrambled to hold his now-crooked and bleeding nose.

Freya took that as her chance to run and tried to squeeze past his agonized form. She launched herself forward with the speed and intention of an Olympic sprinter.

"Not so fast, you little bitch!" An unforgiving hand latched around Freya's neck in the middle of her attempt to run past Tom. His grasp tugged her back and caused her to choke violently as she blindly grappled to remove the fingers that dug into her throat.

Freya desperately kicked backward, and to her surprise, she managed to swing her leg right behind Tom's kneecap. The action caused them both to tumble down to the ground in a flurry of desperate limbs. They struggled in a knot of twisted limbs. Suddenly, Tom lifted his leg and straddled Freya's midsection. He effectively pinned her down with his weight. Tom smiled like the cat that ate the canary and mockingly said, "Bye-bye, little bitch." His hands wrapped around Freya's neck, and Tom slowly increased the pressure. His eyes gleamed with crazed excitement as he held his weight down and effectively pinned Freya to the ground.

"You're a chicken, Tom." Freya rasped out the sentence as she wildly tried to kick and buck Tom away from her body. She tried to move him away so that she could at least get one breath of air into her desperate lungs. Just like when she was underwater in the lake, Freya was starting to see black spots crowd the edges of her vision. Her grasp around Tom's hands weakened as she stared upward into his manic smile. Tom tightened his grip once more around Freya's neck to the point that Freya felt like her head was seconds from becoming separated from her body.

Freya continued to look Tom in the eyes as she thought pointedly, *You're a chicken, Tom. You'll never know what it's like to be brave.* Her vision slowly left her, and a loud ringing was all that was left in her ears. It felt as though she were caught halfway between life and death.

Suddenly the weight around her neck vanished. Freya immediately tried to suck in a large gulp of air but failed as her body was wracked with coughs. Stars continued to dance around her line of vision, and her hearing was fuzzy. Slowly she heard herself as she spluttered for air, as her body remained sprawled out across the cold concrete floor. Freya reached a hand upward to assess the damage and let out a wounded whimper. The whimper itself even hurt the muscles within her throat as silent tears ran down her face. She kept her hand still as it hovered above her throat because it hurt too intensely to blindly assess the damage.

A burst of realization stopped Freya as she checked over her injuries. *Where did Tom go?* There was no way that he would intentionally leave the store before finishing her off. Freya knew too much, and the look in his eyes told her that he was truly enjoying her suffering. Freya lifted her body into a seated position. The action required all of the strength that she had left within her body. Instinctively she grabbed a large hardcover book to defend herself. Her gaze traveled around the store in search of Tom's towering figure, but her nervous glances were only met with disheveled bookshelves.

A loud crowing sound came from somewhere by her feet. Freya lowered her gaze and let out a startled gasp. A furious rooster stood next to her feet and angrily balked at her shoes. It spread its blondish–brownish feathers outward and continued to flap its wings at her. The bird tried and failed to menace her with its futile stature and less-than-impressive wingspan. The rooster then violently pecked on her shoe.

"Ow! Stop it, you little pest!"

Upon closer inspection, the rooster didn't seem that little at all. Freya didn't have a large amount of farm knowledge, aside from the odd visit to the petting zoo, but the bird definitely appeared to be on the heavier side.

Just then, Freya heard the front door open followed by the light clicking of heels. Aimée's svelte figure came into full view. Freya stared at the other woman and had the strong impression that Aimée was somehow an otherworldly being. Amethyst sauntered around the corner and remained a few paces behind Aimée. The black cat wrapped her silky tail around her front paws as her green eyes evenly observed Freya's disheveled form.

Freya's attention was drawn back to the rooster as it let out another ear-splitting crow. Amethyst was clearly not impressed as she let out an angry hiss that instantly halted the bird's show of indignation. The house cat began to lick its paws, as if satisfied by the display of dominance.

Freya remained on the floor and watched as Aimée took another scathing glance at the now-visibly more subdued bird. Aimée looked around the shelves for a moment with a critical gaze. The aisle looked as if it had been attacked by a hurricane with damaged books randomly crumpled and torn pages strewn around the area. Eventually Aimée returned her gaze to Freya and grinned. "The bastard had it coming."

Chapter 8

Freya didn't sleep. She had spent the night watching mindless romantic comedies and had gingerly tried to ice her bruised and swollen neck. Freya had decided that she would skip a visit to the hospital unless absolutely necessary. The marks were such prominent handprints that it would only invite more questions than answers. Freya had a feeling that she knew what had happened in the bookstore, but every logical part of her body reeled back from the thought.

Last night, after ensuring Freya was at least well enough to get home on her own, Aimée had promised to drop by in the morning and explain everything. Aimée was true to her word and promptly knocked on Freya's door at a little past nine in the morning with a disheveled Tanya in tow. One of Freya's guests was most definitely not a morning person.

"Thank you both for coming. Oh, Aimée, thank you for the bread-basket. I'll put the kettle on the stove so that we can have a little coffee."

Tanya let out a grunt in agreement and grumbled, "Just let me eat the coffee beans, ladies. It'll be easier."

Aimée arched an eyebrow, "Perhaps a bucket of Adderall would suffice."

"That's not funny…Unless you have some."

"Prescription abuse is a serious offense. I would never partake in such behavior."

"Well, Aimée, maybe you should."

Freya held open the door so that her two squabbling guests were able to enter. Aimée closed the front door behind her, and they both followed Freya toward the back of the house. Freya looked over to the guest room door that she had carefully closed and locked before inviting the two strangers inside. A baby monitor was discreetly placed on the kitchen counter behind the bread box in case any alarms were triggered in Axel's room. She couldn't put her finger on it, but for some reason, Aimée and Tanya piqued her curiosity.

Three extremely warm cups of coffee were cautiously placed on Freya's rarely used wooden dining table. Aimée gingerly held the artisanal breadbasket as she inspected which piece she wanted to place on her plate. Tanya wasn't as particular and placed two random pieces of bread onto her plate and then proceeded to select the three nearest pieces of cheese.

Tanya mumbled between bites, "I don't know about you two, but this spread is the perfect start to any conversation. Food that's delicious enough to pass an inspection by Ms. Fancy Pants is definitely welcomed by me."

Wow, they act more like sisters than small-town neighbors. Freya watched them situate themselves with mild interest as she patiently waited for them to get comfortable.

To say that Freya had questions after yesterday would be an understatement.

Tanya placed another slice of Brie cheese on her plate and then looked at Aimée expectantly.

"For the record, this is the kind of conversation that merits a strong cocktail, not just a cup of coffee." Tanya took a long sip of her drink as if to add emphasis.

Aimée let out a defeated sigh and replied dramatically, "It's nine thirty in the morning, and you want us all to get intoxicated to make this conversation easier?"

"Honestly a little liquid courage couldn't make this any harder. It's an uphill battle from here on out." Tanya plucked another piece of cheese from her plate and tossed it into her mouth. Her reaction was as casual as if warning the group that it was about to be another predictable sunny day.

Freya looked at the two women arguing over drink choices and exclaimed, "I have a full bottle of champagne and half a bottle of vodka. We can drink both if one of you will tell me what is going on!"

Aimée dramatically wrinkled her nose and agreed. "You have excellent taste. Bring the vodka, please. I can only stomach hard alcohol so close to dawn."

Aimée's face didn't provide the slightest indication that she was kidding. Freya's chair squeaked as she pushed it backward and stood up. "Okay, vodka it is. Would you like anything to chase it with or to make a cocktail?"

"No, thank you. I'll just wash down the liquor with a bit of champagne, if you don't mind."

Freya arched an eyebrow in slight surprise but then turned to get the two bottles. *This feels like stalling. I'm going to hate whatever they have to tell me.*

Tanya chimed. "Damn, woman. I'd hate to see what you can stomach late at night." Aimée only shot Tanya a cool glare as she refrained from entertaining her with a sharp rebuttal.

"Okay, here are the bottles, and here are the cups. Can you both tell me what's going on?"

Just then a large rooster walked sideways into the room and angrily flapped its wings.

It let out a loud crow and then furiously tried to rush toward the group of seated women. "If you know what's good for you, Tom, you'll march your chubby chicken butt out of this room before I make you into soup." Tanya languidly wagged a long and tan finger in the animal's direction as if she was scolding a petulant child instead of a common farm animal.

To Freya's amazement, the rooster fled the room as if its feathers were on fire. Freya looked toward Tanya and Aimée. Freya looked at them as if she was being pranked. Half of her expected Ashton Kutcher to pop out from underneath the table and shout that she was the butt of an elaborate joke. When their faces remained unchanged, Freya asked, "Tom?"

Freya held up the palm of her left hand and exclaimed, "Wait! I need to get a little food in my stomach before you tell me what I think you are about to tell me." She quickly poured out a shot of vodka and then threw it to the back of her throat. She automatically swallowed the liquid and allowed the familiar burn to provide her a small sense of comfort. "Okay, now I'm ready."

Aimée poured herself half a cup of the clear liquid and downed it in three sips. She pursed her lips slightly but said nothing in complaint. Tanya mumbled to herself with her still-untouched mimosa by her side, "White witches are really another type of woman." Freya snapped her neck in Tanya's direction and waited for her to elaborate. Tanya only shrugged her shoulders and replied, "Stupid is as stupid does."

Finally Aimée clapped her hands together and asked, "Freya, have you ever been strangely good at things compared to others? Just knowing things without really knowing them? The incident with Tom isn't the first one like this for you, is it?"

Freya frowned in confusion but replied honestly, "I have a relatively successful business back in Los Angeles, but never thought too much about my ability to connect and understand people. Maybe this is technically the second incident."

Tanya jumped in. Apparently she was not pleased with Aimée's round-about technique to get to the heart of the meeting. "Look, this is going to be hard to believe, but some of us are more tapped into sources of power and energy than others. For example, women generally are more attuned to that other side than men. Women create what is literally called the gift of life. We are givers of life, but we are also, at times, takers of life. Women are the link between the beginning and the end. So this connection allows us to be holders of a little extra gift. Magic, if you want to call it that. In the old times, women were revered for this connection, and that can be seen in what one today calls the Venus figurines…some of the statues date back over thirty thousand years. We let ourselves forget who we are…what many of us really are because men wrote the most recent history of the world and erased half of the population's accomplishments from its pages. Did you know that in Sparta, women who died in childbirth were given the same honors and burials as soldiers who died in battle?"

Aimée nodded her head in agreement with Tanya's strange and historically inclined explanation. Although both women seemed extremely serious about what they were saying, it felt more like a strange April fool's joke than anything true. Tanya let out a frustrated groan when she saw Freya's still unconvinced face.

"Tanya, maybe it's better to prove the truth through action rather than words." Aimée stood up and walked over to the wilted vase of foxgloves.

The purple flowers were even more downtrodden than usual. Freya had discarded most of the condolence flowers a few weeks ago. She had been surprised that they had managed to live so long. At one point, she had been convinced that they were all dying, but then strangely enough, the flowers had all bounced back and managed to live for a few days more. Now Freya was curious if their extraordinarily long life had anything to do with the preposterous claims that Tanya and Aimée were insisting upon.

Aimée looked over to Freya, her perfectly manicured light-pink nails hovering a few inches above the purple flowers. "Freya, I actually try to avoid using my skills on a daily basis. I let them out a little from time to time, but mostly Tanya and I try to live human lives. It's dangerous to be different in a mundane society. But too much magical suppression can actually drive a woman into insanity from pushing down and denying her true power. I could give a compelling explanation for why the majority of women sent to madhouses about a century ago were actually witches, but I digress. Tanya and I knew that you were like us from the second that we saw you, Freya. Now look at what you can achieve when you learn to master that power. Remember, don't be nervous."

Aimée turned her attention to the nearly dead flowers and closed her eyes. Freya continued to stare at the scene with rapt attention. After a minute of watching in silence, Freya turned her face to catch Tanya's gaze. Tanya saw her inquiring gaze and sent her a comforting wink and a small gesture with her hand. Freya interpreted the gesture as something along the lines of *stay where you are and have a little patience*. A trickle of sweat slowly built above Aimée's brow. It was almost imperceptible at first, but the color slowly grew more vibrant within each petal, and the stems straightened upward. Within a few more seconds, the flowers looked as if they were just plucked from a high-end shop. As if Aimée could sense the completion of her task, she opened her eyes and presented the vibrant flowers like Vanna White.

"I've known for years but haven't practiced enough to really be a strong witch. But, Freya, you are newly ascended, and your powers are already immense. They really radiate from you. That's why Tanya and I assumed that you knew what you are. It's not something to speak publicly about, but I don't see the harm in speaking among other witches."

Freya then turned to Tanya. Their initial interaction at the grocery store now made sense. Tanya had been wary of Freya and didn't know what her true intentions were in Wishburn. "How do you handle being a witch in such a closely knit small town?"

Tanya burst out in a fit of laughter to the point that she had to wipe several tears from her eyes. When her laughter had settled down to a jaded chuckle, she said, "I'm a woman, I'm black, and I'm a lesbian. To these small-town folks, the explanation that I'm a witch is easier for them to understand. The only thing that really got me through my teenage years in Wishburn was the beauty that I was able to find in my own diversity." Tanya sat back down at the dining table and took a fulfilling gulp from her previously untouched mimosa. "Welcome to the club, Freya. May you thrive in your differences."

Freya pulled out her own chair and hunkered down as Aimée picked up a napkin to blot her slightly sweaty face. It was nearly comical to Freya to watch her fuss over something so strangely superficial after she had only moments ago cleverly vanquished the visual signs of death. Freya's eyes suddenly widened in slight panic as she whisper-yelled, "Does that mean I turned Tom into a chicken? How do I turn him back?"

Tanya didn't waste a second before she quipped, "Tom was intent on doing worse to you, and he's already done worse to Sally…for years. We couldn't do anything after her parents suspiciously passed away after they got married. They never liked Tom, but there wasn't any proof to say that he did it. He's dangerous to most people. I'd say this is The Rule of Three just evening the scales back to their original state." As she was speaking, her fingers selected another piece of bread and added three random slices of cheese on top.

"I'm not as worried about Tom at the moment now that I know about—" Freya's voice faltered as she mentally struggled to accept a concept that she had watched tons of movies about as a kid. "Being a witch. The real reason I left Los Angeles was for a slower pace. But the motivating factor came from my husband, Axel, falling into an unexplained coma. The doctors don't know what caused it, but I'm starting to think I might. Do you know how to reverse magic? I'm assuming it's more complicated than clicking the backspace on the computer, but I'm not afraid of a little work."

Aimée silently played with the used napkin in her hand. She continued to crunch and roll it around in her palms as she looked deep in thought. "I don't know how to undo something so complex, but I'm sure three souls committed to this endeavor are better than one."

Tanya placed down her drink before seconding, "Yeah, what Aimée said. Let's look into this. There must be some books on this. Hey, Freya, where is your family from?"

"Well, my mom lives in San Francisco—"

"No, like where are your family roots? For example, I know this is a shocker, but my roots are in South Africa. So my magic has a line of power from thousands of years based in African history. It's kind of like how each witch has their own energy signature on a spell, but the magic in your blood is more in tune with a certain type of climate or may call out to a familiar that is more likely from that region."

"Wait, so you're telling me that the magic in my body somehow has a memory of a past that happened before I was even alive?"

Aimée just nodded her head, the slim fingers of her left hand framing the bottom of her face. "Think about it in terms of the way our DNA is encoded with the ability to remember past events. It's like a road map in our souls that guides us in our lives. We are never truly casting a spell alone, darling. I would love to know about your ancestry. There must be more than a few legendary women. You're already insanely gifted, Freya."

"Thanks, Aimée. I know both my mom and dad have roots in Ireland, but that's all I really know about. Guess it's time to find out."

Tom poked his beak around the corner of the kitchen, as if he were an eavesdropping detective instead of an abusive man in a chicken's body. Freya realized that she didn't want Tom strutting around her house when she was gone and let out a startled, "Oh, Tom! I'm going to put you in the spare bathroom. Don't worry, I'll lay down some newspaper and have a bowl of water for you."

She stood up to try to shoo the rooster into the bathroom, but it tried to look intimidating. Tanya pulled out a large pot from underneath the sink and gestured to it with glee. She was having more fun than she could express humbling Tom and his horrible temper. Freya looked at Tanya's emphatic gesture and let out a snicker as the rooster went running. She found Tom cowering in the corner of the bathroom behind the toilet. In his haste to get away, he had left droppings in the middle of the wooden hall-way. She wrinkled her nose in disgust as she placed a layer of newspaper on the tiled bathroom floor and placed the rug on the counter so Tom couldn't make a mess. She then took a small bowl and filled it with sink water before she placed it closer to the door. Freya sighed, but then locked the bathroom door with a key from the outside. The last thing that she wanted was a rogue rooster running around her house and possibly tampering with some of Axel's machines.

The droppings formed a crooked line through the very middle of her hallway. Freya reveled in the irony that the man who claimed he was superior to Sally was literally shitting himself in fear around her house. She opened up the hallway closet and pulled out two paper towels and dabbed one full of Lysol. In no time, the floor was back to its original state of cleanliness, and Freya was able to return to the kitchen. She opened the silver trash can and plopped the debris inside and then went to the sink in order to wash her hands for good measure.

Tanya wiggled her eyebrows at the other women. "Who wants to go on a brunch run? The diner opens in ten minutes, and I'm starving."

Freya let out a snort, but she was already throwing on a floor-length black puffer jacket. The women quickly cleaned the plates in the sink and then placed the remaining bread and cheese away for another time. The cleaning only took a few minutes, given the dedicated six hands working to get to the diner before the morning rush. Aimée plucked her coat from the hook by the door and then handed Tanya hers as well. It looked as if they were all going to different events as Aimée wore a possibly faux fur coat, and Tanya sported a simple denim jacket over her hoodie. Everything about them was different, from their history, to their clothes, and especially their features. But somehow the trio melded together in a strange harmony as they found a commonality deeper than their reasons for division. It felt nice to have a sense of belonging. Even if the group she now belonged to dabbled in the occult.

The girls walked out the door and chatted on their way to town. Their bodies were warm thanks to a sense of community and, in part, because of liquid courage. Freya let out another snort as the girls turned the corner toward Main Street.

Chapter 9

Calming moonlight peaked through the tops of the forest trees. Freya sat on the swinging porch chair, gazing out at her expansive backyard. The well-manicured grass closest to Freya's home slowly gave way to unrestricted bushes and towering trees that led into the entrance of the forest. Wishburn locals apparently had more than one curious story circulating around town where children and women had mysteriously wandered into the woods but never returned. Some even said that the forest was linked to the spirit realm. Freya didn't mind the stories and myths as they only added to the charm of the sleepy town.

The gentle light of the moon was supplemented by the bright glow of Freya's porch chandelier. The industrial iron circle added a modern flair to the log cabin. Without any context, Freya was sure that it looked more like an isolated summer cabin than a home in a small California town. Her lip quirked upward at the idea that she had managed to rent such an odd little piece of heaven.

Freya's gaze was suddenly drawn to movement within the dark woods. A figure low to the ground prowled closer to her backyard. Two bright green orbs shone from the edge of the forest and stayed in its place for the length of two heartbeats. For some reason, Freya could have sworn that she knew those eyes from somewhere. It was strange that such an ominous figure inspired a surge of curiosity in Freya rather than a striking fear. She inched herself closer to the edge of her seat as she placed her feet on the ground in order to put a halt to the movement of the porch swing. The chains above her head rattled in protest as they tried to continue their rhythm. Freya was far too absorbed in her inspection of the woods to be bothered by the annoying clanking. From the height of the glowing orbs, Freya decided that it was safe to rule out the option of a bold raccoon. They frequented her yard during dusk and dawn, but this creature seemed too tall to manage such a generally minuscule title.

All of her senses were focused on the green eyes that increasingly glowed brighter as the figure emerged, inch by inch, from the shadows. Freya drew in a breath at the massive shape and guessed that it must be a lone wolf from its sheer size. Her assumption quickly proved wrong as a massive mountain lion emerged from the woods and stalked into the spacious backyard. A gust of air left her lungs as she focused on the majestic animal. Freya swore that she was losing her mind. The gorgeous beast in front of her looked exactly like the mountain lion that she had almost run over in Los Angeles a little over a month ago. There was no way that it could be the same big cat, but for some reason, a feeling within her gut said that it was. The massive amount of muscle and sheer intelligence in its eyes confirmed her wild suspicion.

Within a few seconds, the cougar had effortlessly closed the distance between them and then held its ground only a few feet away from the wooden porch. It seemed to be observing Freya and waiting for her to make the first move.

Freya tilted her head to the side and exclaimed, "How are you? You really are impressive, but I'm sure that you already know that." As if the cat understood what she was saying, it let out a playful meow and walked up the two shallow stairs to reach the porch landing. The two were now within five feet from each other.

Freya stared in awe and had the strange urge to reach out and pet the cat's fur. She wasn't exactly in the mood to get slashed to ribbons and decided to play it safe and not act on any strange impulsive ideas just yet. "Hi, gorgeous."

The large cougar leaned forward and arched its body so that its bottom was sticking up in a yoga position. Claws nearly four inches long extended from its front paws as the panther stretched outward and opened its mouth to let out something similar to a yawn. The size of its massive teeth didn't deter Freya one bit from her deeply rooted feeling of safety. After a few seconds of lazy stretching, the wild cat padded forward and then elegantly curled itself into a comfortable position below Freya's feet. She wasn't exactly an expert on big or wild animals, but Freya felt that this mountain lion was definitely on the larger size, as its broad frame was too large to comfortably wedge itself completely between the porch swing and floor. Instead the feline inched its body underneath the swing and then managed to lift the porch swing further upward and away from the ground. Freya wrapped a hand around the porch chair chains in order to steady herself. A throaty chuckle escaped her lips as her eyes remained glued to the furry figure literally beneath her feet.

With painstaking patience, Freya placed her hand closer and closer to the big cat. Freya watched the large ears swivel in her direction, as if the big cat couldn't be interested enough to even look at her. She didn't want to spook the mountain lion, so she made sure to place her hand where it could see first. Freya wasn't exactly sure what rule book to play with, so she decided to treat this situation similar to meeting a new stray cat. To her surprise, the feline nudged its large furry head into her palm and began to purr in content. The cat rubbed its face along her hand as she watched with rapt attention. It was definitely one of the strangest events that had happened in her life to date. Not the strangest since the past month of her life had occurred, but definitely a top-ten moment.

A thought then crossed her mind about the importance of the cat in her life. *Maybe this mountain lion is my familiar?* She had heard the girls mention it briefly when they were at her house the other day and wondered if each witch had one. It seemed strange that she would have such a strong and imposing animal as her familiar. All the television shows and movies that had witches and familiars seemed to pair witches with smaller animals like house cats or even toads and rats. Subconsciously Freya wrinkled her nose at the thought of a toad familiar. It just didn't feel right to her.

Another more firm headbutt to the palm of her hand pulled Freya back to the moment. She smiled in content at the peaceful cat and then moved her hand downward to rub underneath its chin. The cat let out a louder purr, and Freya asked, "You're just like a big kitty cat, aren't you? Want to be my new *National Geographic* version of a best friend?" A louder mew of content came from the cat, and Freya assumed that it was a sign of confirmation.

The two sat in silence as they looked out into the forest and enjoyed the calm atmosphere. Freya wasn't sure what time it was when the big cat eventually stood on all fours. The mountain lion wiggled out from underneath the porch swing, and Freya once again gripped the chain on her left like her life depended on it. Freya allowed a nervous chuckle to escape her lips at the absurdity of the situation when the cougar finally readjusted itself only a few feet from her face. It turned its neck to the side and licked her jean-clad knee, as if in goodbye, before it stealthily disappeared back into the forest.

For a moment, Freya wondered if she was really losing her mind and had just imagined the entire scenario. However, the large wet spot on her knee was the only evidence that she needed to prove that she did, in fact, have an extremely friendly mountain lion in her neighborhood. She watched as the last flick of its tail disappeared into the darkness before she stood up and went inside the house to get warm.

She hadn't noticed it, but it was well below thirty degrees outside, and her fingernails were already slightly blue in color. *Well, that explains why I struggled to open the backdoor.* Freya stripped and quickly hopped in the shower to warm up. She closed her eyes and allowed the hot water to pelt against her body. The steam helped to open her lungs, and for a few blissful seconds, Freya stood motionless, reveling in the stillness. A feeling of peace surfaced in her heart and slowly spread outward as she tilted her head up to enjoy the warmth of the pounding water against her chilly skin. After a few minutes, Freya emerged from the shower and changed into one of Axel's shirts. It was more like a short dress on her petite frame, and even though he hadn't worn it in months, his scent still lingered near the collar. It was the first night since she had moved to Wishburn that Freya wasn't going to bed with a tiny knot of anxiety in her stomach.

The walk to the guest room was calm, aside from the occasional temperamental clucking from Tom. Freya had taken the liberty of buying a baby gate after eating at the diner with the girls. The rooster was safely enclosed for the night in the confines of the kitchen so that he wouldn't get into any mischief. Once she was outside of the guest room, Freya took a minute to look at Axel's face.

Freya had so many swirling and juxtaposed emotions every time that she thought of her husband that looking at his face only increased the flurry of feelings tenfold. Part of her fully resented him and wanted to move on. That part constantly told her to accept Scott's offer to go on a date and see where it led. Another part of her didn't like what Axel had done but understood that she pushed him away by focusing all of her attention and love elsewhere. She gently moved onto his bed and mindfully situated herself in a way that wouldn't disturb any of the lengthy wires that were attached to him. She turned on the bookshelf lamp so that she could read to Axel the start of *The Great Gatsby*. Freya carefully placed her head against his chest and listened to his heartbeat as she thought about a quote that she had memorized long ago. It struck particularly close to her heart as she wondered if, in some ways, she too was Gatsby. Was she merely a boat beating against the current, chasing a past that no longer belonged in the future?

Chapter 10

Coffee trickled down into the waiting pot while Freya stared as if each drop of caffeinated liquid was gold. Although she usually preferred to drink tea, she wasn't about to be particular about her wants versus her needs. She needed every drop of energy that she could possibly muster before calling her mother. It had been a few days since they had last spoken. Freya had held off on calling Joan because she knew that her mom could read her tone of voice like an open book. After a few minutes and a hearty gulp of coffee, Freya felt more like herself. She wanted to see how her mom was doing and, if possible, hear about Aidan and the company.

She had tried to reach him twice yesterday, and the line was continually unavailable. When Freya checked the schedule, it listed only two conference calls for the day. Freya generally asserted her agenda and finished each call in less than an hour. So it was odd that Aidan, who had such a gift for finances, would take so much longer to complete the same simple project. To add fuel to the fire of her curiosity, Aidan only texted a reply to her late the night before that he had had a long day and would call her in the morning. Unsurprisingly Freya had no intention of waiting around for a reply and decided to politely attempt to shake down their mother for information before Aidan called. This was one situation that Freya figured she could control by being proactive.

The final drops of black sludge trickled into the coffeepot, and Freya licked her lower lip in anticipation. For good measure, she had brewed twice the regular amount of ground coffee beans. She carefully poured a cup for herself and pursed her lips at the sight of steam escaping into the air. Freya gently blew across the scalding surface and allowed the cup to remain on the counter for fear of spilling it on herself or the floor. The scalding brew burnt the tip of her tongue, even though she had blown over its muggy surface for several seconds. With a sigh, Freya knew that she could no longer delay the inevitable and called her mother. Although it felt like her entire life had changed since their last phone call, she planned to completely avoid telling her strange new reality to her mom.

Joan answered on the second ring and gleefully exclaimed, "Freya, I was just thinking about calling you this morning. I saw a very good article on the book of faces today and wanted to show you."

Freya could only imagine what article her mother wanted to show her this time on *Facebook*. Two weeks ago, Joan had publicly posted to Freya's page an article about dating after the death of a partner. Even worse, ten of Freya's "friends" had liked the post. It definitely did nothing to temper Freya's furious emotions when Joan was acting like Axel was already in the grave instead of indefinitely resting a few feet from the kitchen. Her mom didn't even know about the cheating incident, and already she held an intense amount of animosity for Axel.

As Freya dwelled on the issue, she realized that her mother was never fond of any of the men that she had dated. Even in high school, when she had dated the star quarterback who had a scholarship to Brown, her mom had turned up her nose. It was almost like no man was good enough for Freya in Joan's eyes. Especially Axel. When they first started dating, Joan had offered Freya an all-expenses-paid trip to Hawaii on the condition that she would never see Axel again. At the time, Freya had laughed at the offer and considered it an elaborate joke, but now she wasn't so sure. *What if Joan had offered Axel a similar deal, and he too had refused?*

"Can you hear me, Freya? It's an article about exercising at home when you have to work from home. Maybe you can tone up a little before returning to the dating scene. It sounds very promising. Do you have bad reception right now? Should I call back later? I have a free morning and afternoon since the book club was cancelled. Tiffany got the flu again."

Freya angrily picked at a loose string from her cotton cowl-neck sweater in irritation.

"I'm here, Mom. Thanks, I'll look at it in a bit. How have you and Aidan been?"

A mumbling sound that was Joan's signature sign of displeasure rang through the line. "I'm fine, darling, but apparently your brother had a bit of a day in the office. You scheduled him for not one but two phone meetings yesterday, Freya! They took him three hours each to get through, so he didn't even leave the office until seven at night. Aidan got home to his fiancée and then got an earful about missing dinner. That's just too many long meetings for a single day, Freya! That's not very thoughtful of you."

Freya didn't bother to suppress the indignant snort that had been building at the back of her throat. There were so many sharp remarks that she felt like saying, but Freya decided not to stir the pot. Instead she merely replied, "I gave him exactly the work that I would do within a day. When Aidan calls, I'll help him narrow the issue down and sort everything out." Freya inhaled before continuing, "Anyway, Mother, would you like to come and stay with me sometime? Perhaps for a weekend or so?"

Freya mentally pictured strangling herself at the offer as soon as she had said it. It was true that her mom now had nothing to do in San Francisco as a retired empty nester, but that just left Joan more time in the day to meddle and fixate on her children's lives. But even though she managed to get on Freya's every last nerve like no other person in the universe, Joan was still her mother. For better or for worse. *It's like the marriage that I never agreed to.*

"Oh, that would be wonderful, Freya! I'm busy this week as I plan to have a housekeeper come sometime to help clean up, but maybe in the next week or two. Then I can print out all the articles for you and show you the highlighted parts that I absolutely adore."

Freya's mental self was now trying to throw her off a cliff. There was nothing that Freya hated more about spending time with her mother than reading, line by line, some unmerited hippie doctrine written by disbarred doctors or practicing life coaches who preyed on a loyal following of older people. Joan was such a smart woman, but the articles she enjoyed reading online always managed to astound Freya.

"Okay, let me know which weekend works for you, and I can pick you up from the airport and drive you to Wishburn." The closest airport was in Brighttown, the next town over, since Wishburn didn't have enough people interested in or in need of traveling. Most materials were either brought into the town in truckloads or just ordered individually and delivered by a postal worker. The town was still very remote in terms of access to the outside world.

"Sounds lovely, Freya. I will send you my dates sometime this week using text. How exciting! A mini staycation."

"Love you, Mom, I'll call you another time."

"Love you, little cat."

The line clicked off, and Freya lowered her smartphone to look at the screen. She pulled it back just in time to see Joan's contact photo disappear back into the home screen. The picture was of her mother holding up their scruffy white-and-gray house cat. Mr. Scruffles had to be at least in his late twenties as an aged domesticated feline. Joan was smiling broadly in the photo as Mr. Scruffles made a half-grimace, as his upper lip curled upward to reveal his sharp canines. Joan in the picture had her hair cut in a smart bob and had a pair of reading glasses held by a string hanging across her white knit shirt like a necklace. Freya had taken the photo at her mother's fiftieth birthday party. It had been a rather relaxed affair and had only included around ten people who were mostly neighbors or old coworkers.

Birthdays and other momentous family events always made Freya think of her departed father. She wondered what it would feel like to grow up in a conventional household that the artists and television shows of the

1950s always raved about. Part of her felt that her drive and starvation to achieve so much might have been different if her life had been more financially comfortable growing up. Seeing her mother struggle to support her and Aidan had instilled a strong work ethic and need for control in Freya. She often wondered if that resolve might not have blossomed under a simpler path.

The day before she married Axel, she had wondered what her father would look like a little more aged than when she had last seen him. Would his eyes have crow's-feet from a life full of too much laughter or would his brow be permanently furrowed with worry lines? It was hard for Freya to really make an educated guess. She hadn't known him with wrinkles because that part of his life never fully came to maturity.

Growing up, there had been very few photos of her father available. Not one picture frame included his presence. Freya supposed it was just too painful for her mother to think of the past, and so she avoided obvious daily reminders. Freya never felt the need to pry about the intense sadness that hovered over her mother like a stifling blanket. All of the questions and daydreams didn't really matter in the end. Her father had passed away before Freya had even reached the fourth grade. He was struck by a bolt of lightning on a previously clear summer evening. It was understandable that Joan didn't like to bring him up in conversation, especially given the fact that she had also been outside when he had died.

Freya noticed Meg with two cups. "Well, don't just stand there, child. Help me with your hot chocolate."

Freya's eyes immediately lit up like a kid on Christmas as she eagerly walked forward to grab the chocolaty treat. "Thank you so much, Meg! I take it that you're having a dreary morning?" Even though Freya had half a pot left of extremely strong coffee, Meg's gift held much more appeal. Freya could tell that it was one of the signature drinks from the coffee house on Main Street that she still had yet to explore on her own.

"Just positively dreary, hon. The weather is nice. I found a humming-bird eating from the feeder outside my door this morning and had time for a little bite to eat."

Meg placed her bag on the kitchen counter and sat down on one of the wooden chairs with her own drink in tow. Freya nestled into the adjacent seat, and the two chatted until it was officially time for Meg to begin her shift. It felt nice to talk to someone who wasn't as batty as Joan. Freya secretly dreaded the day that she would start to act like her mother.

Chapter 11

After a brief moment of consideration, Aimée had generously agreed to allow Freya to inspect her private collection of books. There were a few in the back room that had been handed down from her mother, grandmother, great-grandmother, and even great-great-grandmother. It seemed Aimée's Bookstore actually had a deep history as a matriarchal family business. It dated all the way back to the 1800s to right around the time of the California Gold Rush. Established in a time when there were no true laws between travelers. The only true bond was between a person and their spirit as they traveled the unknown sprawling deserts. The rugged adventurers possibly saw the blue Pacific Ocean if they traveled far enough.

Aimée's great-great-grandmother had traveled the vast distance from New York to the land of bright orange and yellow poppies in a covered wagon with about ten dollars to her name. This wasn't exactly her first adventure as she had left England for its ex-colony about a year earlier. Her departure, as she had coyly explained, was due to the threat of religious persecution. Apparently on her first excursion across North America, she eventually settled in the town of Wishburn. In order to achieve her dream of owning her own bookstore, Aimée's great-great-grandmother masqueraded as a man to hide her true identity.

The scheme had been foolproof until she met the owner of the largest cattle ranch in the area. According to legend, not only was he extraordinarily wealthy, but he also was the most attractive man in town. The two met when he ambled into her store, and they ended up talking well into the evening as other customers came and went. After a few months, Aimée's great-great-grandmother eventually revealed herself as a woman while holding him captive at gunpoint. This fact led Freya to believe that a flare for the dramatic was literally in Aimée's blood. A little over nine months later, Aimée's great-grandmother was born, and the rest was history. The couple had fooled everyone into believing that the original owner of the bookstore was extremely eccentric and had sold the bookstore to the cattle rancher on the condition that his new wife look after it. So for almost two hundred years, Aimée's family had accidentally become the only true history keepers of the tiny town.

Freya watched as Aimée opened the padlocked wooden door to the back room. The wooden door swung away and revealed an intricately designed inner room. The wall directly across from the entrance held a row of stained glass windows depicting different women in varying activities and adventures. All of the women vaguely resembled Aimée, with their striking blue eyes and bright-blond hair. Freya realized that these windows most likely were a way to commemorate Aimée's matriarchal lineage. As Freya looked around the fairly sized room, she noticed an oil lantern placed on an elderly school desk that was pushed into the corner. The papers and documents seemed to fill each crevice from one corner to another. The light from the windows generously illuminated the room and made it easier for Freya to maneuver around the massive stacks of books.

Aimée entered the hideaway and explained, "The room is enchanted. That's why you can't see the stained glass windows from outside of the building. There are no light switches here in order to keep the original energy and power flowing through the room without interruption. Don't worry, the light will remain until the sun sets outside. My great-great-grandma was an absolute genius when it came to engineering ways to thrive as a witch without being seen."

Freya nodded her head in awe as she drank in the details of the room. From the antique bookshelves lined with novels and scrolls to the strange candles and herbs hung on hooks near the entrance to the room, it was like an ancient bookshelf. Freya was momentarily rendered speechless, mesmerized by the sight. After several moments of rapt observation, Freya murmured, "I would love to know even half of what she knew."

A tinkling laughter filled the room as Aimée mirthfully replied, "Well, if you read through this collection, you'll be able to know what over four generations of witches learned in their lives. I haven't sat down to really read them all myself, but the ones that I have looked over are very impressive. Let me know if you need any help. I shall be at the counter. I'll come to retrieve you around noon, and we can grab a morsel for lunch."

"Thank you so much, Aimée. That sounds perfect." Freya turned around to fully take in the expanse of the room and contemplated where to start. In the end, she settled upon searching the tallest pile of books nearest to the old desk, which looked as if it had been rifled through the most. The binding of many books in that particular stack was worn, and some of the pages were even poking out. Freya peaked at the spines of various books and realized the most commonly looked through ones were comprehensive blends of magic health care. One of the titles explained how to help a child through common earaches and teething pains with simple herbal remedies often found throughout New England. Freya guessed that the book most likely belonged to Aimée's great-great-grandmother, as she was the only one that Freya knew had lived on the East Coast for a period of time. The second clue to help bolster her assumption came from the knowledge that the book had been manually bound.

After several hours of searching through titles and skimming pages from different promising leads, Freya grumbled in frustration. She wandered over to a stack of books at the far right corner of the room. Freya plopped her head back into the wall and simply took a moment to breathe. There were just so many books, and the information within each book looked just as interesting as the next but didn't really pertain to helping Axel. From the corner of her eye, an unassuming brown leather book with silver cursive on its spine managed to attract her attention. She squinted her eyes in an effort to try and read the title from across the room, but then let out a sigh and decided to just get up and walk the six feet in distance. Something in Freya's gut told her to investigate the relatively thick book. Gingerly she picked up the book and felt the weight of its pages and smelled the old paper as she opened it. The large silver cursive letters read, "The Rule of Three and the Echoes of Divinity." *Maybe this is the winner, hopefully I know how to read Old English.* The longer she stared at the pages, the more Freya was able to realize how perfect the book might be to solve her mounting problems.

Heels clicked into the center of the room, and Freya looked up to see Aimée's curious gaze. "Any luck, Nancy Drew?" Aimée noticed the book that Freya was peering at and made a small indication toward it with her chin.

Freya smacked her lips and replied, "I think this just might be a winner. The only thing is that it might take a bit for me to be able to actually read and fully understand its meaning. The writing seems to be very old and neat, so many of the words will probably be older English. It's just a matter of time, though, before I figure them out and can see if there is anything promising."

"Excellent! Would you prefer I meander to the diner and bring you back a bite, or do you think you can spare a little bit of time for a momentary reprieve and hopefully a slice of apple pie?" Aimée paused and then whispered, "I believe that it's a period craving." As if there was anyone else to hear the normal admission.

Freya let out a joyful laugh at her friend's explanation. It was just too impossible to pass up an offer of lunch and a sweet treat. Freya wasn't going to pass up an opportunity when it presented itself. She stood up with the book still in her hands and then placed it on the wooden desk. "Will it still be here when we get back?"

Aimée nodded her head in confirmation. "Yes, the books usually stay where you place them last, but random items tend to appear and disappear at will."

The explanation didn't exactly make sense to Freya so she prompted, "Wait, so what moves around in this room?"

"Well, the timepiece over there isn't always in the room and neither is the amulet. They kind of come and go as they please, but the books always stay in their place." Aimée shrugged her slim shoulders and then turned to leave the room.

Once Freya had exited the room, Aimée closed the door and locked it as she said something under her breath. She glanced sideways at Freya and explained, "If someone breaks in, it will just look like a tiny storage room. The room has to be called back into existence by a blood relative of the original owner. An ingenious trick, if you ask me. You know, since you've been in town I've had to use my magic more often. I've honestly never felt better. It's almost as if I'm connecting to a previously repressed part of me that I never really knew existed, and this part of me is very peaceful. I repressed my own magic because I was scared of what it would do, without taking into account the beauty it can leave behind. Even my husband has mentioned that my mannerisms are different." Aimée then fixed her already perfectly styled hair, as if having a vulnerable conversation could somehow visually rattle her flawless appearance.

Amethyst blinked her large green eyes in greeting and let out a meow toward Aimée. The blond walked over toward her affectionate cat and rubbed behind its ears. The black cat began to purr and rubbed its head along Aimée's lean fingers. "Freya, Amethyst is my familiar. She's like an extension of myself in a different form, but with equal value. I suppose now that you are more aware of your powers, your familiar may arrive at any moment now. Don't just assume or accept the first wise creature that you meet. There must be a mutual bond or link from the start or the pairing is bound to fail. A weak bond will hamper both of your performances. So select wisely and proudly cultivate that relationship."

With one final caress, Aimée whispered a farewell to her familiar and then locked the door to the shop behind them. "No need for a repeat of last time. I don't believe we would know what to do with another rooster." Aimée sent a playful wink in Freya's direction.

Freya couldn't agree more, and the two women began to talk about more menial topics that if overheard wouldn't send them straight to the loony bin. A rumbling from Freya's stomach helped to confirm the need for a lunch break. Besides Freya figured that she had a long day ahead of her simply trying to understand such tightly written old cursive. *Two cups of coffee, here I come*, Freya thought to herself in determination. After two hours reading through the brown book, Freya looked away from the text to give her eyes a much-needed rest. Her eyes had been twitching for the last few minutes, and with an aggravated sigh, she testily agreed to take a break. It aggravated her that just when the book was starting to provide important information, her eyes were starting to grow exhausted. So far, Freya had learned that The Rule of Three, in its very basic form, explains that anything someone puts out into the world will eventually return back to them times three. Which means any spell or action made in malice or anger would return to the witch, but with an amplified amount of fury.

The information was eating away at Freya's nerves at the realization that she had placed her husband in a coma, and something three times worse than that was lurking in the shadows to bite her on the ass. Even worse, the book had even explained how larger spells that were imposed on other living creatures such as prolonged sleeping or spells of amnesia ran the risk of becoming permanent for the person subjected. According to The Rule of Three, such terrible spells could cause the witch who cast it to gain a "tainted" mark. The book explained that a spell which brought about death or a manipulated state of reality, like a trance or coma, to another living creature would creep into the soul of the witch who cast it and create darkness from within her soul. The thought sent shivers up and down Freya's spine. Now she knew without a doubt that she had somehow caused Axel to fall into a coma, and she needed to rectify the accident as soon as possible.

The book also cautioned against initiating spells that separated a person from their body during the time of Halloween. It went into a detailed explanation against astral projection near Halloween since restless entities had the highest likelihood of entering an unattended body at this time. If a person's spirit was separated from their body for too long, the results would lead to the eventual death of the person. Immediately Freya recognized the warning against astral projections or near-death-experiences and realized the extent of Axel's increasingly dangerous situation.

That evening, Freya went home and decided to learn what she could online about witchcraft. She wrinkled her nose in dissatisfaction and decided to spend a generous amount of time researching the importance of the holiday. Proper lighting had disappeared from the hidden room hours ago with the sun, so she decided that a more modern approach might be able to glean at least a historical perspective on the situation.

Halloween actually had its roots in Celtic history that dated back hundreds of years. In Celtic tradition, they celebrated a festival called Samhain, where the separation between the realm of the living and the dead was at its weakest point. It was a festival where people would dress up in gory or unsettling outfits in an effort to scare away the ghouls or spirits. People would often make sacrifices to try and appease the gods and spirits by burning animals or crops in fires. The three-day celebration marked the New Year for the Celts and also marked a spiritual celebration that explored the concept of death and the afterlife. Freya momentarily looked away from the computer. The information was much more substantive in nature than she had originally assumed. Freya pushed her desk chair back as she grumbled, "Commercial holiday, my ass."

After a brief break, Freya eased into her chair and proceeded to search the web and clicked more promising leads. Although Celts held a reputation as being savages, Freya wondered how much of that was based on truth and exactly how much was created by the eventual victors who wrote the history books. The mild curse *"English scholars"* escaped her throat as she continued to scroll. A small part of her was glad that Meg had left earlier so that she wouldn't have to bear witness to Freya's verbal rants. If a book written thousands of years after the fall of the Celts, was warning her of what was now called Halloween, perhaps there was more truth to this so-called pagan tradition than originally thought. Did the older religions have a closer connection to the universe?

From what she had learned with her Internet dive, the older religions and societies were generally more equal between the genders. Women were revered for their childbearing but also respected and even welcomed in battle. There were even famous female Vikings, as they had not only been allowed but encouraged to participate in raids and conquests. Perhaps the Celts had a similar understanding of the world. *How funny that the people of two thousand years ago understood equality better than the people of today. I am glad that we don't have such intense punishments for crimes like stealing.* A small shiver racked her body at the memory of all of the extreme torture methods that seemed to be at the front of the Celtic arsenal.

Freya recognized some of what she was reading from when she was in Catholic school. She had learned the origins of All Saint's Day, also known as All-Hallows. Apparently when the church was trying to convert pagans in Europe to Catholicism, they adopted some traditions and rituals as a way to help people assimilate. Both Halloween and Christmas were two holidays that melded pagan traditions into the very fibers of Catholic society. Whether it was a willing assimilation or not, that seemed to be a gray line.

A vivid memory of when Freya was in second grade popped into her head. She was with the rest of her classmates at church, and they had all dressed up as their favorite saints for All Saint's Day. Freya remembered the day in detail since it was the day after Halloween, and she had been beyond thrilled to be able to go to class two days in a row with different costumes. It felt like a very special treat, given the fact that she had to wear a white polo and a blue skort most of the time. Joan had spent two long nights sewing her saint outfit since even the costume stores apparently didn't have any child-sized martyr costumes. For two nights, Joan had continued to mumble over her sewing machine about "too much money for this" and "sacrilege." In retrospect, Freya understood Joan's aversion to the entire event, but her mother had allowed Freya to participate and even made sure that she had the best-looking costume out of all of the kids in her class.

The Mass was one of the longer ones since it was mostly second grade children speaking and participating, but it had always been one of her favorite days since she loved looking at the other outfits and trying to figure out which saint each of her classmates were supposed to be. She had attended Catholic school her entire life, and although she was no longer a practicing Catholic, Freya did tend to use the values from the Beatitudes as a general guideline. Her faith in many things was less than desired at the moment. A strange thought then occurred to Freya. *What if my Irish heritage dates all the way back to the ancient Celts? Would that make the magic within me from a stronger source?* It felt like a valid possibility, given the fact that people from the little island of Ireland tended to have her red hair; a distinctive trait of her strong heritage.

Early the next morning, Aimée welcomed Freya into the bookstore. Sunlight slowly faded from the room as the day passed outside at a rhythm unknown to Freya. Inside the room, there was no way to hear what was happening on Main Street or to hear if someone was coming to open the door. The immortality and power of the room continued to impress Freya as she realized just how powerful Aimée's great-great-grandmother must have been to have so much foresight. The more that Freya continued to read, the more she felt her body ache with tension.

The stained glass windows were barely illuminated by the time Freya finished reading the final page. A slightly shaky hand went to cover her trembling lower lip. All Freya really knew was that time was no longer on her side with less than a month left before Halloween. If she couldn't bring Axel back by then, the odds were that he would be lost forever or, worse, possessed by a wandering soul when the veil was at its thinnest. Freya left the room and found Aimée patiently perched on her plush red velvet chair behind the cash register.

"Did you find what you were looking for Freya?" She placed a rather thick book down on her lap and removed her smartly styled thin-rimmed glasses.

Freya felt like a failure but decided that if humbling herself and asking for help would save Axel, then she would do it.

"Yes, unfortunately. I'm going to need help from you and Tanya. I spent some time learning about The Rule of Three and don't think this is a problem that I can solve on my own. Would you and Tanya mind coming over to my place?" The sentences felt like sandpaper against her tongue. Each word managed to bite into her skin and make her more uncomfortable than the last.

Aimée placed her book down, and Freya noticed that it was nearly finished as a piece of red string poked ten or so pages away from the end. Freya didn't doubt that Aimée had started the book that morning and was an extremely voracious reader— it was in her DNA after all. Aimée gracefully stood upward and patted down her long dark-blue dress as she pulled her white teddy bear sweater closer to her body. "Freya, whatever you need, we are here to help. Just tell us how. We know that your husband is a sensitive subject, so let us know what we can do."

Freya took in a deep breath. "Thank you, Aimée. Can I treat you to dinner for helping me out? Better yet, how about I make brunch sometime this week so Layla will be in school."

Aimée let out a cheery laugh as she turned the key in the side door and whispered too quietly for Freya to hear once again. The duo walked together and chatted casually as Aimée mindfully locked the front door of the bookstore. She then turned to Freya and embraced her in a warm and caring hug.

"Hopefully knowledge from the past will help us in the present."

Unfortunately Aimée's words didn't take into account the injustices from the past that planned to come to light in the present.

Chapter 12

A chilly breeze caressed Freya's freckled face as she looked over her backyard in content. It had been a little over a week since Freya had first gone into Aimée's secret library. She had walked over there every day to read as much as she possibly could about witchcraft. Every moment not spent worrying about the company was invested into fretting over Axel. Dark circles clung beneath Freya's eyes like particles of tar stuck to a wounded marine mammal. Along the way, Freya had fallen into a few very interesting books about familiars and the importance of trusting your instincts to direct impromptu spells. Although the knowledge felt off topic, Freya had decided that any information was power for the future.

Droplets of early morning dew shined across the grass as the sun slowly rose to greet the new morning. It was a little past seven, and Freya decided to sit on her porch swing with a cup of coffee. She squinted her eyes as she reviewed the budget for the upcoming year at Freya Designs. She wanted to go over it with a patient and critical eye to make sure that there was no funny business in each department. Being out of the office had felt like torture at first, but now she was slowly adjusting to a routine.

She took a deep breath of brisk morning air and quickly looked at the timer that she had set on her phone. The timer read that there was a little over half an hour before she needed to go inside and take both the chocolate and regular croissants out of the oven. They were premade and only needed to be left out the night before and then baked. It was the perfect amount of cooking for Freya who rarely enjoyed putting effort outside of her office. The admission gave her a moment to pause and realize how little effort she had made.

Tanya and Aimée were coming over to her home, and Freya wanted to have a few breakfast items available since it was still so painfully early in the morning.

Freya flipped over to the next page within the thin one-inch white binder and looked at a new set of numbers. She let out a curious harrumph from the back of her throat and reached for a yellow highlighter. Without thinking, she bit the cap between her teeth and pulled it off with a quick jerk. The bright ink joined the pale paper as she swiftly circled a number that didn't make sense and then placed a sticky note near it. The note reminded her future self to tell Aidan that she wanted more information. A frustrated wheeze escaped her nose as she realized how much more paperwork would now be required to try and further understand the number that was two or three thousand more than the current year's budget. Freya knew most of her numbers by heart, and just by eyeballing the review, she knew that this department request required an explanation. In a strange way, Freya was slightly excited to see if there was a financial mystery. Although Aidan was much slower in closing deals, he was still very competent.

A sudden movement in the forest drew Freya's attention away from her nearly completed preliminary search. An excited smile lifted the corners of her lips as she patiently watched her friendly mountain lion emerge.

Its emerald green eyes shone in the early morning light as it casually padded toward the porch. "Hello, gorgeous gal. How's your morning so far?" Freya remembered that cougars were generally nocturnal, so she found it odd to have a nighttime visitor on such a sunny day.

Not for the first time, Freya was also glad that she lived on a lot that was over three acres mostly in backyard space. She highly doubted that the elderly woman directly to the left of her log cabin house would appreciate such a massive visitor. The thought alone stretched an even wider grin across her face as she imagined Mrs. McCulley's shocked face with her inch-thick glasses pressed into her kitchen window. Luckily the scenario wasn't possible given Freya's massive backyard that was heavily wooded on both opposing property lines. Immense trees made it nearly impossible to even see the white paint of the other homes, even when standing three feet from the hedges. It was a fact that definitely appealed to Freya when she had first agreed to rent the place. A little over two months ago, she had no interest in seeing any of her neighbors, but now talking with the people of Wishburn didn't sound so bad.

Light-brown fur rippled into her vision as the mountain lion leapt over her wooden porch bannister and landed two feet from her pink fluffy bunny house slippers. "Hello, Madam Cuddles."

The feline let out a low growl of apparent protest at the nickname. "All right. I will think of something that fits you better." Freya brushed her red hair away from her face as she continued to watch the big cat. "I must be going crazy." The mountain lion tilted its head slightly sideways as if asking an important question. Soulful green orbs patiently watched her as she placed down her highlighter and binder on the porch swing.

A realization suddenly occurred to Freya as she studied the big cat that was lounging around like a small domestic kitten. She had read yesterday or the day before about familiars. Aimée's private collection had quickly become her favorite place to venture and explore on Main Street. Even though technically the exact location of the charmed room was actually unknown. A few books had explained the importance of a familiar in helping a witch strengthen and achieve her true potential. It was a symbiotic relationship between both parties where each was assisting the other for mutual happiness.

"I accept you as I accept myself." Freya was careful to keep her voice clear and steady. She felt as if this mountain lion was a strange part of her. For someone who prided herself on control and reason, she decided to act purely upon instinct instead.

As soon as the words left her mouth, the mountain lion crept closer, and Freya watched in shock as a furry face came inches from her own. The large feline opened its mouth and licked her across the face with a tongue that felt similar to sandpaper. Its wet and rough texture was foreign since Freya could only vaguely compare the creature to a much larger version of a domestic house cat. A shocked chuckle bubbled from her lips as the mountain lion continued to lick her face and fuzzy white shirt. The large tongue became momentarily stuck in her shirt's loose cotton material, and Freya was near tears of laughter as the sight of such a big cat trying to escape the clutches of her Max Mara turtleneck.

"Come on in. Let's see if I have anything to feed you." Freya had finally untangled the mess and swiftly picked up her previously forgotten pile of work documents. The mountain lion made a slight chuffing sound in the back of its throat as it meandered behind her. Freya opened the backdoor and held it open so that the big cat could enter first. Secretly Freya was convinced that the cat would find a way to get in with or without her help. However, the latter would likely involve a shattered window or a ruined patio screen.

Brown fur rubbed against Freya's upper thighs as the cat padded into her kitchen and then found a corner to curl up next to the heater. The sheer size of the large cat was once again pounded into her brain as she wondered how tall the feline could stand on its hind legs. It was almost half as tall as her on all fours. That wasn't exactly saying much given Freya's petite frame, but the sight was still impressive since mountain lions were generally nowhere as large as the rest of the big cats like lions and tigers. *Guess even my familiar is a strange exception to the rule.*

Freya walked over to the fridge and pulled it open. The light inside immediately clicked on at the motion and revealed an extensive selection of vegetables and soy products. Besides a half-finished bottle of champagne on the fridge door, there weren't too many frivolous items. A hum of discontent filled the air as she tried to think about any food items that might be appropriate for a big cat. Freya had changed her diet almost four years ago to a mostly plant-based lifestyle, but she still enjoyed the occasional steak or burger on a rough day. *Steak!* After she pawed around in the fridge for a few more seconds, Freya pulled out a large New York steak. Meg had always mentioned how much she enjoyed a home-cooked meal and especially steak as a child. Freya had planned to cook dinner for them sometime this week and had bought a practice steak in preparation. Instead Freya just shrugged her shoulders and decided that she would just have to buy a new one sometime this week instead.

She unwrapped the premium cut of meat and then momentarily paused. It was her first time feeding such a wild animal, and she wasn't sure if she should put it on a glass plate or a paper towel. The glass plate would most likely shatter if any amount of weight was pushed into it, and the mountain lion would most likely ingest pieces of the paper towel. With a light sigh, Freya tossed the raw meat onto her kitchen floor. She calmly observed as streaks of blood soiled her clean floor as it skidded an inch or two in the direction of the big cat. The mountain lion was milliseconds before taking its first bite when an angry caw caused it to pause midbite.

Tom stood in the doorway and pecked furiously at the wooden archway. A small splinter of wood separated itself from the house under the perpetual beatings of the relentless pest. A furious growl ripped through the chest of the mountain lion as it bared its impressively sized teeth. Although Freya strongly disliked Tom, she didn't want him to end up ingested by a cougar in her home. As quickly as Tom had entered the room, he disappeared into one of the unlocked areas in the house. Since Freya had her new plucky housemate, she began to lock Axel's room as well as her makeshift office and bedroom. The only room that was still freely open to the constantly crowing creature was the guest bathroom that she tended to lock Tom inside of as a form of time-out.

Freya turned her gaze to the mountain lion after Tom promptly escaped her line of sight and felt her eyebrows rise in shock. The big cat seemed to be laughing as it let out a half-purr and stared at the spot where the rooster once stood. "Yeah, he really is a coward when it comes down to it. We're going to get along just fine, Cahira."

The name just rolled from the tip of her tongue as she looked at the playful and bold cat. Green soulful eyes matched Freya's intent green gaze. "Cahira it is." She barely whispered it into the room, but it felt as if she was solidifying their bond as she spoke it into the open. The words breathed into existence seemed to take on a life of their own. In some strange unspoken understanding, the duo knew that they were now together as witch and familiar.

"It's an Irish name, you know. So now we come from the same place and can head in the same direction together." A hearty sneeze from the kitchen floor was her only reply to the impromptu speech that she had personally found to be so meaningful. Freya watched Cahira as she devoured the massive steak with ease. Her powerful jaw clenched shut and tore an ample chunk away from the bone with ease. Small droplets of blood splattered over her nearly white paws and turned them red. Freya felt great joy in feeding her familiar, even though the sight made her stomach twist in distaste.

After a few minutes, only the large bone remained as Cahira busied herself by meticulously cleaning her fur. The meal was a little messier than Freya had anticipated, but she figured that it was worth it to have such an eager breakfast guest.

A loud ringing caused Freya to jump upward in her wooden kitchen chair. The screen on her phone held a large zero as it continued to chirp and vibrate. Freya leaned across the table and swiftly entered the password to turn off the additional backup alarm. She swiped her finger to the left and watched as the green indicator switched back to neutral gray.

Claws scratched across Freya's kitchen floor as Cahira stretched her body in content.

"I am going to assume that you enjoyed the steak. Don't worry, I'll go out and get more options later this week. What do you think about turkey?" Disinterested green eyes didn't even blink at Freya in response. "Fine, that was a stupid question. I'll buy a few slices and like half a chicken to see which one you enjoy more."

She opened a drawer closest to the oven and plucked from its poorly organized interior a red oven mitt. Freya opened the door and inspected the pastries to try and visually judge if they were ready to be taken out of the oven. They seemed to be perfect, and she carefully took one baking sheet out and then placed it on the stove. She then reached back into the oven and went to pull out the chocolate croissants without really watching her movements.

A sharp yelp rang through the air as Freya retracted her arm in pain. She had somehow managed to burn the upper portion of her arm when she tried to get them from the lower shelf. Freya hastily plucked them out of the oven and then shut the door. As quickly as possible, Freya turned off the oven and sped to the sink. The oven glove was tossed somewhere on the counter as she turned on the faucet and waited in discomfort for the stream to be as cold as possible. Freya placed a cautious hand into the water and was relieved to find it was already chilly, most likely from the cold early morning temperature keeping the pipes near frigid. A groan of discontent left her lips as she placed the upper part of her right arm into the cool stream of water.

Freya inspected the damage and wrinkled her nose at the sight. Her skin was already puckering from the exposure, and angry welts seemed to appear in a straight line across the top of her forearm. A strong nudge to her leg caused Freya to look down and see Cahira with her head slightly tilted to the side in concern. Her observant gaze trailed away from Freya's until they came into contact with her injured arm. "It looks worse than it feels. Don't worry."

Cahira let out a sound similar to a snort. Clearly the large cat wasn't impressed with Freya's attempt at nonchalance. Freya turned slightly and bent down so that she could pet the top of Cahira's head with her left hand. She kept her right hand under the faucet as she twisted herself into a pretzel in an attempt to pet her new companion. Cahira mewled in discontent and pulled her large furry head away from Freya's gentle attention. "What's wrong, gorgeous?" Her question was soon answered.

The strong cat pushed herself onto her hind legs and stood with her front paws placed against the counter. Cahira lowered her head toward the stream of water and lapped just above Freya's arm. A pink tongue darted out and flicked water into her mouth at a rapid pace. Freya laughed at the strange sight and momentarily forgot about how much her arm hurt. After a few seconds, Cahira then turned her attention to Freya's burned arm. She lowered her head and then tentatively licked the wound, as if waiting to see if Freya would say that it hurt.

Oddly enough, the gesture didn't hurt at all. With its small backward-facing hooks, Freya had anticipated that it would be close to unbearable against her burn. Instead the wound felt healed. It didn't make sense, but Freya decided to just go with it since most of her life at the moment didn't exactly make sense either.

Freya slowly pulled her hand toward her face and felt her eyes nearly bulge out of their sockets in shock. Her previously puckered and reddened skin had calmed, and she could no longer see where she had been injured. She squinted her eyes in an attempt to find even the slightest of hints of where the burn had been only a few seconds ago but could only find pale and slightly freckled skin.

"You certainly are a marvel, Cahira. Definitely getting a bit of turkey and chicken for the next time you decide to come back." The big cat pawed at the backdoor in impatience as Freya leaned against her kitchen sink and spoke, "Okay, I'm coming. Thank you for fixing my arm."

Freya walked over toward the backdoor and pulled the door inward to let her temperamental guest leave. Before she silently prowled back into the woods, Cahira rubbed her head against Freya's thigh and let out a loud purr in content. The mountain lion seemed to bow her large head, as if in a sign of thanks, and then looked back toward Freya with a knowing glance. Cahira padded away from the porch and reached the end of the yard in no time. A smile gently lifted the corners of Freya's lips as she watched Cahira's tail disappear into the thick brush and trees. Although off to a memorable start, Freya felt confident that it was most definitely a good one.

She closed the door and made sure to lock it. However, she kept the blinds pulled away so that she could bask in the early sun rays and enjoy the view of the dark forest. *I've never been in a forest alone. I wonder what it's like for Cahira. When the girls come over, I'll ask them. Maybe it's better to keep this secret with me for a little longer, just to avoid derailing the purpose of brunch.* Freya's thoughts seemed to buzz through her head at a mile a minute. She was thrilled and filled with warmth at the knowledge that she had a familiar that seemed so much like herself. The cougar was a tad moody but so smart and thoughtful at the same time. Cahira also had little patience for Tom, and Freya considered it a win in her book.

Freya busied herself with putting her hair into a messy bun so that she could cook a Spanish omelet and a few pieces of bacon for her breakfast guests. An angry gurgle from her stomach only made her chuckle. There was a little over an hour before the girls would arrive, and Freya was glad that she had precut the supplies for her omelet the night before so she wouldn't have to handle so much of a headache in the morning. For a few minutes, she was a flurry of moving plates and chopped potatoes before everything was finally situated and cooking on the stove. The kitchen smelled delicious, and it felt good to finally get some use out of the brand-new appliances. Freya put the croissants back inside the oven to keep warm as she cooked away on the stove. Axel had also ensured that Freya always had a warm meal. It seemed silly, but Freya had always shied away from the domestic tasks. It felt too predictable and matronly. Now she realized that there was nothing gendered about the action and that if she was honest, she enjoyed cooking.

Memories floated to the surface of her consciousness as she prepared the food. She remembered the first time that Axel had ever brought her breakfast in bed and how he had been so nervous that he had made not only waffles but a mozzarella and tomato omelet and a divine cup of coffee. Freya could remember how full her stomach felt after she ate every morsel that he had so carefully prepared. She didn't want him to think that she was ungrateful and wanted to let him know that she loved his cooking by showing him in the most obvious way—eating everything in sight. She had joked with him afterward that she felt so full that she might never be able to eat again. Axel had quickly flipped her on the mattress and pulled her underneath his massive form. He had rumbled in a voice full of passion, "You're not properly full yet." His bright iron eyes were partially hooded as he had gazed intently into her green orbs. The memory alone stirred a longing within Freya's lower stomach that, tried as she might, couldn't be satisfied with food.

A faint knocking sound gave Freya pause as her spatula was about to remove the omelet from the nonstick pan. She listened intently and realized the noise wasn't coming from Tom but from somewhere near the front door. Freya turned off both stove burners and quickly pulled out a few plates so that everything would be ready for the girls. *Oh! More coffee.* The reminder temporarily derailed her search for the tapping as she placed more water inside of her coffeepot. The kitchen and chairs were not completely perfect for company, but Freya figured that nobody would die if they had to serve themselves their own preferred portions.

After she quickly wiped her hands on a dish towel to get rid of any additional oil, Freya padded to the front door. Freya called with unbridled excitement, "I'm coming!" The wooden boards made a rolling sound as she briskly jaunted through the hallway since she figured that she had kept them waiting for long enough. However, when Freya opened the front door, the sight in front of her wasn't the one that she had expected.

Chapter 13

Freya quickly opened the door to her home as an excited smile played across her lips. As soon as she saw what was outside of her home, the excited grin melted into a look of confusion. Tanya and Aimée stood outside but were both holding large sticks with pieces of small branches tied to the ends. The wooden contraptions looked extremely old, and Freya wasn't exactly sure of their purpose.

Aimée easily noticed Freya's face and greeted, "We also brought muffins. Good morning, Freya. May we enter?" She looked as effortlessly chic as usual as she wore a pair of high-wasted black jeans with cream-colored stilettos and a cream chevron-patterned puffer jacket. As usual, she appeared more like a model who was preparing for a *Vogue* photo shoot in Aspen for the winter edition instead of a small-town mother who owned a lovely little bookstore. To add to the chic look, Aimée had her hair perfectly styled into a high ponytail. It was almost obscene how perfectly put together and well manicured she was at nine in the morning.

Freya hated to be dressed down in meetings and always strived to be the most composed woman in the room. It was glaringly obvious that her bright-pink fuzzy bunny slippers were not exactly the same as a pair of cream Christian Louboutin shoes. Freya only shrugged and made a mental note to try and at least put on a pair of proper shoes for their next meeting. Freya decided that she would just have to live without being the smartest dressed in the room. It was an unspoken fact that vigorously ground against her perfectionist nerves.

Tanya held a basket of muffins that looked absolutely tempting. Freya wondered if they were walnut or pecan from their appearance. The mental tangent was a welcome reprieve from the impending stress of their conversation. Tanya clomped her combat boots against the welcome mat to get rid of any excess dirt and the occasional stray leaf as she followed Aimée's figure inside. She wore her long dark locks down in multiple braids that seemed to frame her strong jawline. Tanya wore a deep-red knit sweater and close-to-the-body cargo pants. Although Freya didn't exactly like cargo pants, she took note of the outfit in appreciation as it definitely complimented Tanya's curvaceous figure. Tanya had to be about a size 6 or 8 and seemed to have won the genetic lottery when it came to having curves in all the right places.

"Thank you both for coming! Aimée, I really love your outfit. Please come in. I have a few food options in the kitchen, but what are you both holding?" Freya moved out of the entranceway and held the door open so that both women could pass with their strange objects in tow.

Tanya looked absolutely unfazed by the question and answered, "They're our brooms that we plan to use to clean up your mess."

Freya was about to make a snappy comeback, but then realized that Tanya was, in fact, very right. They were definitely coming over with their brooms to try and help clean her miserable mess. So Freya only slightly nodded her head in acknowledgment of the comments and looked at them both as she bit her lower lip. "Thanks, ladies."

The women meandered into the kitchen together after Freya had closed the front door and locked it. Even though it was a sleepy small town, the entire attempted murder incident with Tom had rightfully kept Freya alert. *Yes, now I just lock the doors to keep my husband, my attempted murderer, and myself all locked in together.* The strange irony of the situation didn't escape her as she let out a snort at how she not only lived with Tom but also fed him. Now that Freya knew more about The Rule of Three, she was extremely hesitant to do anything more to Tom. It would be too easy to feed him to Cahira or to just open the backdoor and let him run wild. The only problem with the second option was that then there was a possibility that he would never return to human form since Freya might not be able to find him. So for now, even though it pained her, she decided that she would keep Tom in her house because there wasn't really another option. Tanya had made several thinly veiled threats that karma for Tom included getting eaten by a large wild animal. Aimée had only nodded her head in agreement with Tanya. Freya wanted some cosmic justice but was hesitant to be the dealer.

"Help yourself. I put the plates on the counter and still have about half a bottle of champagne and a pot of coffee in the works. Hey, what was Sally like before she met Tom?" Freya fought with herself to refrain from asking a million questions a minute.

Tanya handed a white ceramic plate to Aimée and let out a defeated sigh.

"She was so nice and pretty. In high school, I didn't really know her since she was a freshman when Aimée, Scott, and I were seniors. Scott was absolutely smitten with her and always found an excuse to be near her. It wasn't hard to understand why since she was the sweetest and tiniest li'l thing at school. She wasn't too confident, but I figured that was just the awkwardness of puberty and moving from one school to start another. When Scott graduated, it wasn't long before Tom swept her away in his bullshit parade. He was always a dick. One time, he tried to set Scott's dog on fire, but Scott beat Tom's face near unrecognizable, so he backed off. I think that some sick motivation for Tom trying to get with Sally came from trying to hurt Scott. At first, Sally was all excited and chatty when she was going out with Tom. He really made an effort to be sweet, but after about three months, things started to change. By the time Sally graduated, she no longer dressed or walked the same. It was as if she was a scared little kitten. I heard from someone in Sally's grade that it was just like she disappeared in front of their eyes. She stopped talking to everyone and stopped going out to parties. The only place she was seen outside were Tom's football games, and even then, she sat in the front row and told whoever tried to sit or talk to her to go away. Her parents ended up dying a month after she got married to Tom. It was just really awful."

The gears in Freya's mind were almost on fire from the speed that they were turning in an effort to process what Tanya had explained. How could Sally just leave Scott to date and eventually marry someone like Tom? Why would Sally stay? Although Tanya's explanation really helped to provide Freya a bigger picture, it also created more questions than answers. It was also apparent that one of the people who knew the most on the issue wouldn't be explaining the situation anytime soon.

"Sally's parents. Did anyone ever think their deaths were a little too convenient?"

Aimée whipped her ponytail back for emphasis and replied, "Everyone. But Tom's dad was the head of the police department and probably the reason that Scott had so many legal and financial issues. The amount of obscure tickets that man received was close to preposterous."

"What a mess. Have any of you seen Sally since Tom left town?" Freya casually peeked over at the women as she placed a generous portion of Spanish omelet on her plate. A smirk played on the corner of her lips as she waited for them to process what she had implied.

Aimée looked over at Freya with her mouth half-open as her eyes held excitement at the apparent story. "How did you pull off his sudden decision to leave town?" She placed her chin in the palm of her hand like a child settling into a comfortable position before story time.

"I sort of waited for Sally to leave and then crawled into one of her open windows. It wasn't exactly easy since she had rosebushes planted underneath every first-story level. A few thorns later, and I snuck into their kitchen and wrote a letter in his handwriting. I said that he had gotten tired of hurting her and wanted to travel to see other women who would listen to him. It wasn't exactly what I wanted to say, but it was the best thing that would check out if the cops came looking. I haven't seen her in about a week and was wondering if you saw her around town. But I would like to say that breaking and entering is a much-smaller crime than kidnapping."

Black coffee swirled in a circular pattern as Tanya stirred it in mild irritation. The rhythm suddenly halted as she exclaimed. "That is some top-notch criminal activity. Covering your tracks and everything. To answer your question, no. I haven't seen Sally in a little bit, but I'll keep an eye out. She might just be trying to take in the moment and gain perspective on her new situation."

Freya mulled that over. It would be fair to assume that Sally was in her home at that very moment, absolutely confused by the sudden peace. The suggestion that Sally was just charging her batteries and licking her old wounds helped to quell Freya's mind. She made a mental note to go over and check on Sally.

She munched on a piece of bacon and then placed the first forkful of her masterpiece into her mouth. The combination of eggs and potatoes was a classic breakfast dish with a little twist of spice from cayenne pepper and chili powder. Apparently one of her early brunch guests didn't exactly feel the same way as Aimée started coughing profusely. Her pale face turned an angry cherry-red from heat and a light trail of perspiration appeared near her forehead. She spluttered in confusion as she stood up and desperately sped to the fridge.

"I don't have any real milk. But I have cashew and chocolate almond milk if that works for you."

Aimée whipped her face back in Freya's direction in shock. Her face looked as if she had just been told that Freya enjoyed early morning nude walks through the town. Drops of sweat seemed to multiply by the minute as Aimée stood helplessly in the middle of the open fridge.

While the two of them were having a lactose disagreement, Tanya pushed her chair backward and grabbed a cup from Freya's pantry. She then walked over to the left side of the fridge and pressed the button for crushed ice and water. When the cup was near overflowing, she moved it away from the sensor and handed it to Aimée, whose eyebrow arched in incredulity. Aimée wasted no time and chugged half of the glass in one desperate gulp. Even while having a total meltdown from spice, Aimée still managed to look stunning.

Freya let out a snort as she laughed in joy. "Remind me to never take you to any proper Mexican restaurants if we ever go on a road trip to Los Angeles." Aimée jutted her chin upward in condemnation of the playful comment. "Don't worry. We can go to a sushi restaurant and tell them to hold your side of wasabi." A faint smile crossed Aimée's face at the light-hearted jabs.

The women continued to poke fun at each other as they convened back at the dinner table. Tanya looked at her empty plate and stood for a second serving.

A sense of pride filled her chest at the minor action. For almost three years, Freya hadn't cooked at all, and it felt good to be able to get into the swing of things with such a level of positive feedback. *Maybe I should learn a few more recipes so that I can cook a proper meal instead of relying on canned foods like someone in a post-apocalyptic movie.* The idea of learning a new skill in a different environment appealed to her. It felt like a step in the direction of normalcy. A direction that she desperately wanted to cling to now that every moment was anything but ordinary.

Brunch soon drifted to a close as they sat huddled together over the wooden table in hushed whispers and melodious mumbles. Aimée leaned closer to the group and chuckled. "Growing up is a learning curve, from birth to discovering the gift of magic. I do believe that I have an enthralling tale to share with the table."

Freya settled closer and placed her head in the palm of her hand. Her green eyes sparkled with excitement as she encouraged, "Please, do tell."

With an elaborate flourish of her hand, Aimée placed down her coffee cup and began her story. "I know that it may surprise you, but as a child,

I was extremely dramatic. I blame this entire story upon my mother for her strangely uninformative approach to handling puberty. It was October, and I was in the sixth grade when I had my first period. We were playing kickball during lunch, boys versus girls. The bases were absolutely loaded, and it was my turn to kick. It had always been my favorite sport, but I had had a horrible stomachache for the majority of the morning. Tommy rolled the ball to me, and I kicked it with such vigor that it ended up sailing across the wall. As I was running, I noticed that there was blood running down my leg. When I had looked down and saw a small droplet of blood trickle past the vibrant color of my blue Bermuda shorts, I thought that I had managed to hit the ball so hard that my insides had burst and were bleeding out. In that moment, I had felt invincible. By the time that I was rounding third base, I remember thinking that at least I was dying for a just cause, by preventing the boys from having bragging rights until the next morning. The kids from my team had gone wild, and many small hands had eagerly reached to embrace me. One of the teachers noticed my minor incident and walked me to the school nurse. Imagine my surprise when my supposed noble death was actually the beginning of my journey into womanhood."

Tanya playfully butted into the conversation, "But maybe it was the metaphorical death of your childhood that you had fought so valiantly to protect." A smile was evident through her words, and Freya realized that she was the only one at the table hearing the story for the very first time.

Aimée described the memory in such vivid detail that Freya felt as if she was there herself. Cheering Aimée on from the sidelines as she barreled forward toward womanhood. In a way, she had run and spit in the face of death as a new chapter came to life. Luckily Aimée's female school nurse was able to set both Aimée and her very sheltered male teacher straight. That Aimée was not, in fact, dying or bleeding out but starting a new phase of her life that would last about thirty to forty years.

Freya loved the fact that even as a child, Aimée had been drawn toward the dramatic with a passionate will to succeed. It definitely made life more interesting to have her and Tanya around. The house felt more like a home, thanks to them and Meg. *I bet Axel would love them if he could meet them in person.* The thought zipped through her mind at the speed of a bullet train. It came almost out of nowhere and disappeared back into the vast expanse of her other thoughts just as quickly, but it was too late. The pain had already crashed against her heart at full speed and caused her near-giddy mood to come to a screeching halt.

Freya reminded herself of the main reason that she had asked the two brightly smiling women over to her house. She brought the remainder of the cup of coffee to her lips and took a drawn-out gulp. When she finished the entire contents of the cup, Freya let out a breath and realized that there was no other possible stalling tactic available. Freya's face must have shown the shift in her emotions, as the two other women allowed their laughter to tinkle away into the morning breeze that danced out the open kitchen window. The noise quickly faded as two pairs of eyes looked at her inquiringly.

Freya realized that they had been patiently waiting for her to bring up the subject. She took a deep breath to steady herself and said, "I need you both to come and look at Axel and tell me what you think. If what you say about witches having different energy signatures is true, then I would like you both to confirm what I'm guessing. It's the only way to really have a chance to bring him back. To know and explore the root of the problem." The bags underneath Freya's eyes were especially prominent as she rubbed her face in agitation.

Tanya kept her warm brown eyes level on Freya's light-green orbs as she reached across the table. "Sometimes fixing a problem is a lot like trying to fix a tooth. You want to save the tooth because it's important to you. Obviously you want to keep it, and you like being able to chew, but it doesn't work the same when its roots are infected. Eventually that infection will spread and make everything worse, to the point it will probably kill you. So in the end, the tooth is better off being chopped up and pulled out than allowed to further fester and kill the entire body. The tooth is only a part of the body. Don't get the order twisted."

Aimée sniffed in approval. "You know there is an excellent amount of fame and fortune in public speaking, Tanya. It might just be for you if the urge to leave Scott's ever struck." The observation was so casually stated that Freya was willing to bet that Aimée had grown used to Tanya's random spouts of insight. Her word choice was generally direct and free of frills. Yet when the need arose, Tanya knew how to create an excellent speech.

"You could hire me to speak at events in your bookstore. My starting rate is half a grand for an hour."

Aimée rolled her eyes. Freya gestured with her arms and stated, "Follow me. Axel stays in the guest room." Freya pushed back her wooden chair with more effort than usual and stood, sliding her feet into her pink bunny slippers. They looked especially odd to her as the situation felt too heavy for such a fanciful choice in footwear.

Freya stopped so suddenly in the middle of the hallway that Tanya tumbled into her back. Even after getting properly jostled, Freya continued to admire her slippers as she explained, "Axel is in this room. It might look absolutely horrible, and that's because it is. Please just tell me what I already know."

She then scooted toward the doorway on the right side of the hallway and allowed Tanya and Aimée to enter ahead of her. Freya didn't want to see their faces morph into horror as they saw what she was capable of, even if she wasn't sure how she did it in the first place.

Aimée let out such a startled gasp that Freya instinctively bobbed her head upward to look at her friend. What Aimée saw visibly shook her statuesque frame. Tanya hesitantly inched closer to the twin-sized hospital bed, as Aimée remained rooted to her spot. Tanya cautiously hovered over Axel's motionless form and then craned her neck downward, as if to get a better look. Instead of looking and scanning Axel for any visible signs of magic, Tanya's eyelids fluttered closed, and she opened her mouth to take in a deep breath. She held the air within her chest for a few moments and gradually released it as she kept her eyes closed and continued to lean over Axel's unresponsive figure.

Freya was about to ask Aimée what was going on, but Aimée intercepted her question and placed her hand into the air in a halting motion. Freya bit her lower lip and decided to remain silent as she anxiously observed Tanya take in another large gulp of air and hold it. Tanya repeated the process for several seconds before she finally released the last inhale of air and opened her eyes.

Tanya stepped away from Axel and then turned to look at Aimée. Tanya and Aimée seemed to be having a conversation with each other without saying a word, and Freya hated every second of it. She felt like she was anxiously waiting for a verdict in her own murder trial, and the judge and the jury were taking their sweet time in sharing their verdict. Freya rubbed her thumb against the inner palm of her hand to try and quell her nerves. She had dealt with several high-stakes multimillion dollar contracts before, but this was an entirely new level of stress. Money was one thing, but finding out you might have condemned your husband to a shadow version of his previous life was a totally different type of anxiety.

"Tanya, I'll tell her." Aimée looked over at Freya with a look of trepidation. She licked her bottom lip before she proceeded, "Freya, we can feel your energy signature on him."

Chapter 14

That was all the confirmation that Freya needed to grab herself around her waist. She held her belly with such intensity that if someone didn't know better, they would assume that she was trying to hold all of her organs in place. *I did this. I almost killed him. It was so foolish to assume that it was something else in the first place.* Freya thought a dozen angry different variations about how dull she was to hope for even a second that she wasn't the reason Axel wouldn't wake up. Of course, it was her.

"But there is also another energy signature surrounding your husband that we don't recognize. It seems as if the two magic signals somehow are battling. It appears that they ended up cancelling out." Aimée looked so confused as she tried to explain what Tanya and herself had discovered.

"You might not recognize it, but every witch has a different energy signature that surrounds their body. It's sort of like having a magical version of a fingerprint. You'll probably be able to know for yourself around Halloween since most witches tend to come into their powers around that time. Magic signatures leave a mark whenever you cast a spell and other witches can 'see' it. Tanya can get a better perspective on signatures than I can because she receives magic signatures through all of her senses to get a fuller picture. But there is most certainly your signature and another witch's around Axel. Which is good and bad, depending on how you wish to perceive that information. Since it's not a coma caused by normal circumstances, the odds are that when we lift the spells, he will be able to wake up."

A strangled sob of relief ripped its way from Freya's throat. It felt like she was finally able to breathe again at the knowledge that there was at least the slightest bit of hope to be able to wake Axel up. "Is there any way to find out who the other witch is?

Tanya shrugged her shoulders as she kept her arms crossed and leaned against the neutral-colored wall. "The best way would be to think of people who may have wanted to hurt you or Axel. Was anyone mad about the two of you being together or was anyone upset about your success?"

The question immediately created an image of an extremely likely suspect in her mind. She didn't want to say it out loud just yet because it seemed so absolutely preposterous. "Is it possible that if I come from a long line of Celtic witches, that my mother is also a witch? Would my brother be able to have some witchcraft?"

"It's very likely that your mother is a witch and that she knows. And if she is, your mom probably hoped that your powers would remain dormant and decided not to tell you. No, magic doesn't really work that way as women are the gatekeepers of life. Men are viewed as important but unable to have the same gifts. They don't have the ability to connect as strongly to the universe with their Y chromosome…and toxic masculinity in common culture has definitely helped to lessen any chances of a connection. Your brother is simply mortal, and if you have a son, then he will also be fully mortal."

The conversation was beyond strange, and Freya stood in silence and looked at Axel. His face was peaceful and appeared as though he had just fallen asleep. It felt like he had been away for so much longer than about a month and a half. The intense longing was strange since she rarely shared more than a random phone call and their bed together. She had completely taken him for granted and pushed him to the side. Not only had she left him emotionally for dead, but she had almost left him on death's door. Freya rubbed her lips together and continued to mull over the last night he was awake. She still felt the stabbing agony of betrayal within the pit of her stomach and wanted to punch him in the face.

Even if they were able to wake him up, Freya wasn't sure if she would take him back. There were just too many emotions swirling around for her to definitively know what she would do if he were conscious. All she knew was that her new mission was to save Axel's life. She'd just have to accept and prepare for each day as it came. Otherwise Freya was likely to just lose her mind and start only talking to Tom. Although both options were the most logical explanations as to why someone would try to hurt Axel, they felt too simple. Placing someone into a coma wasn't the same as turning down a dinner invitation.

Axel's hand felt different than Freya had remembered. It reminded her of a lofty anchor as its weight continued to pull her hand downward. "I'm not letting us sink." Freya solemnly promised. The silence gave her a moment to search through a very short list of possible culprits. After a moment, the most obvious suspect was Joan. Her mother had always disliked Axel and was only too happy to see Freya move on.

Freya tiredly rubbed the palm of her hand over the middle of her forehead. "How do I cast a protection spell? It's possible that someone still has unfinished business. I'm going to have an Irish coffee in the other room if anyone wants to join."

She bit her lip to try and stop herself from losing her composure and then turned around to make a strong cup of coffee. It wasn't exactly a professional way to cope, but Freya highly doubted that there were a set of guidelines on how to manage with the guilt of accidentally turning your husband into a 210-pound vegetable. *It's like every gold digger's dream. This is my worst nightmare, besides the one dream where I lost the Freya Designs,* Freya thought miserably to herself. Freya grabbed the pot of coffee that was still about halfway full and poured herself a generous helping into her favorite coffee mug. A giant black cat was curled around the mug and now held a different symbolism than just the simple fact that Freya considered herself a cat person. The smell of freshly brewed coffee helped to focus her thoughts as she tried to brainstorm a list of who could have possibly placed a spell on Axel, besides her mother.

Two distinct sets of footprints strolled from the guest room and into the kitchen. Tanya squinted her eyes as if she wanted to say something else but wasn't exactly sure how to phrase it. She turned toward Aimée, as if asking for help, but rolled her eyes in apparent frustration at her own inability to spit whatever she wanted to say out of her mouth.

"Freya, if you think it's someone from Los Angeles, the easiest way to find out would be to see them in person. That way the energy signature is immediately visible, and then there is no room for guessing. But that is extremely risky given the situation, so we might be able to scry for the answer instead. Each witch has a set of skills and excels in certain areas. Like Aimée has a crazy memory and the ability to siphon energy from different sources. She's kind of like a human generator but with an unlimited battery. Who knows, you might be able to scry, and then we can take an educated guess from there."

Although it did sound like scrying was a good option, Freya didn't want to take any chances. "That's a valid point. Would you be able to teach me how to scry? I need to know who placed the spell on Axel without a doubt. Otherwise everything we do will just waste our time and resources. My mom said she was coming to visit me this weekend. So I'd be picking her up in three days and be able to arrange a lunch or meeting where you two can tell me if there is a match."

Freya licked her lips and then took a sip of her coffee before she realized that she was missing her special ingredient. Aimée picked up her old wooden broom and then handed Tanya her own.

"Freya, we might not have known each other for long, but you risked your life to save my daughter. I wasn't there for her, but you saved her and brought her back. I don't know how you did it, but your magic was all over her when we were at the edge of the lake. It was coated to every strand of her hair and on her skin for days. Helping you with Axel is the least that I can do." Aimée had unshed tears threatening to spill from her bright-blue eyes. Her voice caught within her throat a few times as she tried to explain as eloquently as possible how grateful she was to Freya. After, she cleared her throat. "So at least for now, Tanya and I will clean away any ill will from around Axel's bed and search for protection charms like the one that's placed on the door handle of my bookstore."

For some reason, Aimée's explanation dug up a memory and connection that Freya had been unable to grasp until now. She reached into the neck of her shirt and retrieved the necklace that her mother had given to her over a decade ago. Freya squeezed the insignia within her small palm and then let it go so that it was revealed to the morning light. "Would you be able to tell me what that symbol means? My mother, Joan, gave it to me when I was sixteen and said it was a symbol of protection from the old land. I haven't been able to find it anywhere online."

Aimée squinted her eyes and then let out a small grunt in annoyance that she wasn't able to see it clearly from across the kitchen. Her heels clicked across the wooden planks as she approached the table and then pulled out a chair. Aimée sat down in the seat nearest to Freya and then inspected the ancient-looking symbol. Aimée crept closer to the necklace but refrained from reaching out and touching it.

She let out a hum of recognition. "Yes, that's the exact one that my ancestor placed on the bookstore doorknob. It's an extremely ancient sign of protection that dates all the way back to the Celts and has a very strong amount of power. I realized that Tom never entered the shop on his own, even if he saw her in the shop window. Sally sat in my shop on more than one occasion when she was trying to avoid Tom and even mentioned that it was a place that he never wanted to enter, even to go get her. Freya, you must have opened the door for him so that you could both enter. That symbol around your neck might also explain why you are all right and Axel isn't. Some witch bitch might have tried to put a spell on both of you, but it failed to get you, thanks to that necklace. Objects that are older and that have lived and experienced life with their owners have a way of remembering too, you know."

In response, Freya reached forward and took a chocolate muffin from the basket. She took her time as she chewed her first bite and used that moment of silence in order to collect her thoughts. The more that she learned about this world of witchcraft and mystery, the more that Freya wished there was something like an online course. It felt as if she was traveling blind and bound to make countless mistakes since there was so much room for error. As Freya read and learned from Aimée and Tanya, the more obvious it became that magic had different gradients. It wasn't just black and white. There was no such thing as purely good and fully evil when discussing people. Freya only hoped that she was able to do more good than harm in order to keep on the positive side of The Rule of Three.

"Yes, I had opened the door for Tom to enter your shop. I literally let the fox into the chicken coop on that one. Once Axel is all right, I will have to circle back on dealing with Tom. In the meantime, can I watch both of you clean the ill will from around Axel? Are there certain rules? Where did you get the brooms?"

Tanya let out a delighted laugh and continued to cackle so much that she leaned on her broom for support from her crouched position. "You were definitely top of your class in school. I bet you hated to lose even by a point. Yes, you can watch, but it's not as interesting as it sounds." Tanya straightened her athletic build after her laughter lessened to sporadic chuckles and continued, "Sometimes the art of a spell is more about what you can't see. There won't be any bright lights or crazy Fourth of July style fireworks, but you'll probably feel a change in the energy of the room as we work."

Without any preamble, Tanya turned around and then headed out of the kitchen and down the hallway. Aimée winked at Freya and said, "Looks like we are getting to work now. Not a visually dramatic spell, but it will definitely do the trick. Let's proceed to the next room before she decides to start without us."

The three women spent the remainder of the morning hours cleaning around Freya's home in case there was any residual negative energy. They then placed a protection spell around Axel's bed as well as both the front and back doors to try and prevent any unwelcome guests. The morning had drifted into the early hours of the afternoon as a scratching sound from the front door attracted Freya's attention. She stopped her teasing about Tanya's apparent distaste for chocolate and listened closer for the strange sound. There it was again! Freya was relatively sure that it wasn't Cahira since she had already paid a visit earlier in the morning. That and Freya figured that if the big cat wanted in, she would just create a way to enter.

"Hold on, do you hear that?" Tanya pushed the chocolate muffin that Aimée was holding away from her face as the three of them tried to listen. A faint clawing came from somewhere outside the first level once again.

Aimée was the first to unfreeze and walked out of Freya's bedroom in search of the mystery disruption. Tanya and Freya followed a few paces behind in an effort to find answers to the persistent noise. The trio sped down the stairs and realized that the sound was coming from directly outside the front door. Aimée reached for the door, but Tanya made her stop before she could reach the handle.

"Have you lost your mind, woman? There could be a very sloppy wannabe murderess outside of that door." Tanya's eyes were almost doubled in size as she emphatically waved her hands in the air.

Aimée let out an embarrassed chuckle and then pulled the strands of her hair within her ponytail tighter in an effort to keep a handle on her composure. "I'm relatively confident that Amethyst is outside. She gets antsy when I'm gone from the bookstore for too long." A frustrated mewl rang out from the other side of the door and helped to bolster Aimée's explanation. "Amethyst has been my familiar for almost twenty years. It's come to the point where I can sense her general location since we're bonded." Aimée wrapped her slim fingers around the door and opened it to reveal a perfectly sunny afternoon and an extremely disgruntled black cat. Amethyst's fur was full of leaves, and its tail continued to whip furiously from one side to another.

"Oh, darling. I'm so sorry that you're filthy. Come here, my little love." Aimée immediately knelt down and reached out to pick Amethyst up. She tenderly cuddled the traumatized feline into her. chest. The black cat settled into a more comfortable position with her paws placed on Aimée's shoulder.

As Freya looked at the small little cat that Aimée so clearly adored, an interesting thought came to mind. She violently bit down on her bottom lip in order to avoid bursting out into laughter. *Cahira, I don't think that I'll ever be able to pick you up like a baby.* The mental quip did little to quell the waves of dread that continued to crash against the shores of Freya's serenity. Was it really possible that Joan hated Axel so much that she was willing to kill him to get him out of Freya's life?

Chapter 15

"Freya, do you have any Tylenol?" Joan inquired from somewhere at the top of the stairs.

"Yes, Mom. I'll bring them to you."

Freya walked out of the kitchen and padded toward the half-bathroom down the hallway. She passed Meg as she diligently changed Axel into a different set of clothes. Meg looked up and sent Freya a playful wink. Joan had been in the house for less than two hours and was already driving them both batty. As soon as Joan had entered the master suite, she had very politely insisted that the furniture was arranged incorrectly. She had then proceeded to move the accent chair toward the window and away from the vanity, where Freya liked to put on her makeup in the morning. Freya had bitten her lip and tried to contain her rapidly rising temper. She was a grown woman with an extremely successful career as well as a husband. But somehow Joan viewed her as too incompetent to even properly decorate her own bedroom at thirty years old. Normally Freya would have given her mother a strict no, but this time, she made sure to hold her tongue. Freya didn't want to get into an argument or disagreement that had the potential to spiral before Tanya and Aimée arrived for lunch.

Immediately after Joan had finished rearranging the furniture into chaos, she had turned around and commented on Freya's apparently lacking attire. Freya took note of her outfit and thought that her high-waist black skinny jeans and slightly cropped white knit turtleneck were a perfect outfit. Part of her felt like the comment was specifically directed at her fluffy pink house slippers. There was also no way that she planned to change her shoes just to appease her mother, who had already destroyed the layout of her bedroom.

Freya had placed her mother in the master bedroom for more than just the obvious reason of being a good daughter. Her bedroom was up the stairs and furthest away from Axel's room, and although there was now a strong protection charm around his bed, she wasn't in the mood to take any risks. The sound of steady footsteps from the floor below helped to quell some of Freya's anxiety.

Meg was downstairs taking care of Axel's intravenous drip. She had told Freya earlier that it was one of the stranger cases that she had worked in her long career. When Freya had tried to pry for detail, Meg had only shrugged in response. After a little more vigorous prodding, Meg had mentioned that Axel was able to breathe on his own and didn't require intubation, like many more serious patients that she had assisted. It was almost as if he had just fallen asleep one night and never actually been able to wake up. The comment only strengthened Freya's anxiety at the knowledge that that was literally what had happened. He had fallen asleep after their fight and never woke up.

As Freya listened to Meg bustle around Axel's room, Joan had already waltzed up the stairs and momentarily left Freya with her thoughts. There was no point in trying to beat around the bush with Joan. Her eyes had been on Freya like a hawk to prey since the minute Freya had picked her up from the airport. The question that Freya was dying to ask felt like it was causing the hairs on her neck to stand on end. Luckily Meg's presence felt like a blessing. At least there was a buffer so that they couldn't have an in-depth conversation about Freya's strange behavior.

Aimée and Tanya had agreed to come over for lunch under the guise of introducing themselves to Freya's mother. In reality, they were coming over to see if Joan had a magical signature and if it was the same one that they had found on Axel. Freya had immediately thrown the idea of trying to cook for five out of the window. Instead she had meandered over to the wooden cabinet closest to the fridge and retrieved a paltry stack of delivery menus. Apparently there were only three restaurants that she knew of that actually delivered in the sleepy town of Wishburn. Freya had thumbed through the options, relieved to have a task to distract herself with, if only for a brief moment. She eventually settled on a family-owned Italian restaurant that was about three streets away. Freya wasn't exactly sure what everyone would prefer, so she decided to play it safe and ordered a cheese-and-spinach pizza, pepperoni pizza, fettuccini alfredo, and a generous house salad.

Freya pressed the disconnect button on her phone and then looked at the screen. It was only five minutes away from noon, and Freya realized that she just had to last another forty minutes before she would have an answer. She anxiously chewed her bottom lip and listened to the ongoing sounds within the house.

The shifting of weight upstairs told her that her mother was still getting settled and most likely still unpacking her multiple bags. Joan was notorious for overpacking to the point of it being criminal. Or at least, it felt criminal, given the pricey overweight baggage for which Freya had had the pleasure of paying.

Freya remembered around the time she was fourteen when they went on a family road trip to the Grand Canyon. The trip had lasted only a week, but Joan had packed enough for at least a month, if not two. They'd had to rent a large Escalade SUV for the sole purpose of fitting Joan's entire luggage collection. Joan had insisted Freya learn to drive it when the road was more isolated between towns. Freya had complained and threatened to jump out of a moving car if Joan made her drive. She had shouted something like, "If you love me, then you won't make me learn to drive!"

Of course, Joan had only replied something to the effect of, "I love you enough to teach you, even if it ends up making us crash." The only reason that she ended up safely seated and buckled in the driver's seat was courtesy of a generous bribe.

Aidan had bawled his eyes out in the back seat for the entire hour and a half that Freya had anxiously attempted to drive. Freya had learned to drive a tank of a car with an inconsolable child screaming and kicking the back of her seat. When Freya had told Joan to make Aidan stop, her mother had flippantly replied, "Stress and distractions build character." It seemed apparent that Joan had no idea what caused a majority of car accidents.

The memory was still fresh in Freya's mind as she waved back to Meg and walked further down the hallway. She could hear Tom angrily clucking away from the other side of the door, and the thought of him complaining about his time-out sent her into a mild fit of giggles. She had caught him trying to peck through the drywall around five in the morning and had placed him in the bathroom in an attempt to limit the damage. The noise was horrible, and Freya was furious at the sight of her hallway in shambles. She was more than tempted to make fried chicken and waffles for breakfast, but had decided to refrain since she already had one major mess to clean up before the end of the day.

She opened the door to the bathroom and stuck one leg into the gap in order to prevent Tom from running out and pestering Joan. An option that Freya wasn't completely opposed to, but she didn't want him meddling with Axel and Meg. A sharp peck to her shin caused an angry yelp to escape her lips. It tumbled halfway through her mouth before she bit down on her tongue in order to keep quiet. The last thing she needed was an angry rooster and a nosy mother who possibly put her husband in a coma under the same roof. *Now I need some Tylenol too*, she thought to herself in frustration. The sound of ruffling feathers alerted her to another impending attack. Freya swatted her leg outward in order to prevent Tom from successfully pecking her a second time. She heard the sound of ruffling feathers and swiftly burst into the room before she closed the door.

Freya leaned down so that she was closer to Tom's line of sight.

"Listen here, you pest. If you don't behave, you're going to find out how mean I can really be. I've been very patient with you. Especially given

145

that in human form, you were the redneck devil. If you want to stay alive as a chicken and not a cockroach…behave."

Tom suddenly found a speck on the tiled floor to interest him. He continued to look down as Freya remained crouched and opened the cabinet below the sink. She reached into the drawer and pressed down in order to open the child lock. She had placed child-lock doors in the entire bathroom in order to thwart her tiny guest from any sneaky plans. She rifled through the cabinet and found the large emergency kit that was extremely full of items from face masks and gloves to Tylenol and hydrogen peroxide. Freya took the bottle of Tylenol out and decided to just leave it out on the counter for easy access throughout the weekend. She placed the emergency kit back inside the drawer and gave one more meaningful look to the silent rooster.

Freya let out a large sigh and decided to get her mother a glass of water from the kitchen before heading upstairs. She quickly grabbed two of the tallest glasses and filled them both to the brim. The two pills of Tylenol were relatively simple for her to toss back without water, but she decided to follow them with water for fear of them getting stuck in her throat. One of her friends had taken antibiotics without water and had ended up in the emergency room with a burned esophagus. The story sent a shiver of discomfort down her spine. Even though she could easily swallow two tiny pills without water, she made a point to use water in order to avoid the same fate as her dear friend. It was all that Adrianna had talked about for an entire summer, and there was no way Freya planned to deal with such agony with two possible attempted murderers under her roof.

An hour later, Joan was in the middle of explaining why the upstairs office needed to have a better flow when a loud ringing reverberated around the first floor and trilled its way up to the second. Freya wasn't sure if her mother was referencing feng shui or just didn't particularly find Freya's bedroom appealing. She decided not to dwell on the possible reasons. *Thank the stars. This furniture fight was set to be the end of the McLoughlin family.*

146

Freya barreled down the stairs two at a time and raced to the front door. The arguing voices hinted at the newcomers outside.

She could faintly hear, "At least tuck the charm necklace inside of your shirt, you idiot. We're supposed to be undercover. This isn't *CSI Wishburn*. There will be no police report if we go missing."

A slight frown of confusion crossed Freya's face as she cracked the door open and poked her head out to greet both Tanya and Aimée.

The duo instantly grew quiet as Freya greeted, "Thank you for coming." Lowering her voice to a whisper, she continued, "Please, remember this is just a casual lunch. At least until it no longer works out that way." The sound of footsteps on the wooden stairs alerted Freya to her mother's approaching presence, so with one final look at Tanya, she fully opened the door and exclaimed, "I'm so glad that you could both make it and meet my mother!"

Joan allowed a genuine smile to grace her lips as she stepped forward and motioned for the two women to enter the house. "Thank you, Mrs. McLoughlin." The women walked into the foyer and proceeded further into the house.

A pinched nerve seemed to mar Joan's host-like smile at the comment. "You both can call me Joan. I actually insist. Even my daughter needs to refer to me as Joan or Mom when speaking with other people." The comment was casually thrown into the air, but the suggestion was clear.

Freya shifted in discomfort as she moved to close the front door. Her mother had always hated being referred to by her last name. It especially became an issue of extreme contention after Freya's father had passed. Joan had even mentioned changing her last name, but then Freya and Aidan had thrown multiple explosive fits at the thought of no longer sharing the same last name with their mother. At the time, the change felt like a symbolic desertion of their father. In the end, Joan had yielded and kept the last name, but she had made it clear that she preferred to be addressed by her first name. Freya assumed that it was too painful for her to hear even the slightest reference to her dead husband. Freya was finally beginning to understand Joan's aversion.

Aimée glided into the rarely used living room and perched on the cream sofa. The seating arrangement was shaped in a half-circle that showcased the stone-laden fireplace and massive window. A perfect view of the large tree in the front yard warmly greeted the cozy room and added a sense of peace to the tense group. Tanya walked over to Aimée and claimed the spot next to her on the sofa. Aimée inclined her head to Tanya, and they both leaned forward to shake Joan's hand in greeting.

Tanya and Aimée each held a bouquet of flowers and handed them to Freya's mother as they were introduced. It wasn't hard to tell which bouquet was from Aimée, as it was an elaborate assortment of roses. Tanya's arrangement had several flowers handpicked from her personal garden and was neatly wrapped around the middle with a bow. The personal touch didn't escape Freya as she knew that Tanya enjoyed spending the majority of her time cultivating her notorious green thumb. Freya wanted to hug Tanya and Aimée for their thoughtful gesture. Even if their main motive was to discover if Joan was guilty, it still felt nice that they were giving Joan the benefit of the doubt. Something that Freya begrudgingly acknowledged seemed to grow more and more difficult.

"Mom, these are my two friends that I have been telling you about. Tanya and Aimée. They have been helping me get to know the town and cope with Axel." *If only you knew how much they were helping me with Axel.* Freya gestured with her hand to each woman in turn and tried to keep an observant eye on her mother. If Joan was a witch, then she would most likely have the ability to sense Aimée and Tanya.

Not for the first time, Freya wished that it was past her first Halloween as a witch so that she would be able to come into her own abilities and use them. It was extremely frustrating to have to rely on other people because she wasn't strong enough to use her own magic.

"Oh, let's go meet Meg. She's with Axel at the moment, but I'm sure that she won't mind. Meg was my first friend in Wishburn and helped me when I ended up with a little chill." Tanya let out a loud snort. Freya sent a sharp glare in her direction. Freya didn't want her mom to know about her near-drowning adventure. Joan would just insist upon Freya moving in with her if she knew. Freya felt like a kid all over again as soon as her mother walked through the door. It was like she was ten years old and had to resort to scheming and half-truths in order to have her way. That and Joan was just as overbearing now as she was when Freya and Aidan had lived with her growing up.

Tanya instantly realized her mistake, and in an effort to make amends, she stood up and clapped her hands together. "That sounds great, I haven't really had the pleasure of talking much with Meg." Tanya practically crawled over Aimée's lap to be able to escape the confined space between the blue sofa and wooden coffee table. Tanya led the charge toward Axel and Meg without further explanation as she sped out of the room.

Aimée picked up both bouquets and added, "Yes, let's greet her, and then I'll place these flowers in a vase for you, Joan." She bundled them into her arms and then walked at a much more leisurely pace down the hallway.

Freya and her mother remained facing each other in the living room. Joan arched a singular eyebrow in the exact fashion that her daughter had learned from years of familiarity. Joan then stood up and flicked imaginary flecks of dirt from her clothing. "They're certainly more enthusiastic than your friends in Los Angeles. Must be their lack of exposure to proper social settings."

"Mom!" She let out a sharp hiss and stood up to follow behind her friends. *This is going to be a long weekend*, Freya thought miserably.

Chapter 16

Tanya sent Freya a conspiratorial wink and went back into a heated conversation with Meg. Freya could only understand bits and pieces of their passionate conversation since she had walked into the middle. Apparently they were disagreeing about the best place to grab coffee in Wishburn.

Joan walked into the room and squeezed Freya's shoulder. Freya's eyes widened in response to her mother's subtle gesture. It wasn't very often that her mother displayed signs of affection. It was a small gesture of support that warmed her heart with joy. The knowledge that everyone had gathered to officially find out if Freya's mother was guilty of putting Axel into a coma provided a newfound sense of anxiety. Freya's stomach felt as though it was made out of lead as she tried to remain calm. Freya watched Aimée squint her eyes in concentration. The blond continued to look between Axel and Joan with a look of stern calculation upon her delicate features. Although Tanya tried to be subtler than her counterpart in order to gain back brownie points from her living room debacle, Freya could still tell that she was also trying to analyze something mainly invisible.

Freya felt her heartbeat suddenly thrum inside of her ears. It surged in her chest until it was the only sound that she could hear. She thought of every time that her mother had brushed off meeting Axel and told her to just adopt a dog if she was lonely. Joan insisted that getting married was a last resort for lonely people. Joan had only met Axel six months before they had married because Joan had continued to insist that the relationship wasn't serious. Freya felt as if she was finally putting together the last chapters in a crime novel as her head swam with memories. Instances where Joan didn't approve or made pointed jabs at Axel throughout their marriage. He had always politely rebuffed Joan and told Freya in private that Joan wasn't really attacking him in general. He was convinced she had a strange aversion to men. But what did Joan have to gain if she successfully killed Axel? Did she want more time with Freya? Did she want Freya to sell Freya Designs or hand the company off to Aidan?

None of her guesses made sense.

A movement near Axel's bed caused Freya to settle back into reality. Tanya slowly shook her head in a negative manner as the two made eye contact. Freya felt sick. Bile rose in the back of her throat and into her mouth. *Now we have no suspects and no clue how to undo the spell before Halloween.* If Joan was the culprit, at least they would have known where to start. Without a clear lead, there was nothing that the trio could do. Freya didn't really know what to feel as a large part of her was relieved that even though Joan didn't like Axel, she didn't hate him enough to end up killing him.

"Are you okay, Freya?" Meg stopped fussing with Axel's blanket and turned to look at Freya's visibly pale face. The color had drained away and left her freckles as the only sign of pigment across her high cheekbones.

"I think that I just need some water." Freya did her best not to stutter as she practically raced out of the room. She needed space in her now-crowded-up-to-capacity guest room. Freya entered the kitchen and turned on the faucet to as cold as possible. She stuck her slightly shaking hands under the cool flow of water and just watched the liquid dampen her shaky palms. Freya cupped her hands and then threw the collected water onto her clammy face. A deep breath released itself from her chest as she looked out of the kitchen window and into her backyard. *How did I get here?* The question seemed to taunt her as she stared out the window as cold water carelessly trickled into the drain.

"We need to talk, Freya. I know what you did."

Joan came into the kitchen with her arms protectively crossed over her chest. Her observant gaze looked over her daughter as she licked her upper lip with disdain. Joan looked as calm and collected as any other day, but there was an aura of sadness around her that was extremely unusual.

"I know, Mom." Freya mustered out a simple reply before she turned off the faucet and headed back to join the rest of the group.

Meg and the girls had left about ten minutes after they all had shared a more relaxed lunch. Freya was glad that she had the foresight to order delivery so that there was one less thing she had to handle. The lunch had been relatively calm, given that the girls now knew that Freya's mother wasn't the culprit behind Axel's situation. Under better circumstances Freya was convinced that Joan and Aimée would have gotten along and been relatively good friends. The two had exchanged witty commentary more than twice over catered Italian food.

Joan and Freya were just about finished with putting away the leftovers when Joan let out a frustrated sigh. She closed the fridge and looked at her daughter with evident irritation that she had so tactfully held back for the entirety of lunch.

"Would you like to talk, Mom?" Freya placed the last dish inside of the dishwasher and then started the machine. She wiped her hands on the dish towel and then placed it on the handle of the already-humming contraption. *No point in procrastinating now.*

"I'm not sure how you figured it out, but our family has a long and deep line of gifted women. Your new friends must have helped you to better understand some things, I assume. Clearly not everything, as you geniuses assumed I was a suspect."

The verbal quip was sharp and stung Freya as intended. "You never told me that we were witches. I had to learn everything without you. You're the only other choice besides me that I know of. Now that we're finally talking about this, why did you never tell me?" Freya's face flushed red in frustration. She had been going in circles for weeks to try and better understand herself and her true identity without anywhere to start. She crossed her arms over her chest and dug her fingernails into the skin of her upper arms in anger.

"I'm not going to discuss that with you."

"If you don't want to discuss what we are and why you didn't want to tell me, you might as well leave now and never come back. I need answers, Mom."

Joan stood still for a moment as her eyes widened in shock. She took a moment to compose her facial features before she finally relented. "Let's sit in the living room."

The two women stiffly walked into the other room and sat down on chairs opposite to each other. Freya sat down on the sofa and pulled her legs up to her chest. She wanted to be comfortable for this conversation as something told her that it would take some time. Joan settled onto the plush blue chaise lounge and took off her shoes. Freya wasn't surprised that her mother wore thick black socks that went past her ankles. Joan hated feeling chilly or anything frivolous like multicolored socks.

"We come from a very long line of powerful witches, as in one of the very first recorded claims of witchcraft in all of the homeland. Our first known descendant was named Alice Kyteler, who was born around the year 1280. In her time, Alice was an extremely gorgeous and well-connected aristocratic woman. However, tragedy befell her when her husband died. She remarried a total of three more times, and each husband passed away. Suspicions grew around her name, and she gained the title of a witch who lured men with her beauty and then killed them. The town accused her of killing all four of her husbands in order to gain their wealth and property."

Freya suddenly interrupted, "Wait, so we are related to a woman who killed all four of her husbands?"

Joan let out a snort and emphatically shook her head no. "There was very little in the way of medicine in Europe at the time. It would have been strange to have four husbands die but definitely not impossible. The fact that she was a gorgeous and popular aristocratic woman, no doubt, led to rumors spurred on by hatred and envy. It was well known that she turned down more than one powerful man. Alice maintained that she loved her husbands and that she was innocent of their deaths. She swore that she was somehow marked with death. She was able to escape before men arrived to kill her. Her many powerful close friends believed in her and were able to smuggle her away in order to save her life and our bloodline."

She paused, and her face pinched in a way that made the crow's-feet around her eyes more prevalent. "Alice had a dear friend and personal maid that wasn't so lucky. Her name was Patronilla De Midia, and she was accused of being a witch mainly by association. Alice wasn't able to get her contacts to warn Patronilla in time. The poor girl never stood a chance. The dark ages weren't too keen on strong women, and that's not too far off from today's America. I had hope for the future for eight short years, but things look darker than ever now. It wouldn't surprise me if the current wannabe in charge was placed there by witch hunters to try and exterminate us once and for all."

"Mom! You're doing it again." Freya cocked her head to the side and waited impatiently for Joan to get back on topic. Her mother had a habit of getting derailed when it came to topics that she was passionate about. Not always the most convenient when in the middle of a tense conversation about their family lineage.

"Right. Alice escaped and eventually found love, according to the rumor. They were able to live together until they both died of old age. Something relatively extraordinary as we age and heal differently than mortals once we finally come into our powers. You see, a woman may be a witch at birth but never develop her potential due to repression. A witch that believes she is inferior or refuses to allow emotional experiences to teach her difficult lessons will be unable to grow. Believe it or not, giving birth, for many women, actually connects them to the world and to their powers, even if they never showed signs before. The magic of life. You know about mother's intuition? It's a little more than that, but few women actually realize to what extent. That's the truly sad part. In the past, it was common for women who never had a coven to slip into madness. Repression of your magic can and will cause insanity since it's like shunning and ignoring a part of your soul. Less than a hundred years ago, many cases of women in asylums were from unaddressed depression and postpartum, but there were also a fair amount of cases where the break with reality came from women who repressed their true powers until they snapped. You see, we are one of the first recorded line of witches in European history, but that's not to say we are the only ones. Covens in Africa and Asia can trace their roots back just as far or, in some cases, further as their cultures and societies helped to foster nature. We answer to a higher power where men are not the singular masters of the universe. I could really go all day and bore you on this."

Freya hadn't noticed, but she had subconsciously shifted herself to the very edge of the sofa as her mother spoke. Her feet were planted on the floor in order to help her balance. Her elbows were pressed into her thighs and looked more like an invested sports fan than a daughter listening to the stories from her mom.

"It's fine. Whatever happened to Patronilla and her family?"

Joan shrugged her shoulders. "It was understood that she had been killed, but very little was really known about her or her origins before she came to work for Alice. It was likely that she was poor and fell into a bit of luck to be able to work for Alice." The explanation didn't exactly sit well with Freya. If Alice and Patronilla had been close, then it would have only made sense that they would eventually talk about their pasts together. They seemed like close companions for a few years. At least from Alice's first marriage until the time Alice was accused of being a witch. Maybe they had, but it just never made it to the oral story of their family lineage. It felt more likely.

"Wait, so our family line has remained in Ireland for hundreds of years. What made you and Dad decide to move to the United States?"

Joan looked away as if she was somewhere other than Freya's cozy living room. She stared somewhere just above her daughter's head and said, "Jack insisted we leave. I was so in love with him that I agreed to leave my family for him. Eventually I lost all contact with them. Freya, do you remember what I told you about your father's death?"

The question took Freya by surprise. She hadn't expected an origin witchcraft story to begin with the death of her father or for her mother to mention his passing so openly. She had never spoken about him so bluntly in the past. It had always been like pulling teeth just to gain the slightest information about what he was like.

"Yes, you told me that he was struck by lightning and that you were there." Joan suddenly looked much older than her sixty years of age. Her frown lines seemed more pronounced, and the crow's-feet in the corner of her eyes seemed to pinch the skin on her face. Her hands were slightly wrinkled on the top of her palms, and there was the occasional age spot that Freya hadn't noticed before. It seemed as if it was the first time that Freya had really taken the time to look at her mother.

"I'm going to tell you a story that you can never tell Aidan. When you were both very young, I had to work long hours at the hospital. I was a nurse and tried to pick up as many shifts as possible in order to support our tiny family. Your father was a mechanic and worked regular hours, so when I was on night shifts, he was able to watch you both. It was the perfect parental plan."

Joan let out an angry bark of laughter as her eyes glazed over in thought. She was caught up in the memories of a past that Freya could only vaguely remember. After all, her father had passed away before she was even thirteen. Freya remained silent to allow her mother time to gather her thoughts and continue when she was ready.

"One night, I got home early from a shift. My gut was already screaming at me before I had even parked the car. I have always had these strange gut feelings about things from when it's about to rain to how warm it was going to be the next day. But nothing ever worth truly noticing. I had walked into the house and—and Jack was beating Aidan with a belt. Both of their pants were down, and Jack was yelling at Aidan to take off his boxers. My poor baby was screaming in agony, and I hadn't been there to protect him. It was like some other force took over my body. I can't really explain it, but it felt as if everything in my body had shattered and rebuilt in an instant. I yelled at Jack and told him to get out and die. Aidan was curled up in terror underneath the kitchen table, so I grabbed a broom and started to beat Jack with it. He was so shocked, I guess, that I had come home early and caught him that he went out the front door. I was screaming at him, and all of a sudden, a storm came from nowhere and drenched us. The rain was torrential, and to this day it's on record as the worst recorded flash flood in Los Angeles. The lightning came out of nowhere and struck him down. He was dead before the ambulance even reached him. I remember it like it was yesterday. How the hairs on the top of his head were slightly scorched and how I just felt relief when he crumbled to the ground." Joan had tears streaming down her face as Freya sat in shocked silence. She never knew that any of that had happened. Suddenly every time that Joan was furious with her for trying to talk about her father or ask about him made sense. He was a monster.

"Does Aidan remember?"

"He never mentioned it to me afterward. I tried to get him to talk to a therapist about everything, but it was like he had wiped it all from his memory. It's possible that it was so traumatic that he really has suppressed those three months from his memory. Freya, that man was a demon and not right in the head. That has nothing to do with you or Aidan. He was only your father by blood. I realized that after I had his death on my hands that I was a witch, just like my mother. She had told me when I was sixteen and given me a locket of protection as a gift. I passed that locket down to you on your sweet sixteenth. But I never had any of the signs like she did. It all just came to me at once in a fit of fury. It had never happened to me before, and then suddenly I murdered Jack out of the blue. But I would do it again."

Joan looked at Freya with such a burning conviction that Freya had to look away. It was so full of honesty and rage that it shot through Freya's heart like an arrow. The two women sat quietly together as they processed the words that had been spoken between them. Eventually Freya looked up at her mom with a look of confusion on her face.

"Mom, Axel is nothing like Dad. Just because something horrible happened with one man doesn't mean that they're all the same. It's not fair to write him off or try to convince me to give up on him. I love him."

Joan reached over the coffee table and grasped Freya's hand. "You don't understand. When I killed your father, it tainted a part of my soul. A crime against other creatures takes away a piece of your soul and twists it into something dark and unnatural. It's similar to The Rule of Three. I suppose that in some cosmic way, his death was accepted as an evening of the scales for everything he made Aidan endure. I can't accept Axel, not because he's a bad person but because I don't want you to get hurt the same way. But I would never kill your husband, Freya. You're my daughter, and I love you. I know that it might not be expressed in the best way all the time, but you and Aidan are my everything. I can't just leave you both to fend for yourselves. I'm always going to care."

Freya felt a tear slip out of the corner of her right eye. Her lower lip trembled as she replied, "I love you too. I wish that you would have told me sooner, but I understand." She stood up and crossed the room to give her mother a hug. Her heart was aching, and even at thirty, a part of her desperately yearned for the comforting embrace of her pain-in-the-butt mother.

She crawled onto the blue chaise lounge as Joan shifted her body so that there was more room for both of them. They both held each other and cried in a moment of shared grief. Bringing up the past was almost like exhuming her father's grave. Every time that she had yearned to hear more about him or for Joan to keep a picture of him up around the house now felt so accidentally cruel. All the times when she was growing up and had wished for her father to be there with her flashed through her mind.

To realize that the image that she had created of her father was actually infinitely better than reality hurt a part of her confidence that she didn't even know could be injured. It shattered an image of her happy family and made her feel foolish for yearning to meet him for so many years.

Freya allowed another flurry of sniffles to escape her nose as she tried to wipe away her remaining tears on the sleeve of her top. "Mom, I need your help. Axel is under a spell, but I don't know who did it or why. If he's not back before Halloween, the odds are that—that he won't come back to me."

It was the first time that Freya had really said it out loud and asked for help. She was in way over her head and needed to rely on the guidance of three other women to get her and Axel out of this alive.

Joan untangled her limbs from her daughter and stood up from her curled position on Freya's furniture. Freya watched her mother's retreating figure as Joan hurriedly left the room, only to return with a box of tissues. She held the full box out to Freya and made an entreating gesture with her hand for her daughter to take a few. Freya easily obliged and grabbed two. She folded the first one in half and blew her nose like her life depended on it. The sound trumpeted around the relatively silent house.

"We need to find a way to wake Axel up before Halloween. It's the day that you'll officially ascend after getting your powers. Usually witches have an entire year to ascend as powers usually come into existence a few days after Halloween. Did you receive your powers or realize you had special gifts around the same time that Axel fell into his coma, or a little bit before?"

Freya let out a breath that stuttered a few times as it escaped her chest. "I realized for the first time the morning that Axel wasn't waking up, but the night before, the light bulbs in the chandelier had shattered when all of the electricity in the house had caused everything to go haywire. I didn't really think much of it and figured that it was a result of old wires. The house is a little over one hundred years old, so it was a little easy to explain it away. I was so busy panicking over Axel that I didn't really think about it. Mom, the night before Axel fell into his coma—we got into a fight. I was so mad, Mom."

Tears fell from her face, and Freya couldn't be bothered to wipe away her shame. She had left for a small town to try and restart her life. But strange incidents not only followed her but also intensified tenfold. Joan reached out a slightly weathered hand and used her pointed finger to smooth away the water droplets from her daughter's agonized face. They both sat together in silence. It was the first time in years that Freya could recall her mother just sitting with her in an attempt to comfort her. Even when Freya had gotten her first period or had broken her arm, Joan had been aloof at best. It was comforting to see a new side of her mother. Joan wrapped her arms around Freya, and the two held each other.

The previous hope in Freya's chest felt deflated. It was as if she was an excited child at a fair, and someone had taken a needle to her brand-new shiny balloon. The air was trickling out, and she didn't have any idea how to stop it from dying. Although asking for help had always felt like grinding sandpaper against her tongue, she was more than ready to put her ego aside in order to save Axel. If there was one thing—no, if there was one person that Freya had always desperately loved, it was Axel. It only took the near-certain knowledge that Axel would not survive past Halloween for her to understand just how important he was to her.

Freya removed one of her hands away from her vice-like grip on Joan's arm in order to rub her fingers over her tired and swollen face. She could feel how warm her face was and moved her hand to cover the skin right above her heart. In the silence, she could feel her own heartbeat as it thundered in anticipation of the future. It was a future that continued to barrel straight toward them. She thought of ways to find out who wanted Axel dead and decided to research the best private detectives and see if they were able to find any hidden vendettas against either of them. It wasn't much, but it was the best plan that she could come up with after crying her heart out with her usually stoic mother.

"Freya, I'm always here to help you with whatever you need. You just seemed so together with Freya Designs. Even now, Aidan tells me that you're running a tight ship and that he's struggling to keep up, even though he has the home field advantage. I'll do some digging for you and help you with Axel on one condition."

"What's that condition?"

"Tell me why you have a rooster locked inside of your downstairs guest bathroom?" *So much for being sneaky*, Freya thought to herself.

Chapter 17

The screen continued to cast a bright glow around the tiny office. Although it was supposed to be one of the additional rooms, Freya had to squeeze and awkwardly shuffle sideways to be able to have access to her desk. She stretched her tired arms upward as the glow continued to wash over her tired eyes. Freya cast a tentative gaze toward the corner of her computer screen and let out a tired groan.

It was almost midnight. Freya had spent almost five hours straight in her budget-friendly white swivel chair. Her back felt slumped, and her shoulders were tense from the hours of inactivity. Usually the vast hours online wouldn't even bother her, but she had spent almost an entire work-day prowling the Internet for answers and had found nothing. The Internet was apparently a place more akin to the occult and fanatics than historical truths. The best she had found were many Wiccan sites that explained how to make spells for wealth and love. Wicca, as she had learned, wasn't even related to the old customs. It was created in the twentieth century by an English man who had plucked different aspects from various cultures and placed them together.

Unfortunately Freya had only discovered her researching folly after about an hour of intensive note-taking. A rush of air escaped her nostrils in a semblance of a laugh. *If only I could have told myself a year ago that I needed to find historic evidence of witches and accurate spells.* That's it. Freya locked her computer and then turned off the screen. She decided that it was best to come back to her frenzy of open tabs at another time. With a fair amount of effort, she wiggled around the cumbersome desk and walked out of the compact space. Tom crowed at her approaching presence and then made an attempt to charge at her feet. Freya vigorously stomped her feet, and the intimidating motion almost immediately halted the attack. Instead he cowered away in a flurry of feathers. Freya walked down the stairs fully intent on a light late-night snack but halted in her tracks. There was about a two-inch hole near the bottom of the wall. Tiny specks of paint and drywall littered the floor.

"This bird is literally a gift from hell. He's so lucky that I'm trying to behave. If I lose my deposit over him, I'm making chicken and waffles," Freya angrily mumbled to herself as she ran her finger around the glaring imperfection.

She really enjoyed her new home and wanted to do everything in her power to keep it in the best condition possible. Freya knew it wasn't logical, but she always felt that a person's home was a representation of their mental state.

"On second thought, maybe a house in shambles is an accurate depiction." The dark thought escaped past her lips as she narrowed her eyes and thought about her changing reality. Maybe she really had lost her mind. That would definitely explain her conviction that she was a modern-day witch. It felt ridiculous to be a witch and drive a car. It just didn't make sense to Freya. She had always read about witches from the perspective of Salem or the witch hunts, but never in modern times. The current parallels still made it easy for Freya to understand why women with extraordinary skills or powers would try to remain anonymous. Society feared powerful women.

Either she was truly losing her mind, or she was about to face the biggest challenge in her life. Part of her hoped that she was really going crazy because at least this nightmare would all be in her head, and Axel would be alive and well. But a different part of her took pride in her growing powers and was excited for the opportunity to bring Axel back to the land of the living. Part of her also craved revenge. After all, attempted murder was a crime, and although it wasn't something that could be taken to court, she still believed that there needed to be some sort of retribution.

Freya padded into the kitchen and took her minihandheld vacuum from its perch underneath the kitchen sink. She cleaned up the mess in the hallway and then decided a little fresh air would hopefully help to provide her with a much-needed break.

"Nope." Freya let out a surprised yelp as she felt the brisk wind whip against her exposed neck. She decided to change into warmer clothes and then brave the cold weather a second time. She was glad that Aimée and Tanya weren't there to judge her inability to tolerate cold temperatures. It was freezing, at least for Freya, who was used to temperatures that averaged around the seventies and sixties. She grabbed her long winter coat and admired how it just barely brushed her ankles. It was supposed to be calf-length, but her petite size ensured that the jacket kept her fully clothed. As if on principle, Freya switched out from her comfortable pink bunny slippers and into thick socks and tall snow boots.

For the second time that evening, Freya padded outside and into the chilly evening.

She arched a skeptical eyebrow in approval and then closed the door behind her. A chilly puff of air rattled around the wind chime and drifted away into the night sky. The porch swing swung back and forth in the steady breeze. Rivulets of red hair spun around as Freya situated herself on the bench. She looked around the backyard and took a moment to just enjoy the greenery. The night held a certain energy that seemed to radiate all the way from the individual blades of grass and out into the air. It was almost as if it was a sacred place where anything was possible. Just like at the start of any visually tantalizing fairy tale. That or Freya was definitely exhausted and stressed. It also didn't help that there was less than a week before Halloween. There were only six days left since it was technically early in the morning.

A rustling sound drew Freya away from her negative train of thought. She peered into the forest and noticed a large figure as it stealthily moved through the undergrowth. Freya had a pretty good idea of who it was.

"Good evening, Cahira. How are you?" she confidently called out into the dark night. A rumble somewhere near the forest replied to her inquiry. A smile edged its way onto her lips as Freya leaned forward off the porch swing in eager anticipation. She squinted her eyes because she couldn't really differentiate the strange lifeless shape that was clenched between Cahira's powerful jaws. *Please don't let that be a rabbit or a small raccoon. I really don't want to insult her by not eating her gift*, Freya fretted to herself. In less than a minute, Cahira had easily crossed the grass and stood with her head tilted to the side in inquiry. Freya looked into the big cat's eyes and noticed that her familiar seemed to know something that she didn't. It was a look that Cahira had given her on the night that they had first met.

Freya stood up and walked over to meet Cahira on the dewy green expanse. She felt compelled to care for the cougar's comfort and decided that Cahira had done most of the work crossing the backyard, so the least that she could do was walk down three steps.

Crumpled fabric became visible as the light from the patio illuminated the previously hidden item. It didn't seem like something that Freya had made in her textile factory. Even though she hadn't been there to personally green light the newer items, she had an amazing photographic memory and knew that she would have recognized it right away.

She walked closer to Cahira and knelt down to get a better perspective.

Cahira's warm breath caressed Freya's chilly hands as her knees grew cold from the condensation on the ground. Freya grabbed the fabric and realized that it was a shirt that she had seen before. It was Delilah's shirt. She could still smell the lingering scent of her ex-assistant's absolutely vile perfume. As if Cahira could read her mind, she let out several catlike sneezes and rubbed a massive paw over her wet nose. Freya absentmindedly petted Cahira's soft fur as she continued to stare at the shirt in confusion. "Why did you bring this to me, gorgeous? It must have been a real journey."

The longer that Freya held onto the shirt, the more it seemed to burn her hand. She couldn't put her finger on it, but the fabric seemed to rub her palm raw. The discomfort motivated her to walk up the porch stairs and open the backdoor for Cahira. Freya made an entering motion as she held open the door. Cahira let out a chuffing sound and leapt onto the patio in one bound. She seemed to have grown in size since the last time she had visited Freya. The muscles in her back shook as Cahira bounded over the expanse of the entire patio and landed one pace away from the doorway. She casually waltzed into the kitchen and headed toward the living room.

Freya closed the door and locked it as she called out, "Where are you going?" Her question was quickly answered as the mountain lion walked back into the room with a white knit throw blanket gently gripped between her teeth. The sight was definitely one that Freya would remember as the blanket trailed behind Cahira as she struggled not to rip it in the move. She placed it right next to the heater in the corner of the kitchen and then curled up into a comfortable ball. She looked more like an oversized house cat than a cunning and intelligent wild feline with over one hundred pounds of muscle.

A hiss of pain escaped her lips as Freya dropped Delilah's shirt to the ground. The material had somehow scalded her. Upon further inspection, Freya realized that the palm of her hand was aggravated. *I must be going crazy.* She riffled through her cabinets and easily found a paper bag from one of her new favorite clothing boutiques on Main Street and unceremoniously tossed the shirt inside and placed the bag on the dining table. Freya then washed her hands in case there was any residue.

"Did you get any on you?" Freya felt her brows crease together in concern as she crept closer to the comfortable cougar. Sure enough, there was a bare patch around the bottom of Cahira's chin where her fur was partly missing.

"I can't believe that I'm about to do this."

Freya then reached forward and pulled on Cahira's upper lip so that she could inspect the big cat's massive teeth and gumline. Inflamed skin immediately came into view, and Freya reflexively let out a hiss. She could only imagine how tedious it was to carry that shirt over two hundred miles over the span of multiple days when Freya could barely tolerate holding it for a few minutes. She walked over to the sink and placed a little water on a rag before she settled next to her unflinching counterpart. Cahira opened her mouth and revealed her massive teeth and irritated gums. In any other situation Freya would have run for the hills at the first sight of such large death mushers, but this creature was her responsibility. Gingerly she dabbed the water-soaked cloth over the irritated areas and hopefully soothed a little of the discomfort.

"Freya, what's all the fuss?" Joan called down the stairs in a voice filled with sleep. The distinct sound of footsteps on the wooden stairs caused Cahira to swivel her ears like a radio searching for the perfect frequency.

Joan entered the kitchen with large pink rollers in her hair and a floor-length white silk robe. She looked as if she had escaped from a 1950s Hollywood film and mistakenly wandered into a log cabin. Her eyes were slightly blurry with the remnants of sleep but instantly perked up when her previously dreary gaze landed on Cahira. Joan's eyes widened into saucers as she exclaimed, "That's a pricey familiar to feed!" She then strolled over toward the coffeepot and began to prepare an extremely early morning brew.

For some reason, the underwhelming reaction was somewhat expected. Freya then opened the fridge and found the half a pound of turkey that she had purchased earlier in the morning as well as a cooked half-breast of chicken. Cahira looked upward in excitement at the smell of fresh meat.

"Yes, these are for you. Thank you for the gift, even though I'm not really sure what to do with it."

Freya placed the slices of turkey on a plastic plate that she had purchased just for Cahira and then filled a new bowl to the brim with water. She realized her mistake of filling the bowl too early as she cautiously tiptoed over to the comfortable feline. The water sloshed around and constantly threatened to spill over the edge but remained just shy. Freya let out a sigh of relief that was short-lived as Cahira eagerly lapped at the water and spilled it everywhere. Freya rolled her eyes and checked on the chicken that she had tossed in the pan. She had thought about just tossing it in the microwave but decided against it. The taste wouldn't be the same, and she didn't want to spoil Cahira's first taste of chicken. *This kitty already has me wrapped around her paw.*

Joan finished pouring Freya a cup of coffee and then grabbed a similar cup for herself. Freya's mother looked somewhat more alive for someone who had been fast asleep only a few minutes earlier. After their heart-to-heart conversation, Freya had decided to let the past go and stay in the guest room closest to Axel.

"Freya, what's in that cheap bag on the kitchen table? Don't tell me it's another top from a store around here. They're positively kitsch." Although Joan mumbled the last part, it didn't escape Freya's hearing. She struggled to refrain from rolling her eyes at her mother. Even though Joan had made it clear that she loved Freya, there were times when Freya struggled to really feel that love.

"You know we used to be poor, Mom? A fact that you love to forget when it comes to whatever I wear or do."

"That's not the point. Is it so wrong of me to only want the best of you? I'm just concerned, sweetie, just because your husband is in a coma doesn't mean you need to buy wrinkled shirts."

"Mom! Stop. Cahira brought me it as a gift. It's my ex-assistant's shirt." Freya pointed behind her as she placed the warmed chicken on the same plate as the sliced turkey. She let out a youthful giggle as Cahira elegantly lifted up her nose to smell the now-properly prepared meal.

Within a few seconds, Cahira eagerly devoured the chicken. The crunching and cracking of bones filled the air as Joan disdainfully peaked into the bag and inspected the wrinkled shirt. Freya watched Cahira curiously sniff the chilled slices of deli meat. She then curiously stuck out her tongue and gave it an experimental flick. Cahira seemed to approve of the results from her initial taste test as she happily devoured the morsels.

Joan's sudden silence caused Freya to turn around. It wasn't like her mother to suddenly become silent in the middle of one of her notorious rants. Freya instantly noticed that Joan's complexion had grown pale as she covered her gaping mouth with her left hand. She looked as if she had accidentally opened Pandora's box.

"Freya, who was your assistant?" Joan's voice was high-pitched, and the question grated against the air like nails on a chalkboard.

"She came highly recommended. We worked together for a few months before everything fell apart, why?"

The tension in the air was palpable as Joan slowly removed her gaze from the content within the bag. Joan looked across the room to her daughter. Her face held a look that was just about two steps below panic. Cahira seemed to notice the change in the room as her tail restlessly flicked back and forth to display her mild agitation.

"This shirt is a perfect energy match to the one that mostly surrounds Axel. Your assistant is the one who tried to kill Axel? Why?"

A jolt of fear slammed into Freya's rib cage at the new information. She had foolishly thought that Delilah's attitude problem the last few weeks that they had worked together was a result of personal issues. At the very worst, she had assumed that her assistant had grown too stuck-up for her job and no longer had the decency to behave herself. But to know that Delilah had attempted to kill Axel left her with more questions than answers. Why did Delilah pick Axel? Was he just convenient, or was there more to the story? Who really was her devious assistant that Freya had so naively invited to drop off reports at her home more than once. *That's most likely how Delilah met Axel, I served that idiot up to her on a silver platter.* The thought didn't sit well with her, mostly because she still struggled to process the feeling of betrayal that slithered within her stomach at the thought of her husband with another woman. A strong sense of violation also crept through her body at the understanding that she had unwittingly invited a murderess into her sacred sanctuary.

"At least we know who did it. Now we just have to find out who she is. Something tells me this is not going to unravel as simply as I had hoped."

Joan let out a loud snort. "You think that a witch who, for no apparent reason, wants to murder your husband is a relatively simple spell to resolve? This is going to be a very difficult job, not only because we need to know more about Delilah but also because we are going to need at least two more cans of coffee to get this mended before Halloween."

Freya only nodded her head in agreement as her memory desperately tried to recall every detail about Delilah. If that was even her real name. Freya left the kitchen in a flurry of movement that was so unexpected that it startled Cahira into letting out an aggravated hiss. In less than two minutes, Freya returned with a copy of Delilah's old résumé that was still warm from the printer. She cracked her neck in a circle and mumbled, "That's a start."

The patter of soft paws drew Freya's attention away from the make-shift evidence table. Cahira rubbed her large body against Freya's over-sized winter coat in a gesture of affection. Freya looked down and let out a chuckle. She hadn't even had time to remove her snow coat or boots. With a few impatient tugs, the jacket was soon removed and placed on the hook nearest to the backdoor.

"You're very powerful for a new familiar. It's not very common for witches to discover their familiar before their first Halloween. This is very strange but in the best way possible."

"Mom, where is your familiar?" Freya turned around in sudden curiosity. She had completely forgotten until now to ask Joan about her familiar.

Joan smiled mischievously at her daughter as the crow's-feet by the corner of her eyes crinkled to add a hint of aged wisdom to her features. "You've met him before."

It took Freya a moment to think of the answer. Suddenly the answer came to her as clear as the Los Angeles skyline after a week of rain. "Mr. Scruffles. That explains his unusually long life."

"He doesn't like to fly, so I gave Aidan strict instructions on how to take care of him. We found each other a month after the anniversary of your father's death. After we bonded, my magic had more control. When did you and Cahira find each other?"

The question brought a frown of displeasure across Freya's features. She rubbed the palm of her hands against her black sweatpants in discomfort. "We met before any real incident with my powers happened. I almost ran her over when I took Mulholland Drive to get home. She was in the middle of the street like she had come out of the wilderness just to greet me. At the time, I thought it was just an extremely rare stroke of luck, but now I think that it was her way of officially introducing herself to me."

In true Joan fashion, Freya's mother chose to interpret only the most negative part of her explanation. "Freya McLoughlin, I taught you better than to speed recklessly through the hills. Were you texting? I will take your car keys away from you."

Freya let out a sigh as she looked upward in an attempt to salvage her patience. If Joan had indirectly taught Freya anything, it was how to keep herself together when dealing with difficult people. "Mom, the point is, I met Cahira before any of my powers had even manifested. She knew before I did and found me first."

Her mother continued to mumble incoherently about driving as she pulled out a kitchen chair and sat down. The bright-pink rollers in her hair as she continued her rant only made her look closer to a strange cartoon character. Each roller was a slightly different size and thickness than the last. A smile lifted the right side of Freya's mouth as she looked at her mother's nightly routine.

"Cahira, welcome to my daughter's home. You will make a lovely family member." Joan looked over to the cougar who had carefully placed its large head on Freya's lap.

"I'll have to see if it's possible to put a strangely large dog door on the backdoor since this is a rental. Maybe we will just change out the doors while we're here. I'll just place back the original when the lease ends."

Cahira let out a loud yawn in response as she stretched out her front paws and extended and then retracted her massive claws in one powerful motion. The big cat rubbed against Freya's legs as she strolled toward the direction of the door. Cahira looked at Joan and slowly dipped her head in a formal gesture of goodbye.

Freya walked over to open the door and lovingly ran her fingers over the rather coarse brown fur. Cahira let out a contented purr as the two played a game of cat and mouse around the kitchen chair. *She's stronger, better-looking, and better-mannered than I am, but at least my hair is redder.*

Joan strode over and placed a comforting hand on Freya's shoulder as they watched Cahira leisurely wander back into the dense forest. In less than five heartbeats, the mountain lion had soundlessly prowled back into her home. Freya looked upward at the sky and let out a sigh of exhaustion. The surrounding area was nowhere as dark as it had been when Freya was outside earlier in the evening. They had spent at least a few hours up and squabbling about Delilah's shirt. It wasn't sunrise just yet, but Freya had a feeling that it was already around five in the morning.

"I'm going back to bed. As soon as it's morning, we can dive into a plan to weed out Delilah's true identity. Something tells me that we're going to need to work very hard to bring down this bitch of a witch."

Before Joan was all the way up the stairs, she turned around and called out again, "Oh, and Freya? Put the shirt somewhere no one can get it. Preferably not close to Axel. We aren't sure what that would do." Joan paused for a third time when she was halfway up the stairs. She turned around to look her daughter in the eyes and said, "I'm proud of you for finding Cahira. Or for Cahira finding you. She'll be a lovely addition to the family."

With that said, Joan turned around and headed up the remaining final stairs to the master bedroom that she had so passionately redecorated. Freya wrapped her arms around her chest and allowed the words to wash over her body. It was extremely rare for Joan to say anything positive and encouraging, and she wanted to bask in the words of encouragement for as long as possible. She knew it wasn't very logical, but in some ways, she still really wanted to receive words of approval from her mother. Even at thirty years old, Freya wanted to make her mom proud. Which, at many times, had seemed absolutely impossible when she and Aidan were growing up. It now occurred to her that Joan's inability to mother in a style that she had needed and craved wasn't a result of a lack of affection for her daughter but from Joan's darkened soul. Now that Freya knew about her mother's past, the childhood full of sparse encouraging words and infrequent hugs made sense. It wasn't a reflection about Joan's love for either of her kids but more a result of her accidentally tainted soul.

After she had cleaned Cahira's little mess in the kitchen and put away the bowls, the sun was moments away from peeking through the horizon. From the kitchen window, Freya was able to see the faintest traces of orange and pink hues as they playfully intermingled across the dark sky.

Freya only had one conference call at noon today, so she wasn't exactly in a hurry to rush to bed. Usually she would have three to four calls a day and stacks of paperwork to sift through. Although Freya didn't want to admit it, having more time to herself felt amazing. If it was under any other set of circumstances, she was sure that it would be the perfect way to recharge.

Without putting much thought into where she was headed, Freya soon found herself outside of Axel's bedroom. She reached into the top of her shirt, but then retracted her hand and hesitated. *I need to put that shirt away.* Freya quickly sped back into the kitchen with her snow boots that she had yet to remove and grabbed the bag. She placed it inside of her temporary bedroom, underneath a stack of books, and then closed the door. Finally she returned back to Axel's room and left the door ajar. Freya felt guilty for keeping his door locked, but she wasn't sure how else to protect him if Tom or someone else decided to dabble in a bit of mischief. She also opened the window curtains and allowed the sparse morning rays to trickle into the room. Freya gently traced Axel's sharp jawline that was covered in a generous layer of early-morning stubble.

"I love you. I'm sorry that it took me almost losing you to be able to show that." She looked at Axel's face and willed him with every cell in her body to wake up. He remained stoic, just as he had for almost two months.

Freya threw her snowshoes near the entrance of the door and then picked up her new copy of *The Great Gatsby*. She flipped toward where she had left a blue bookmark and prepared to continue reading. They were almost halfway through the story, and although Freya had read it several times, she always managed to immerse herself into the plot as if it was the first time.

"I really hope that I'm not Gatsby in our story, Axel."

Chapter 18

Tanya managed to find more information in two days than the two private detectives that Freya had hired combined. She managed to put two paid professionals to shame using only the Internet and a smartphone low on data. Tanya had called Freya about two hours ago and insisted that she was coming over with information. She also added that she planned to pick up Aimée in about an hour. About halfway through the call, Freya could hear Scott as he pestered Tanya to get off the phone in the middle of checking out a customer.

Tanya hollered close enough to the phone so Freya overheard, "But this is a matter of life and death. Scott, go bag the groceries!"

With less than forty-eight hours to be able to save Axel, any information was welcome. The last few nights, Freya had woken up from multiple restless attempts at sleep. After two nights of anxiously grinding her teeth, Freya felt like her jaw was about to break. Her clear mouth guard never stood a chance. Although she hadn't ground her teeth in years, the negative habit seemed to have come back with a vengeance. Freya was excited to meet everyone and took the stairs two at a time to throw on a pair of pants without gaping holes near the crotch. She doubted that two-day-old sweat-pants would present the proper image.

"Freya, why are you pounding up the stairs like an elephant?"

"Mom! Tanya and Aimée are coming over in a bit. Tanya called and said that she found some information on Delilah last night." Freya walked into her old room just as she secured a clean pair of bottoms around her waist.

Freya didn't have to say anything else as Joan immediately stood upward at the news. She left the comfortable bed and walked over to give her daughter a large hug. They remained there for a moment until Joan pulled away and furiously blinked her eyes. Freya felt a tinge of guilt as she remembered how she had so strongly assumed Joan was guilty of hurting Axel. But at the time, her mom was the only guess that made sense. Joan had always lacked the presumed warmth of a mother, but now she seemed to be making an effort.

"Well, now I have to call out for food. It's almost lunchtime, and we can't have people over without food. That simply can't be done, even if the world is going to hell in a handbasket."

Freya nodded her head in agreement and left the bedroom. There was no point in arguing against the food. Besides Freya was a little hungry since she had accidentally skipped breakfast and opted for two cups of black coffee. *A bite of food would help to make a proper plan of action.*

As she was fixing her hair in the bathroom mirror, she let out a groan. A bright streak of yellow ran down the top of her chin to the side of her neck. Freya had just finished the preliminary budget for next year, thanks to the figures that Aidan had sent back to her.

She turned on the sink and furiously scrubbed in an effort to remove the remaining highlighter marks.

Furious clucking drew Freya's attention away from the mirror, and her gaze wandered to the floor. Tom was just as unruly as usual as he tried to peck at Freya's feet. Luckily she had thrown on a pair of flats, so it wasn't as painful in comparison to the few times that Tom had attempted to peck away at her bare feet.

"Good morning to you too. I'll let you walk around the majority of the house today, if you promise not to be such a menace."

The only sign that Tom even heard her was that he begrudgingly backed away from her now-slightly throbbing toes. He ruffled his feathers and shuffled his feet in impatience and sulkily strolled out of the room with his busted ego in tow.

"Glad to see that we are on the same page."

The doorbell rang and caused Freya to turn around one more time as she pointed her finger in Tom's direction and threatened, "Behave." The doorbell rang again and continued to persistently trill to the point that it almost sounded like a song. Freya opened the door and found Tanya bouncing on the heels of her feet in excitement as Aimée stood about a foot back with her arms crossed casually across her chest.

"In case you're wondering, Tanya was pushing the doorbell to the theme song from the television show *CSI*. Before you ask, yes the one with the lyrics that are like, 'Who are you—'" Aimée stopped herself as she realized that she was about to burst out into song. She composed herself back into her usual calm-and-collected demeanor as the faintest tint of red invaded her cheeks.

Tanya let out a snort as she waved her hands in the air and walked into the kitchen. She held two manila folders that were nearly bursting with various papers. Tanya smiled from ear to ear as she spread out the contents of the first folder that had the title "Delilah the Demon Witch Part 1" in bold black Sharpie.

Joan walked into the kitchen, and it didn't escape Freya's gaze that her hair was perfectly curled and styled, thanks to the randomly sized rollers that she had used earlier that morning. *At least I'm wearing real pants.*

"Ladies, I ordered Thai food, and it should be here in about an hour. Tanya, I'm told that you have some exciting news."

"More than exciting! Delilah is a witch and not just any kind of a witch. Apparently she's more like a siren. She inserts herself into relationships and feeds off the pain and sadness from the loneliest partner. In a way, she seduces them with her magic and then uses their pain to keep her young. Ultimately after sirens have sex, it kills the lonely partner and moves on in search of a new victim. I had to look up some information about this kind of witchcraft and found out it's very rare but has its roots in dark magic. Delilah must have been keeping tabs on you and Axel for months. Freya, I think that she was at the end of draining Axel and that you walking into the room was actually a very messed-up good thing—"

A sharp chime of the doorbell caused Tanya to stop midthought. Freya stood up and motioned for the women to wait as she walked over to the door. As she pulled it open, her eyes widened in surprise. *That's definitely not Thai food.*

Chapter 19

Freya quickly managed to suppress her shock. Instead of Thai food, Sally stood outside in a pale-pink down jacket, and her hair was neatly combed. There were no apparent bruises on her face, and for the first time, she seemed to have an air of calm radiating from her body.

"Sally! It's so good to see you. What brings you over?" Freya made sure to practically shout the first part so that the women seated around the kitchen table in the back of her house were able to hear. She heard the faintest shuffling of papers as she continued to smile at Sally. If she hadn't been intentionally searching for the sound, Freya was sure that she would have missed the movement.

"Hi, Freya, I was wondering if it was a good time to maybe talk over a cup of coffee? If not, that's okay."

"I'm so happy that you came over. Please, come in. You can meet my mom and Tanya and Aimée since they're all in the kitchen too. We ordered too much for lunch, so you actually came at the perfect time. Now we don't have to throw anything out!"

Sally's face practically beamed in joy at the invitation to have lunch with the other women. She was more at peace than Freya had ever seen the petite girl. The years that had previously aged her face seemed to have subtly melted away, now that Tom was no longer scaring her and depriving her of peace. Freya led the way to the kitchen in an effort to partially block the view in case there were any stray papers from the files on Delilah strewn about the room. To Freya's relief, the kitchen table now had four cups of warm coffee and thin chocolate wafer cookies on a large white plate.

"Look who is joining us for lunch! Sally stopped by, and it's the perfect timing so that we can all catch up. I'll be right back, Sally. I'm going to get another chair from the living room."

Freya walked down the hallway toward the front of the house and entered the living room, just in time to witness Tom trying to rip apart bits of the sofa.

"I told you to behave! That's it. Go to the kitchen, you pest, or you'll spend the rest of the week inside of the downstairs bathroom."

Frey picked up the rarely used blue-accent chair in the corner of the room and walked closer to the rest of the group. Easy laughter and friendly banter rang throughout the house and helped to put Freya's mind at ease. From the first time that she had met Sally, the small woman made her feel a strange sense of protectiveness. The instinctive emotion proved correct now that everything with Tom had eventually come to light. *I wonder if in the future, Scott—*

The thought was placed on the back burner of her mind almost as quickly as it started.

Freya walked into the kitchen with the rather large chair held precariously in the air. Tanya was the first to notice her precarious struggle. Immediately she stood up to help lessen the burden.

"Thanks for the lift, Tanya."

After rearranging the furniture, Freya thanked her friend and then sat down on the blue chair around the table. She settled into the semicircle of chairs as a bubble of laughter burst through her lips. Freya had sunk down about three inches into the chair that was already much closer to the ground than the other seats. The top of her red hair and joyful green eyes were just barely visible above the table. The situation reminded her of simpler times when she was a child just learning to sit at the "grown-up" table. A snort escaped Tanya as she searched in her purse for her phone. Freya was relatively small even for a woman, and the chair created the illusion that even Sally was at least a head-length taller than her.

A few seconds later, and Freya's height debacle was clearly documented. Aimée let out two or three giggles and then pulled out her cell phone from her purse. She took a few quick photos as Freya tried her best to pose appropriately. For the last photo, Aimée decided to take a selfie of the group. Freya wrapped her arm around Sally and pulled the other women closer to her as everyone smiled brightly. When Aimée showed the group the photos, the last one sent everyone into a new round of hysterics. Sally towered over Freya, and the mousy brunette had the largest smile that Freya had ever seen. A warmth spread within Freya's chest as she absent-mindedly rubbed a circular pattern over her heart.

An angry clucking interrupted the group. *Tom, you are really almost as bad as a rooster as you were as a man.* When he turned the corner and noticed Sally, he let out a furious crow and attempted to charge her. Freya jumped in shock as Sally reflexively thrust her purse toward the irate bird. Tom flapped his wings in panic as the purse connected with his chest with a medium amount of force. It was enough to stun the bird as well as all the other women within the room. While Sally was busy unwittingly chastising her husband, the remaining table members exchanged looks of shock. Unaware of the situation, Sally exclaimed, "I didn't know that you had a chicken, Freya!"

She turned around in surprise once Tom settled in the corner closest to the backdoor. The rooster turned to face the wall as Sally continued to stare intently at him. She ran her fingers through her neatly combed brown hair and waited for Freya's reply.

"I hadn't planned to get a rooster, but he kind of appeared out of nowhere. He's really a pain, and I'm not really sure how to deal with him, to tell you the truth."

Although Freya tried her best to speak with an air of indifference, a hint of color crept over the top of her shirt. There was no easy way to try and admit that she had turned Sally's husband into a bird.

"I have a chicken coop in my backyard. It would be no problem at all for me to take care of him for you. That way he can roam around the backyard, and it will give your furniture a break. He seems to have already made his way around the kitchen."

Sally was right. There were several holes now around the room, thanks to the temperamental beast of chaos. Chunks from the wooden doorway were missing, and the once-new walls were already full of scratches about five inches above the wooden floor. "Sally, I don't want to impose and give you another pet to have to look after."

"I don't mind. I was fixing to buy a rooster, so this would save me some money, unless you really want to keep him. Then in that case, I'm sorry to have even asked. I just wanted to help."

It didn't escape Freya's observation that Sally had yet to stutter in their conversation. Less than a full month without Tom berating her, and Sally was slowly gaining back some of her confidence. Although she was still overly apologetic, the improvement since they had last talked was immense.

"I would love for you to take T—this rooster off my hands and keep him outside in your backyard. Hey, I haven't seen Tom around town recently. How have you been?"

The ghost of a smile crossed her gentle features. Years of pain that usually seemed to reflect so brightly just behind her eyes was duller than usual as she brushed a stray strand of hair away from her face.

"He's gone. I came into the kitchen one day and his wallet, phone, and car were gone. The note he left was a little harsh, but it really gave me the motivation to have some closure. I didn't really want him around for some time now. To have him gone and to feel comfortable at night—it feels good." The faintest moisture seemed to press against Sally's eyes as she spoke, but she managed to keep her composure and avoid crying in front of the group.

"Wait, so he just got up and left? What did that no-good dope have to say?"

Instead of acting defensively, Sally let out a small chuckle as she looked over at Tanya. "He said that he was bored and that he'd found some other woman to bother. That I was too tough and didn't fit into his idea of a woman since I didn't do everything he wanted. I have never been so glad to be called tough or insulted in my entire life. It was like a backhanded compliment. Did you know that he even worked up some divorce papers and left them on the counter?"

The rooster crowed with fury as Sally finished her speech. Tom flapped his arms and tuned to glare at Freya as if she was the devil herself. Freya only sent the bully a sly wink in return. It had taken some work and craft, but she had gotten a good family friend and top divorce lawyer to legally and financially free Sally. Freya's hunch proved correct as she passively watched Tom throw a fit at the knowledge that he no longer had claim to Sally's assets.

Freya had done some digging, and it turned out that Sally's parents were extremely wealthy when they had passed and left everything they had to their only daughter in their will. Although Freya couldn't prove it, the timing was too convenient. They were both found dead a week after Sally had married. It was written off as a home invasion gone wrong and never inspected further. Freya had always believed in coincidences, but some were just too unbelievable. When Tom stepped into the role of Sally's husband, he took control of all of the money by convincing Sally to move everything into a joint account with both of their names. Sally had listened to him and had even agreed to put his name on the deed to her home. For years, she was financially, emotionally, and psychologically a prisoner to Tom. It only felt fitting that Freya helped to undo the damage with the little magic and wit at her disposal.

Tom continued to throw a fit and pecked his beak against the wall in petulant protest. He was apparently less than thrilled by the news that he had officially lost his hold over Sally and her money.

"I'm glad that he's gone. Now you have more time to hang out with the girls." A ring at the front signaled the arrival of food. Joan stood up and helped Freya carry in the generous serving portions.

"Thank you for thinking about lunch, Mom. Thai food sure beats grilled cheese sandwiches for such a nice casual and totally not suspicious gathering."

Joan only shook her head at her daughter and replied, "Mother knows best. If it weren't for me, this entire place would be a mess."

Freya bit her tongue, but as soon as Joan was further ahead and out of earshot, she mumbled, "Mother knows I like food. She doesn't know everything."

Sally chatted with the group for a little over two hours before she finally stood from the table. Her smile and positive energy proved infectious as they all stood to hug the little brunette farewell.

"Thank you for having me at the last minute. I'd love to stay longer, but I really want to get groceries and explore town."

The obvious implication was that Sally rarely went into town when Tom had made sure to keep her under his thumb. Before Sally left, Freya was only too eager to help maneuver the rooster into a cat carrier so that Sally could take him to live in her backyard. When the tiny brunette finally left with the screaming bird, Tanya said, "I haven't seen her smile so much in years. In fact, I haven't seen her so happy since she was dating Scott way back in high school."

Freya nodded her head in agreement, although her mind was far away in thought. She hoped that Tom wouldn't give Sally too much trouble, but something told her that she'd be fine. Sally had easily controlled the situation in the kitchen earlier and put Tom in line without so much as a quiver in her voice.

From her seated position at the table, Aimée chimed in. "You know, this might just be the most twisted sense of universal justice that I've witnessed. Freya, you are a real terror when motivated. Remind me to never incorrectly cross your path." Aimée finished the last sentence with a gentle teasing, but Freya returned a short glare in response.

Freya had spent almost a month thinking that her magic had sent her husband into a coma, and two months convinced she had, in some way, contributed to his miserable state. Axel cheating on her with her snake of an assistant had really awakened a new side to her that she didn't understand. That lack of understanding had caused her many sleepless nights. The last thing she wanted at the moment was to actually be responsible for using magic against another person. But try as she might, Freya's entire body seemed convinced that Tom deserved it and more. After all, he abused Sally for years and had tried to kill Freya to keep her quiet.

The women waved to Sally and Tom as they walked across the street to the other side of the cul-de-sac. Once Sally had entered her home, Freya closed her own front door and turned around with a playful smile on her lips. "We had a wonderful guest addition to our detective party, and now we're free of one destructive plucky pest. Now, Tanya, what do you have for us?"

Tanya practically bounced out of her chair like she had waited the entire lunch to hear that question. She swung open the oven door, although Freya had sworn that it was turned off. Tanya reached directly inside without any hesitation. Her long black hair touched against the oven door, and even though Freya knew that it was off, she felt herself recoil from imaginary pain. Her questions were quickly answered when Tanya reappeared with two thick folders in her hand.

"Nice improvisation." Freya nodded her head in approval at the unconventional but also rather genius hiding spot.

"Here in the first file, it explains a five-year pattern where she lived under three different aliases. The first time that I found Delilah, her name was Sammy, and she mysteriously broke up a couple at her work, and the woman suddenly died two weeks later from a heart attack. The second time was about two weeks later, and her name at the time was Megan. Under the name Megan, she engaged in an affair with this accountant, even though she had a family and everything. Get this, the poor woman also died less than two months after meeting Megan—well, Delilah. I have so much to share."

A shaky hand crept its way upward and covered Freya's mouth. Her tongue felt like lead, and her mouth felt as dry as the Sahara as Tanya provided concrete evidence of Delilah's malice. She couldn't believe that she had been so blind. Freya had failed to see Delilah for the true evil that she was to her core. Freya always prided herself on her ability to read people and see their true intentions, but somehow she had let a monster have full access to her life. Her lower lip wobbled from a combined sense of fury and unjustified failure.

"Do you know how she had access to Axel? If they had met at the office or at a dinner event?"

"A month before everything happened, Freya had instructed Delilah to drop off some files and samples at my home. I wanted to look them over before an upcoming trip. It didn't seem like anything at the time. I just needed her to give me some materials, and I knew that Axel was home since he always came home earlier to make me dinner. Dinner that I never bothered to prioritize."

"Dang, talk about a darker spin on *The Devil Wears Prada*."

An invisible vice seemed to tighten around Freya's chest as she acknowledged that Axel tried most nights to prepare dinner for them with the constant hope that Freya would leave work at a reasonable hour. He never gave up on her. Freya had told Axel countless times that he didn't have to feed her, but that never deterred him from trying to show his affection through his time and effort. The last week before he fell into a coma, he had made Freya promise to come home in time for dinner because he had planned to make one of her favorite dishes every night. Reliving the memories made Freya feel like a complete jerk. She had assumed that Axel was always going to wait for her on the sidelines of her life. Taking him for granted and treating him as less than her equal had placed them both in a perilous position.

"Earth to Freya. Girl, we still have plenty of hours to pull a plan together and make everything turn out okay."

Aimée nodded her head in agreement and asked, "Tanya, didn't you tell me on the way that you had discovered a book that contained a few possible spell options?"

The not-so-subtle hint of hope helped to bring a more confident smile to Freya's face. She angled her body to face Tanya's direction with a look of eager interest. If that were true, they would at least have a good idea on how to work on finding the right spell. Tanya nodded as she opened her large purse and shuffled her hand around. She looked as if she was rummaging toward the very bottom of the earth. After a few seconds and three mints, one wallet, and a jar of black paint were deposited on the kitchen table, Tanya finally retrieved a large leather book that had bold letters indented into the cover.

"It's from my family collection. This one was created in New England a few years after my great-great-great-grandma was kidnapped from Africa. She had been a revered figure in her village for her strong connection to nature. The men of the tribe had grown jealous of her influence and had sold her into slavery. There are more terms from the old land written in it than from here. I'm finally glad that I spent most of my Sundays listening to my granny tell tales from the old land. I wouldn't recognize half of the words without those stories."

True to Tanya's explanation, Freya could only understand about a third of every page as she hovered over Tanya's shoulder to try and gain a better look. Tanya confidently flipped through the book until she was almost a third of the way to the end. Tanya looked at Aimée and Joan so Freya wasn't able to gauge the expression from her position. However, from the two faces that Freya was able to see, there was something that Tanya hadn't said that made the group anxious.

Freya asked, "So what's the catch, Tanya?"

There was a moment of hesitation before Tanya smacked her lips together and replied, "The book seemed to be organized in order of difficulty. The easiest spells are in the front and the more complex ones in the back. We are going to have to perform a spell near the end of the book, and I've never really tried to perform a spell before. I always just kind of freewheeled my magic and hoped for the outcome I wanted in my head."

The news was less than positive, but Freya had anticipated that Aimée and Tanya would have little formal experience with spells. They had both tried to live their lives as mortals for the majority, and it only made sense for them to avoid casting actual spells. Freya released a breath and took her time counting to three in her head. After she took a moment to process, Freya shrugged her shoulders.

"We can work on a starter spell together as a kind of test run before we perform the main spell for Axel. Maybe we should try a spell to levitate one of us in the air. A spell that requires all of our collective efforts and attention, just to see how well we can work and communicate together."

Joan nodded her head in agreement as she placed another helping of tofu pad see ew on her plate. They had left out the tray specifically on Joan's request because she claimed that it was a dish that was best on the day it was made. Freya knew that the truth was that Joan tended to be a nervous snacker. Joan munched away on another helping, but her mind seemed to be far away from her food as she listened intently to the conversation.

"That's a good idea. I think there was a spell about levitation closer to the beginning of the book that we can try together. There are a few more things that I need to really make clear. It says in the books that manipulating people usually has a countereffect. The book says something about three rules. Basically if we bring Axel to life, something needs to happen in order to balance the scales. We can't control what happens, but the book points out that the price of life is death. Sounds ominous because it is.

However, I think we can shimmy out of that because Axel technically isn't dead. Is everyone willing to take that risk?"

Freya knew her answer immediately. However, she bit her tongue to refrain from barking out her loud and emphatic yes. She didn't want to pressure anyone. If there was one thing that Freya understood, thanks to her crash course in magic, it was that there was no spell that could be executed without clear thoughts and harmonious intentions. Every time an action was negative, it seemed to only dig Freya into a deeper hole. That meant that when they cast the spell to free Axel, they couldn't cast something to harm Delilah at the same time. It was an indirect piece of information that rubbed Freya the wrong way. She wanted to make that viper of a woman pay for everything she had done, not only to Axel but to all those helpless and unsuspecting couples. Freya knew that she had to come to terms with her thirst for vengeance, or the spell would backfire and lead to another unforeseen disaster.

"Okay, let's get to work on learning how to make someone fly. I vote we pick anyone but me."

Aimée let out a chuckle and replied, "That's funny. I was about to nominate you, Freya, as our magical cheer flyer. You already have enough skin in this game. Besides what could possibly go wrong?"

Chapter 20

"Please don't drop me. I know that the pizza was late, but you can just write me an angrily worded text message." Freya nervously chuckled as her body levitated almost ten feet from the ground. Although a drop from this height most likely wouldn't kill her, Freya wasn't in the mood to get a sprained ankle.

"I birthed you. Dropping you would be a waste of paying for private schools for over fifteen years."

Joan sounded as if she was rolling her eyes, but Freya couldn't be sure since she kept her eyes locked on the ceiling. The log-lined detailing looked even more impressive up close. Freya was grateful that they decided to try the spell in her foyer where her ceiling was tallest. Her body had jolted several feet in the air, and Freya assumed the burst of movement would have caused her face to smack into a wall anywhere else. They had pulled off both the queen-sized and twin-sized mattresses and placed them underneath Freya's floating body.

The room was bathed in gentle candlelight as the old book had advised. Getting back to the roots of magic proved simple enough. All of the cell phones were moved to the back of the house, and the lights remained turned off. The women didn't want anything to interfere with their first attempt at a joint spell.

Aimée commented, "I believe that we are an excellent mix of skills."

Just then a loud sneeze ripped through the room, and Freya felt the air around her body suddenly thin. She let out a startled shriek as her body flew backward at an incredible speed. The mattresses did little to stifle the blow to her bottom. Freya rubbed her sore body as Joan's face entered her field of vision.

Tanya sheepishly mumbled, "Sorry, Freya. I forgot to take my allergy pills before coming over. I guess some of Tom's feathers are still around, even though he's gone."

"It's okay. The bottom line is that we did it. Let's all just make sure we avoid sneezing or getting a random cold before tomorrow night. I'm really happy with how this turned out. We might have some hope after all. We just did something that would probably take most witches weeks to work up to as our starting spell. That's promising."

Joan continued to lean over and fuss over Freya. Once she was content that there was no permanent damage, she crawled off the mattresses and mumbled under her breath, "My investments were almost wasted."

Freya mustered her composure and managed to only flare her nose at the offhand commentary. Joan succeeded in making almost every maternal endeavor into something practical and disinteresting.

Aimée uncrossed her legs from her position on the floor and still managed to look like a woman from an old Hollywood film set. Freya wondered if she was somehow related to one of the starlets from the height of the film era. Not Marilyn Monroe, but another one possibly less known, with just as much ability to catch the attention of the cameras.

From her seated position, Aimée mused, "I was reading a little about the best place to cast such a spell, and one of the options was a place where your familiar is most comfortable. But that doesn't seem like an option. Another recommended spot was somewhere in nature so that we can better commune with the forces that brought us these powers."

At the mention of a familiar, Freya's ears immediately perked up. She knew the perfect spot that fit both of those criteria. She'd have to call out to Cahira tonight and see if her cougar was somewhere within earshot. Something told her that the big cat was never far from her or Axel.

"Actually I recently bonded with my familiar. She doesn't stay at home with me since her spirit isn't one for small enclosures and wooden walls. We should try the spell from within the forest. That way we have a better connection to the earth, and it's also a place where my familiar won't mind to venture."

The group nodded in approval. Tanya stood with her arms closed tight over her ample chest for a moment. Her dark hair flowed with each tap of her heel onto the floor. Finally, she spoke. "Wait, so you haven't even shown us your familiar?"

Freya quipped, "You show me yours, and I'll show you mine."

"Ugh, you're such a boy sometimes."

"Boys and men only dream of the power we have. If they had it, there would be no world left for us to make gross comments about."

Aimée pushed her blond locks back from her face after her impassioned commentary. Unsurprisingly there were no words of dissent about her critical analysis. The men in small villages, the church, and the royal family had managed to kill more women during the European witch hunts than was even quantifiable. They had blind fear and toxic male egos. Even though it was over five hundred years ago, it was still a justified moment in history to feel vexed about. The estimates of lives lost generally tallied around fifty thousand in a time when the overall population of men and women wasn't even a hundred million. Just because Aimée loved her husband dearly, it didn't make her blind to the errors of the patriarchy.

"Okay, so what time should we meet tomorrow evening, and what do we need to bring?"

The women spent a little over an hour crouched around the two mattresses in deep discussion. They finally settled on a time and the necessary tools to properly execute the magic. Freya agreed that it would be extremely difficult to successfully create such an elaborate spell but remained hopeful that four witches were better than one. There was nothing else she could do to help Axel. Freya told herself the best she could do was remain positive for tomorrow.

Tanya and Aimée were almost out the door when Freya hollered, "Wait! What if we try and scry for Delilah right now?"

Aimée effortlessly whirled around on her heels and exclaimed, "That's perfect! The four of us absolutely can concoct this spell."

Joan poked her head down the hallway and agreed, "Yes, that's the best and safest way to get to know what witch bitch we are dealing with." She walked over to the group of younger women and inquired, "What do we need to make this work?"

Less than ten minutes later, Freya was in the middle of removing her large wall-length mirror from the inside of her closet. It took a little bit longer than she had anticipated, thanks to Joan's redecorating spree. The bedroom looked more like something completely upside down than Freya's usual living environment. She took a deep breath and brought the mirror into the living room. The plush curtains obscured the view of the massive tree outside, and the furniture was arranged away from the front corner. "This reminds me of a hostage video, Mom."

"Well, little cat, that's because we don't want any distractions when we peer into the mirror. The blank walls just help to avoid any identifying information. This Delilah won't be able to see us, but we will be able to gain glimpses of her day as she passes reflective surfaces. If we keep practicing, then eventually when we scry, then we will be able to see the individual we are searching for, just like we see ourselves in the mirror."

Tanya chimed in. "There's no time like the present! Okay, girl, you need to concentrate since you're the only one that has seen her face and been around her presence."

Suddenly Freya remembered the shirt that Cahira had brought back from her travels in Los Angeles. She riffled through her makeshift hiding spot and smiled brightly. "Would this shirt help us to focus our combined powers on her?"

Aimée clapped her hands together in satisfaction and agreed, "That's superb. We can focus to find her magic signature and follow your lead."

After they placed a circle of salt around the impressively sized mirror, Freya squinted her eyes in confusion and inquired, "So are we assuming Delilah is a slug? Or am I missing something?"

Tanya allowed a little wave of laughter to roar throughout her body. "Look, the salt creates a circle of protection so in the worst case scenario that Delilah tries to come back to us, we are protected. It's better to just avoid ill intentions and invite warmth into our lives by keeping the door closed to demons."

"I highly doubt that my daughter hired a demon."

An awkward silence settled around the room as three women exchanged worried glances. Freya felt her face grow pale at her mother's casual brush-off.

"Ladies, stop procrastinating! Come form a circle and focus our intentions as pure. Don't get too confident from our last spell as this one requires more precision."

Freya repeated Delilah's name over and over as they all held hands around the mirror. Slight condensation seemingly appeared out of thin air and began to creep from the furthest corner of the mirror inward. If Freya wasn't watching it with her own eyes, then she would have assumed that the mirror had just been removed from a steamy bathroom. The mirror steamed intensely, but upon further inspection, Freya realized that the water was somehow coming from the other side.

A quick movement from the other side of the mirror caused all four women to jerk back in shock. Freya instinctively gripped both Aimée and Joan's hands tighter out of reflex. However, the reaction seemed to be mutual, given two sharp squeezes immediately cramped her hand in response.

Delilah's face came into view, and it looked almost as if she was staring directly back at Freya. Delilah's dark hair was damp and clung to her face in a manner more becoming of the child from *The Ring* instead of a hapless assistant. Freya realized with a jolt that Delilah must have gotten out of the shower and was just staring at her own reflection.

However, Delilah cleared her throat and spoke aloud, "Hello, little relative of Alice Kyteler. I hope your husband is enjoying his new life six feet under. I would love to stay, but I have to go rectify the Patronilla name."

As mysteriously as Delilah's image had grown in clarity, she was suddenly gone. Delilah's image slowly grew enshrouded with mist, and when it cleared again, the mirror finally reflected Freya's living room.

Joan quickly broke from the circle and smashed a chair against the surface of the mirror. Shards of glass shattered into the air, and Freya released a startled shriek as Joan mercilessly beat the mirror until the shards were finely ground and generously shattered around the room.

"I'll get you another mirror. But we need to collect the pieces and then bury them in your backyard as a precaution. Delilah wasn't able to see into the room, but she obviously comes from a powerful-enough line to be able to sense your presence, Freya."

The room seemed to pass in a blur of confusion as Freya watched Aimée and Tanya help to clean up the broken shards of glass. Freya placed a hand behind her neck and continued to watch. She needed a minute to process the name that Delilah had mentioned. A giant light bulb went off in Freya's mind as she exclaimed, "Delilah is related to our relative Alice Walker's staff member! She must have a grudge because of our family history. But I thought that Patronilla was murdered?"

Aimée allowed a sigh to pass through her lips as she mumbled, "Revenge is a dish best served ice cold with over two hundred years of animosity included."

Joan clapped her hands after she turned off the vacuum to better hear Aimée's self-directed musings. She replied with ease, "At least we know who we are dealing with. It's a valid explanation and means that she most likely knows more about us than we know about her. Let's even the playing field."

Chapter 21

The evening grass felt cool and damp against Freya's exposed feet. Water trickled down the face of an impressive rock as the night air helped to soothe her tight chest. The silk fabric of her long black dress stirred around her ankles as a calming summer breeze lazily stirred around the clearing. Cahira had led them to a break in the forest where the foliage was least dense, and a small waterfall dominated the location. It held a calming presence that seemed to hold a thin shroud between the mortal and supernatural realm. The trees were glowing in the powerful beams of full moonlight. Water from the miniature waterfall reflected around the enclosure like beams of light bouncing off a diamond. Steady streams of crystal-clear water pooled into the petite plant-lined basin. It appeared so shallow that Freya was almost sure she could touch the bottom at its deepest point. However, nothing was exactly as it seemed in nature or witchcraft.

A soft nudge to her shoulder caused Freya to look down into intelligent bright-green eyes. Cahira rubbed her large body against her thigh in an attempt to help provide a sense of comfort. Instinctively Freya reached down to lovingly pet the fur between Cahira's large ears. A guttural purr answered her dotting behavior and caused a soft smile to grace her anxious features. It was almost ten at night, and the group of women had gathered in the forest with their familiars. Joan was able to bring Mr. Scruffles, thanks to Aidan who sent the feline on an airplane. But the domestic grump was less than pleased with the proposition of being out so late. He was well over 120 years old in cat years and had a passion for napping in windowsills for the majority of the day. Joan held her petulant pussycat in her left arm as a mother might hold a child. The cat's front legs were secured around her neck like the arms of a babe, as its head propped on her shoulder and continued to glare at Freya.

"So glad that you were able to make it on such short notice, Mr. Scruffles," Freya lightly goaded as Cahira continued to purr against her leg. The tiny cat finished its fit and then sent a small wink her way before it moved onto another victim to harass. *My mom definitely found the right familiar. No doubt about that.*

A brightly colored bird entered the clearing as Tanya called out to it in greeting. The orange-and-black bird looked around the clearing to observe the varied group before it flew over to a higher perch. Freya had never seen Tanya's familiar, and she had to admit that the small creature was extremely adorable with its bright and curious gaze and subtle air of haughty confidence. Freya thought it was genius that each woman had a mirror image of her own personality within an animal kindred spirit. It was one thing to understand in theory but an entirely different one to experience firsthand.

"Tanya, your familiar is gorgeous."

In response, the little bird sang out a merry tune that Freya assumed was meant as thanks.

Tanya replied, "Thank you. She's a hoopoe from Africa. I found her when I studied abroad. Sneaking her past customs had been a nightmare."

Comments between everyone were sparse as they focused on drawing a large pentagram on the damp earth. Pebbles were carefully organized in the intricate symbol and checked twice by each woman to ensure that there were no gaps. The pentagram was about six feet in diameter, and as soon as the circle was connected, the air instantaneously crackled with energy. A strange glow momentarily appeared on the rock before melting away into the darkness.

The small hairs on Freya's entire body immediately stood at attention. With less than two hours before All Hallows Eve, there wasn't a moment to lose. Freya was running a mild temperature since the early hours of the morning and knew that it wasn't a random bout with the flu. The closer the clock ticked toward midnight, the warmer and more miserable she felt. If Freya hadn't known any better, she would have assumed that she was suffering with an intense bout of hay fever caused by visiting Tom in Sally's chicken coop.

Freya took a point of the pentagram and continued to clench her hands around the bag that contained Delilah's shirt. Cahira stood a few paces behind with Amethyst. The shirt and five dollars' worth of string were the two main items for the spell. It seemed ridiculous that their only tools were such small and utterly mundane items. Freya had somehow assumed there would be a need for more obscure items or at least more. *So much for eye of newt and tongue of rat.* As far as Freya was concerned, television had failed at educating her about witches.

Finally they were all arranged around the pentagram. Freya glanced individually at each woman. Her look hinted that they could still back out now. Finally Freya locked eyes with Joan and felt all the years of tension and misunderstanding wash from her shoulders. Joan apparently felt similarly as Freya's mother slightly bowed her head and encouraged, "We're ready, Freya."

With that confirmation, Freya took a deep breath and then confidently strode into the center of the pentagram. She plucked Delilah's shirt out of the bag and flung the open bag away from the circle. Cahira caught the bag with ease and pulled it away so that it wouldn't blow back into the circle with the evening breeze. Freya sent a wink toward her familiar and then attempted to ground herself in the moment. The constant stinging of Delilah's shirt against her bare hand helped to solidify Freya's resolve to free Axel. She kept her mind on that pain and let it sharpen her intentions as she deftly retrieved the string from inside of the only pocket on her dress. She grasped the thin piece of material so tightly that her fingers started to turn red. The rough material did little to distract her from the constant sting when holding Delilah's shirt. Oddly enough, all of her faith was dependent upon a craft-store purchase.

Freya started to chant in Latin. The words felt strange as her tongue caressed each syllable with care. The foreign words had taken some time to put together, and Freya was extremely glad that Aimée's daughter had decided to take Latin instead of Spanish. They had all gone over to Aimée's house and spent the better part of an hour taking a lesson from a more-than-eager Layla. The dead language was apparently very much alive and well when it came to strong incantations.

Freya had spent hours memorizing the simple two-sentence chant in an effort to make sure that the spell wasn't derailed by poor pronunciation. The words roughly translated from Latin to English as, "Return to us what you tried to steal and allow Axel to come back and heal. Bind Delilah's magic into this shirt, in order to prevent future hurt." Three voices from the outside corners of the pentagram slowly added their own will to the spell. The words grew lyrical as they repeated the two sentences and thought of their intentions with every word.

Freya continued to lead the chant as she meticulously wrapped string from the bottom of the folded shirt to the top. She took in another gulp of air and projected her voice into the clearing. As she worked her way to the middle, the fabric became increasingly warmer as if each fiber was growing irritated from the spell. Freya held her voice steady, as if nothing was happening. When Delilah's shirt was over halfway wrapped with string, a strange aura started to emanate from the piece of cloth. It was as if the shirt itself was solemnly devoted to stopping Freya from finishing the spell.

The skin on her fingers steadily began to change color from a pale cream to an irritated and throbbing red. It looked like an irritated sunburn. When Freya's fingers reached the top of the shirt, the pain was almost unbearable, and it almost felt easier to drop the shirt than to have to continue the last three or four rotations around the garment. *Focus on the words, Freya. Make your intentions clear to the universe. Get Axel back home and do no further harm.*

Irritated sunburns quickly escalated to raw patches on her fingers and blisters where her skin was in direct contact with the unwrapped portion of the shirt. Freya took large gulps of air to center herself between repeating the two sentences; she tightly wrapped Delilah's shirt and ensured it was securely bound. For good measure, Freya proceeded to tie both ends of string together with three separate knots. *Three knots in recognition for The Rule of Three.*

Freya placed the bound shirt down into the middle of the pentagram and stepped away. She looked intently into the symbol and waited for something to happen. After about five minutes of waiting, Joan mumbled, "Maybe there are no lightning bolts for this one. Maybe it worked, and the only way to know is to go back and see Axel."

The idea did seem to make sense. They weren't trying to do anything vengeful or magnificent, so it didn't really make sense to receive an elaborate sign. Freya just wished that there was something so that her heart would stop trying to beat out of her chest. She was sure that Cahira could hear it continue to anxiously thrum in her rib cage as large ears continued to swivel toward Freya's chest. One of the straps on her black silk gown slipped down her slim shoulder, and Freya let it dip toward the ground. Her ample chest prevented the top portion of the dress from following the instructions of gravity and fully exposing her body to the gentle moonlight. But it didn't matter. Freya already felt naked.

Slowly Freya nodded in acknowledgment to what Joan had suggested. She stepped into the circle and dug a hole directly in the center. The indent in the pentagram was about three inches deep. Freya placed the wrapped shirt into the soft earth. Then she vigorously covered the hole with the displaced dirt and marveled at the symbolic grave. Hopefully it was the death of Delilah's terror streak. The earth looked so new in the center as it was the only upturned soil within the clearing. Freya decided to clear the area of any true signs of witchcraft and rearranged the small rocks. The other women quickly jumped into action. They soundlessly moved the pebbles around the clearing without a single word. Not one of them dared to talk for fear that it would ruin all of their hard work.

A soft breeze swept across Freya's face. Her breath began to come out in frigid puffs, and there was a communal sense of relief once the rocks were no longer so obviously arranged. The last thing that they needed was a curious hiker or a group of kids stumbling into the clearing and playing with forces that they didn't understand.

The walk into Freya's backyard felt more like a funeral procession than the end of an occult ritual. Not one of them really knew what they had been looking for in the clearing after the spell, but some sign of confirmation would have been comforting. Once the four of them cleared all of the branches and carefully padded into the mouth of her yard, Freya spoke, barely above a whisper, "Please come in if you would like. I'm going to check on Axel and then brew a pot of coffee."

She couldn't bring herself to say that she didn't want to be alone. But somehow the message was interpreted without confusion. Her friends and mother were luckily able to read through the lines and agreed to go inside in order to be Freya's last line of support in case the unthinkable happened. Once the little group was firmly away from the last remaining tendrils of the forest, a steady stream of mindless chatter birthed itself into existence. Usually Freya didn't mind participating, but it was as if her mind and soul were sitting on the chair next to Axel's bed and waiting for her body to catch up. Freya jerkily opened the backdoor and allowed everyone to enter. She was about to put out a few snacks for the four familiars, but Joan put a hand over Freya's as she tried to open the fridge. That was all the indication that Freya needed to bolt out of the room and check on Axel. Freya opened the door to his room, and not for the first time, Freya's heart plummeted to the floor.

Chapter 22

Freya wasn't sure what she was expecting to find, but the odd sight in front of her definitely wasn't it. Nearly two inches away from Axel's body were strange floating particles that were somehow perfectly suspended in the air around his entire form. She paused to observe the supernatural scene.

"Maybe that's Delilah's magic," Freya whispered to herself.

The thought caused a bubble of hope to rise from her chest as she tentatively walked closer to the bed. After two minutes, she noticed that the strangely milky particles appeared to be breaking apart and floating into the atmosphere. When the last visible speck disappeared, Freya reached out a hesitant hand to touch the air where were only moments before.

Her eyes scanned over the empty room until they landed on the digital clock that was placed near the bookshelf. There were only two minutes left until midnight, and all of Freya's previous hope quickly shifted into panic. Freya's voice was thick with emotions that she didn't know how to properly convey with words. "Please come back, Axel. I did everything possible. We did everything possible to save you."

A strange sob ripped through her throat as the clock remorselessly turned to midnight. All Hallows Eve had officially arrived, and Axel was doomed to remain in an eternal sleep. Freya leapt from the chair and wrapped her arms around Axel's body. She continued to sob as large drops of water cascaded down her agonized features. Freya leaned down and chastely kissed Axel on his forehead as she whispered, "I'm always going to love you. I didn't properly appreciate you when I had the chance, but I know that now, and I am so sorry."

Freya remained hunched over Axel as she continued to sob. Months of pent-up frustrations and fears finally broke free from her hold without any regard to who could hear. Her next sob was suddenly cut short when a strangled gasp shook her body. Freya's eyes widened in disbelief when she realized that the sound didn't come from her own lips. Her eyes remained fixed on the window above Axel's bed as she sent a prayer to the universe, to whatever higher power would listen, to please help her make things right.

Blurry gray eyes peered up at her with a mixture of curiosity and exhaustion. It felt as if it was an unbelievable illusion or an extremely lucid dream. Freya was afraid that she would wake up at any moment and once again be greeted with the harsh reality of the situation. She stared at those miniature thunderstorms that she had missed so dearly as her body precariously hovered over Axel. *If this is a dream, please don't wake me up.* A thousand wild thoughts seemed to battle for her attention and gain priority, but as she kept unrelenting eye contact with her husband, all of those ideas slowly turned into one. A whine escaped the back of Freya's throat as her tear-streaked face once again prepared for more waterworks. "I forgive you, Axel, and I'm sorry."

Axel opened his mouth and an irritated wheeze escaped from the back of his throat. He scrunched his eyes closed in what Freya could only assume was discomfort as he tried once again to speak. Axel tried to move his hand upward to grab his dry throat. The attempt was short-lived as the wires yanked his arm back toward the bed.

"Stay there. I'll get you some water and be right back." Freya scurried into the kitchen and barely registered the glum faces that surrounded her.

Before she was completely out of earshot of the kitchen, Freya hollered, "Please call Meg and tell her Axel is awake."

A flurry of excited hollers echoed from behind Freya as she barreled down the hallway with a cup of water that was full to the brim. A trail of water followed her hasty movements. Slim rivers of water dribbled down her elbow and pelted the wood floor. For once, the floors and state of the rental home was the least of her concerns. Freya slowed her pace and gingerly helped Axel with the cup. He couldn't seem to lift himself into a seated position, so Freya arranged them both so that most of his weight rested against her chest. Freya held the glass of water as he took a few tentative gulps and watched with rapt attention as a sprinkling of water trickled down his stubble. It didn't get far as the water was promptly wiped away by small and observant fingers.

Freya then pressed her body against Axel's and drew him impossibly closer into her trembling arms. The wires and cords did nothing to deter Freya from trying to gain the comfort and assurance through her firm grasp around her husband. In that moment, watching him spill water on his chin was the most beautiful sight that her eyes had ever seen. Her heart felt as if it had expanded twice its size in her chest, and she wondered if all the magic in the world could ever compare to such a feeling of peace.

Chapter 23

Pristine snowflakes sporadically pelted against the bedroom window. The snow arrived a little earlier than usual for Wishburn and made it possible for Freya to have her first Thanksgiving with real seasons. Los Angeles remained a city of consistency, even during the usual chilly months, and the change of scenery reminded her of classic winter movies that she used to watch when curled up on the sofa with a cup of hot chocolate as a child. The weather wasn't the only obvious change within the warm log cabin. Large arms wrapped around Freya's slim waist, and a firm chest gently pressed against her back.

She cooed, "Good morning, sleepyhead. How did you rest?"

Axel placed a light peck to her temple in greeting as he mumbled, "It was perfect. Felt good to hold you. But I can do without sleeping in since apparently, that's all I managed to do for three months." A tinge of sadness laced the end of his words as he mentioned the still unexplained to him gap in his life.

The question of when to tell Axel about her powers crept about the corners of her mind on a daily basis like an unwanted houseguest. Freya decided to tell Axel about her powers once he could stand for at least ten minutes without getting winded. There was no point in adding more emotional and mental baggage to an already-grueling recovery. It also didn't hurt that Freya was still pondering the best way to break the news to him. Preferably he'd find out before Christmas since she knew firsthand how family secrets had a way of pushing people apart instead of together.

Freya untangled Axel's left hand away from her stomach and brought the outer part of his palm to her lips. The gesture reminded her of a role reversal on a debutante dance where usually, the gentleman kisses the knuckles of his dancing partner. Freya kissed the now-soft skin of his knuckles from so many days of disuse and breathily replied, "You're here now and so am I. We're lucky that you were able to escape such a freak accident. Let's just avoid crazy amounts of stress for a little bit longer."

Losing Axel had given Freya a new perspective on life. Asking for help was something that had pained her in the past, but life had a funny way of pressing on the wounds that were most sore. Freya had realized that without the help of her mom and new friends, she never would have been able to save Axel or discover her true powers.

New gifts and talents seemed to emerge everyday as Freya slipped away when Axel was in physical therapy. While Axel diligently worked to improve his physical strength, Freya now focused her attention on gaining mental stamina. Sometimes Tanya and Aimée even joined forces to try and combat against Freya's spells. However, each day emphasized Freya's unbridled potential as her spells easily overtook the duo's best efforts when sparring.

Even in the chaos of a full supermarket, Freya could now sense the energy of the people around her. Vibrant colors seemed to obediently follow each person around, and some signatures were just brighter than others. Freya now understood why it was so obvious to Tanya and Aimée that Freya had powers all of those months ago. The first time Freya had looked at them, there was a unique energy that emanated from them. It was similar to Freya's own aura since their signatures were completely different from everyone else in town. Their power invisibly radiated from their bodies like the leisurely lapping of waves after a windless afternoon. The signatures were there, but they were not overbearing. Unlike Freya's own mark that seemed to fill a room before she even arrived.

She knew that eventually, she'd need to make a trip to Aimée's Bookstore to find a spell that could conceal that power. Just in case she ran into another witch in Los Angeles. The odds were high that returning to such a densely populated area would bring about the discovery of at least one other witch. But that was nowhere in the near future as Freya had only traveled twice into the city for Freya Designs since Axel had woken up.

If Freya had told herself a year ago that she would be living in a log cabin and remotely managing her company, she would have laughed in her own face. Now the idea actually gave her peace of mind so that she could enjoy her life in the moment.

"I have something for you, Freya." Axel untangled his arm from her petite waist and slightly wrinkled white shirt. He reached into his pocket and retrieved a folded piece of paper from what Freya assumed was his jean pocket. Axel placed it level with her eyes. "It's nothing crazy, but I remember that you said that you wanted to be able to find a way to read more so Aimée agreed to help me."

Freya unfolded the white sheet of paper and read over what was obviously Axel's penmanship. It was the most organized that she had seen from him, and it read, "Welcome to the book club! One year of classic novels brought directly to your door. A book will be provided at the start of every month for the elite Freyel Book Club."

A snort of disbelief escaped her as she read the cheesy title. "Is this title a combination of our names?"

Axel shuffled his feet, and Freya felt his weight shift from one leg to the other as he replied, "Yes, but seeing as you're the CEO of the company, if you hate it, then feel free to change it."

Freya turned around in his arms and bent upward. She stood on the tips of her toes to catch Axel's lips in a slow burning kiss. Afterward she replied, "It's the most thoughtful gift that I could ask for. Thank you for creating Freyel."

A bright lopsided grin spread across Axel's features as his gray eyes gleamed in joy. The last month felt as if they were on their honeymoon all over again. There were moments when it was obvious that their relationship had progressed from that night, but that only made intimate moments much more special. They were comfortable with each other, and even though there were three glaring months of pain and hardship, in a strange way the difficult time became a blessing. The marriage had died out into embers years ago, and realizing what both of them were missing rekindled it into a passionate blaze.

Axel casually asked, "What time is it?"

"We don't have time, Axel. The girls will be over in about ten minutes. Meg and Sally were the only ones who said they couldn't attend. You met Meg when you were coming out of your coma. She was the smart woman who always checked in on you."

The only part of her explanation that Axel replied to was, "I can be very good at time management when motivated."

Freya couldn't contain her laughter at Axel's comment. "Yeah right, you consider half an hour your version of efficiency," she playfully goaded.

A wolfish smirk overtook his features as he explained, "Well, guess we will have to be very thorough when we finally have the house to ourselves again."

Freya's stomach filled with butterflies as she nodded her head in agreement. There was no point in using her voice since the answer was bound to escape in a breathy whisper. She refused to admit defeat to her very convincing husband. Even though the idea was excellent and exactly what she was hoping for later in the evening.

A loud chime echoed over the wooden walls, and Freya let out a stream of laughter as she wiggled free from Axel's embrace and ran to open the door. Shrieks of excitement bounded through the entryway as Freya embraced both Tanya and Aimée in a group hug. "Finally! I was feeling so left out. I can't believe that I'm the last person to officially meet your husband."

"Tanya, Aimée came over last week to bring me a new book. I wanted to read a book with Axel when he was awake. We still haven't left the house yet. We are supposed to take it easy." Freya whispered the last sentence to avoid Axel overhearing and growing self-conscious. Axel had remained mostly in bed for a week as his periods of consciousness gradually improved. He had only stayed awake for a few minutes on Halloween, but that was enough for Freya to know that their spell had worked. Although the coma was caused by magic, it still took time for Axel to recover, just like one not caused by supernatural forces.

Aimée exclaimed, "Let us enter and officially meet your beloved partner that we all toiled so intensely to revive!"

Tanya clamped a hand across Aimée's mouth and whisper-yelled, "He doesn't know yet, you drama queen. Keep it on the down low."

An hour had passed, and the group was settled into a comfortable pattern of conversation. Axel was his kind and confident self and managed to maintain a steady stream of energy, even though Freya was sure that most of it was really being mustered by sheer willpower.

A strong arm lazily pulled Freya's chair away from the table. She looked to her left and saw Axel's signature lazy smile as he sent her a playful wink. Freya cozied up to his shoulder and whispered, "Let me know if you're tired. We can have a safe word."

"I really like your new friends, Freya. Glad to see that you still have great taste."

"You have to say that I have great taste since I married you."

Axel allowed a grumble of approval to reverberate through his chest. She'd understood his pointed remark that somehow managed to give both of them praise at the same time. The reverberations from Axel's chest pressed against Freya's back as she enjoyed the blissful moment of serenity. After over a year without a close bond with her husband, it was strange to finally feel as close as they had on their wedding day. Freya had insisted that they hold the ceremony at the Jamaican Bay hotel in Marina Del Rey. It wasn't extremely chic, but it was where they had their first kiss, and that memory felt extremely special to the both of them. It had taken them three dates because they both had been so terribly tongue-tied with each other. At one point, Freya had been convinced that she was dating someone who was extremely out of her league because Axel was playing soccer for the Los Angeles Galaxy soccer team and spent most of his free time helping with women's shelters. He wanted to allow those who were hurting to have a second chance. Needless to say, Freya had been convinced that he was the bleeding heart between the two of them. He felt too good to be true.

And as Freya grabbed Axel's hand and observed Aimée's phone conversation with her daughter, Layla, Freya knew that he was the best choice that she had made so far. Freya knew that she wanted to start her own family.

Freya had an epiphany as she observed the moment almost from a third-person perspective. She realized that she didn't have to choose between her husband or her career. A support system had always been at her fingertips of strong and powerful women, if only she decided to ask for it. All she had to do was remove her ego.

A ring from the doorbell caused a temporary lull in the conversation as three pairs of curious eyes turned to Freya.

She only shrugged and replied, "I swear this is at least five times the visitors that we had in Los Angeles. But that's five times the excuse to break out the champagne."

A tiny weight leapt into Freya's unsuspecting arms as soon as she opened the door. Freya pulled her face just far enough away in order to recognize the stranger. Sally's smiling face beamed up at her from a new haircut. The layers emphasized her heart-shaped face and softened the visibly difficult years. Freya had a sneaking suspicion that the relaxed appearance had more to do with Tom's disappearance than a simple beauty trick.

"I'm glad you could make it, Sally! How was Brighttown?"

"It was wonderful! Oh, I brought you these flowers. Would you believe that I've spent my entire life in Wishburn and never visited the town over until now? I didn't want to stay overnight and decided to surprise you. It's so great to be able to meet Axel."

"I love sunflowers! Thank you. What was your favorite part about Brighttown?"

Sally shrugged her slim shoulders as her peppy smile never faded from her face. "I suppose I just really like the newness of it all. Maybe one day, I will stay overnight in a hotel or something like that. Scott offered to go on an adventure with me outside of town for next weekend."

That took no time at all, Freya thought to herself in glee. She had the sneaking suspicion that Scott had never stopped having feelings for his high school sweetheart. Even if he had tried to date Freya for a short period of time, it wasn't the same affection that he had for Sally. Instead of ruminating on the possibilities of the future, Freya ushered Sally into the kitchen and made room for another seat at the table.

"I need to order another set of kitchen chairs before we end up with the entire neighborhood crouched on the floor." Although Freya's quiet complaint came out harsh, the cheerful glint in her eyes clearly contradicted her attempt at solemnity. Axel grabbed the back of his chair for support as he stood upward to greet Sally. Freya had told him earlier that it wasn't likely the little woman would attend, but it didn't take a genius to figure out that statement was now incorrect.

When everyone was finally resituated around the table, Tanya looked over toward Freya and Aimée with a mischievous glint in her eyes as she inquired, "So, Sally, how is that plucky rooster treating you?"

Sally placed her cup of tea down on a white saucer as a shade of blush rushed from her neck and traveled into her cheeks. Her hand grabbed the tea bag string as she idly began to dunk it in the water.

"That rooster was very mean. He kept hurting my other hens. It was like he was getting a real kick out of it too. I couldn't have him hurting my hens." Sally let out a deep breath and explained, "So I got rid of him." The air felt heavy with the weight of her words. Sally continued, "I made him into soup. I'm sorry, Freya. It was just like he was born mean."

Oh, if only you knew how evil that plucky bird really was, Freya thought to herself. She felt her grip tighten around Axel's hand underneath the table but couldn't be bothered to lessen her talons as they nearly punctured his skin. Axel seemed unbothered by the grip as he continued to look intently at Sally, as if he expected some further explanation. Tanya's honey-colored eyes nearly popped out of her head as she blew rivulets of warm coffee through her nose at the mention of chicken soup. A strange half-choking and half-coughing sound came from her parted lips, and she looked like a fish out of water gasping for breath. Tanya didn't even bother to clean the scalding coffee from her chin as it proceeded to dribble onto her shirt. Axel looked inquisitively around the table until his gaze eventually landed on Freya.

He leaned downward and attempted to ask a question, but then seemed to think better of it and closed his mouth. Axel's lips were nearly indiscernible as he nibbled on his lower lip to keep himself from bursting with curiosity. They had never even gone camping together as a couple because Freya had found the idea to be too survivalist, and Axel didn't want to shower in cold water. The news of her having had a pet rooster felt almost inconceivable. Freya sent a silent prayer to whatever greater being was above to give Axel the common sense not to ask for details while Sally was a good second or two from bursting into tears.

Instead he rhetorically questioned, "You had a pet rooster?"

"Don't worry about the rooster, Sally. I didn't know how to care for him, and you did a perfectly normal farm activity. The circle of life."

Tanya muttered, "Oh, this is throwing me for a loop, all right."

Freya sent Tanya a look that could practically scare the shell off a hermit crab, but if Tanya noticed, she didn't seem to care. Instead she placed her dark locks behind her ears and poured another cup of coffee. Without saying a word, Freya retrieved a bottle of whiskey and placed it on the table.

Aimée nodded her head in thanks as she poured a little into her cup and then handed the bottle toward Tanya without even bothering to look. Apparently the news of accidental cannibalism was enough to warrant an extremely bold afternoon beverage.

Chapter 24

Joyful teens hollered across Main Street as they basked in the excitement of starting Christmas break. Freya watched as the kids chatted in clusters that were mostly headed in the direction of the diner. A few young couples stole themselves away in the edges and corners of the building in order to provide some sense of privacy with their paramour. As Freya recalled, young love, and especially a first love, tended to be the most irrationally passionate. As the eager teens seemed incapable of remaining apart, it brought a smile to Freya's face.

A small child of around ten years old managed to draw Freya's attention as the little girl cautiously approached. Her long dark braid swished from one side to the other as her tiny legs continued to dawdle closer. The little girl's mother sent a sweet smile toward Freya that held a secret conversation between two caretakers of life. Freya nodded her head at the woman who was snuggly bundled up with a white puffer coat to her ankles. According to the news, it was only meant to snow until the later parts of the afternoon. Freya could tell that the little girl wanted to say something as she continued to steal glances between Freya and her patiently waiting mother. Freya lifted the corners of her mouth into a welcoming smile that successfully put the kid's mind at ease.

The friendly glance incentivized the youngster to pick up her pace so that she was no longer painfully dawdling inch by inch. "Hi, miss. I'm told to ask three strangers if they want to have our school carolers go to perform at their house tomorrow."

"That sounds lovely. You'd really make my day with some Christmas cheer." Almost immediately, the little girl turned around to face her mother and hollered at the top of her tiny lungs, "Mom! She said yes! That means I only have to ask two more people for choir class. Can I please have a cookie now that I finally asked a not-scary-looking person?"

Freya watched the interaction between the tiny family. She unconsciously moved her right hand in calming circular patterns across her stomach. She wasn't exactly sure yet, but something had felt a little different for the last few weeks. The pregnancy test in her shopping bag seemed to call her name, and Freya had to talk herself out of heading into the nearest shop to use their restroom. At the first whisper of motherhood, years of patience earned through countless tedious meetings, somehow fell to shambles.

She clutched the shopping bag a little tighter to her chest as she relived the encounter with Tanya. When Tanya had checked her out at Scott's Supermarket, her friend's eyes grew to the size of saucers. Freya had quickly leaned over the register to clamp a hand over her mouth in order to prevent the impending shriek of excitement from informing the entire store of the possible news.

Freya had placed a finger to her lips and mumbled, "I'm not sure yet. So I'll let you know when I figure that out." Her eyes danced with a merriment that conveyed to Tanya her deep sense of excitement.

For years, the thought of starting a family with Axel had only been a passing idea. It never felt like the right time, but Freya realized that there was no such thing as the perfect time for any large life choices. Life is something that no one has the ability to control, and the best that even a modern witch can do is keep her loved ones close and enjoy the ride.

Now Freya felt confident that a new direction in her life was possible. Freya didn't have to deny herself the pleasure of starting a family just to avoid distractions that would divide attention away from Freya Designs.

The walk home from town never felt so long as the light layer of snow sporadically spattered the ground. Trees that were bare of their leaves and held their frosted branches upward to the sky as if in defiance of the chilly weather. Eventually the vibrant colors of spring would return to help the trees attract nesting birds and busy squirrels. It was a continuous step in the infinite cycle of creating the next generation.

Although Freya was excited to start a new chapter, a shroud of doubt continued to weigh across her mind. *How was Delilah able to discover my lineage? Was it personal to get revenge for something that I've done or simply generational? Are other members of the De Milla family still alive?* The questions seemed to taunt her with a feeling of impending dread because Freya couldn't bring herself to put forward any logical explanations. A hunch that solidified itself within her gut continued to whisper that Delilah had planned to torture Freya, and it was only a matter of time before the snake reappeared in her garden.

Freya walked into her warm log cabin home and called, "Babe, I'm home! How are your contracts coming?"

Rushed footsteps hustled down the stairs and Axel's filled-out form swiftly threw Freya over his strong shoulder. "It was good. Might have a contract in the works with 24 Hour Fitness as a partnership where I provide a few workouts and tips. But we might have to push back the release until I'm in better physical condition. Look, I have something to show you for lunch."

Freya noticed the flicker of insecurity that flashed across his features and replied, "Axel, your body looks amazing from any angle. But especially from this angle." She brought her hand down to Axel's bottom as a playful *thwack* resounded around the hallway. Tendrils of red hair whipped around as Freya allowed Axel to carry her upside down through their house. The wooden floor changed into white-spattered blades of grass. The pressure on her waist increased as her limbs were flipped around, and her booted feet were finally reintroduced to land. Instinctively her hand reached out and firmly grabbed Axel in order to anchor herself to his stable form.

"What are we doing outside, Axel?"

He let out a chuckle and thrust his arms outward to emphasize his grand idea. Freya turned in the direction of Axel's outstretched arms and found what seemed to be a pillow fort. Two large blankets covered the top of a camping tent. An outside heater was thoughtfully placed right next to the magical little fort. The elaborate scene reminded her of a miniature circus tent. It was obvious that the sweet gesture had taken several hours for Axel to put it together.

Freya wrapped her arms around Axel and whispered, "I love it. A perfect way to spend a Friday afternoon."

She then pecked him on the cheek and rushed over to inspect the homemade tent more closely. Freya lifted part of the blanket away from the opening and saw a string of battery-operated tea lights strung about the upper poles. It was a camping tent converted into every kid's dream hideout. It was just spacious enough for two grown people or at least two adults, plus possibly a tiny bundle of cells. Freya didn't want to consider the possibility any further than that and quickly untied her boots. She placed her shoes outside of the little creation and eagerly wiggled her way into the center.

The heater helped to keep the quaint nest warm and blocked out the early chill of winter. Even so, Freya unzipped her long coat and placed it across her lap like a makeshift blanket. Axel's head of spiky blond hair came into view, and he looked down into Freya's eyes. He leveled his joyful gray eyes with her excited green.

"Axel, would you like to keep the door open?"

"It's okay. I'm not concerned about being trapped with you. I've apparently been confined for months, so this should be easy."

Freya nodded her head in agreement and then leaned over to place the zipper down. She paused in the middle and allowed a partial view of the outside to enter into their cozy scene.

After months without meeting Axel's bright stormy gaze, the action felt extremely personal and left Freya feeling oddly naked, even though her body was thoroughly bundled in layers of clothing. She let out a shaky breath but refused to be the first one to break the intimate moment. Axel sent her a wink and placed a large pizza box in the middle of the tent. He then retrieved a blanket from the furthest side of the makeshift tent and handed it to Freya.

"Thank you, Axel."

"A meal fit for a queen. Cheese pizza ala outside heater. Don't worry. The weather report said that it would be a mild evening."

"It's better than anything that I managed to cook without you. I'm sure you can think of ways to keep me warm, even if the weather gets cold."

"I know. The bar was so low that I really didn't have any pressure. Freya, what kind of husband would I be if I let you freeze?"

Freya burst out in a fit of giggles and pecked Axel on the lips. She half-heartedly chided, "I could definitely get used to this."

A look of regret passed over Axel's face as he paused from opening the pizza box and confided, "I wanted to make the most of our time before we go back to Los Angeles. You're the most important thing in my life, Freya. Modeling is fun, and I loved playing soccer, but it's not what I want to be remembered by when I'm gone. It's not where I want to dedicate my entire life."

Freya felt a nerve in her face twitch downward as her heart felt touched by his honesty. "What if I told you that we could have plenty of those adventures on Fridays in Los Angeles. Maybe even a few beach days and trips? Not as many as here, but at least a weekly adventure of your choice? You are one of the most important people in my life."

Gray eyes glistened with tears as Axel cleared his throat and proceeded in a shaky voice, "I would like that, Freya. But what do you mean one of the most? Do you mean besides Joan?"

"I'm taking a pregnancy test later tonight. So you might have to get more creative with the tent designs in order to accommodate three. If you're up for the challenge."

"Any challenge with you is the adventure that I want to live."

Freya leaned her head closer to Axel and allowed the calm to seep into her entire being and eradicate the remaining tension within her heart. It was the first consistent snowfall of the year in Wishburn, and Axel wanted to make sure that it was a special moment for them both. They had an unspoken agreement to repent for their lost years spent living parallel but not actively intertwined lives.

Axel was right, whatever happened, they would have to face it together. What if her secret would be too much for him? Freya desperately hoped that he wouldn't mind living with a volatile witch in training. She was still the same woman that he had fallen in love with. But now she was stronger and accidentally an accessory to murder. Additionally she was now possibly a moving target for Delilah whenever she decided to reappear. *I just won't mention Tom right away since that might send the wrong message.*

Freya gulped and tentatively turned to Axel, "I have one more thing to share with you."

Chapter 25

Bright welcoming string lights were strategically hung from almost every snow-dusted roof in Wishburn. The occasional reindeer and Santa display welcomed the random passerby. New Year's was less than a week away, and the decorations were at an all-time high. Main Street was a joyful sight as Freya carefully turned her car and made sure not to jostle Meg's Christmas present. It had taken several weeks, but Freya had finally found the perfect gift.

Freya placed a hand over her slightly swollen stomach as she locked her Jeep and headed into Aimée's Bookstore. It was almost time to receive her January edition for the Freyel Book Club, and she was hoping that she would be able to retrieve the book a little earlier than expected. She knew Aimée was heading out of town to celebrate the start of the New Year with her family, so it was either ask now or wait until most of January was over.

Freya's competitive nature made it difficult for her to be able to accept defeat. Mostly Freya just really wanted to begin an activity with Axel, especially one that he knew meant so much to her. In the evenings, Axel and Freya would curl up together on the blue sofa near the stone-layered fireplace and read about a chapter from their assigned book. The tradition was only a week old, but Freya really liked having an activity to look forward to after a long day full of phone calls with Aidan and the usual mountain of paperwork. Luckily December tended to be one of the slowest months of the year, so there was plenty of time to explore the town and peruse over dusty spell books.

A well-loved book from Tanya's private family collection had explained that women with active magic were extremely likely to give birth to little girls with gifts linked to the supernatural. It was still too early for Freya to know the gender, but a little voice in her head continued to whisper about a redheaded baby girl with striking gray eyes.

Although she was only a few months along, the added weight and discomfort had already begun. Nearly every morning, Freya was greeted with the lovely sight of the inside of her toilet bowl. It had come to the point that Axel had even brought in a pillow so that she could more comfortably kneel on the bathroom floor. Each time, he'd come and sit right next to her and grin like an idiot as she hurled her guts out and mumbled threats to the toilet water. Freya wasn't a huge fan of an audience but decided that she didn't want to discourage his attempt at supportive behavior. On her mental checklist, the pro column had narrowly beaten the cons. A bit of information that caused her to grip the toilet bowl a little tighter in indignation every time she looked over and saw Axel's pale face. He had wonderful supportive intentions and a much-weaker-than-expected stomach.

Amethyst's lazy mewl pulled Freya back to the present from her stomach-turning memory. She waved in greeting to the regal feline and walked the few paces to scratch behind its furry ears. A throaty purr of content caused a small smile to creep onto Freya's chapped lips. The winter weather wasn't exactly as easy as she had assumed. With the heater constantly blowing throughout the night, the air in her bedroom managed to feel consistently bone-dry.

"Where is Aimée? Don't worry, I'll find her myself."

Freya winked at the fluffy feline and strolled by one of the bookcases toward the charmed storeroom. She looked upward toward the sign and chuckled at Aimée's inside joke. A tastefully ornate sign hung above the book aisle and read proudly, "Magic and Fantasy." The words perfectly lined up above the door, but to anyone searching the store, it was just another sign to explain the contents of the aisle.

"I love an excellent pun." Freya laughed to herself.

She walked toward the door and felt the energy field around it ever so slightly shifted. Freya reached out her left hand and twisted the doorknob to the left. To her surprise, it opened without so much as a creak of a protest. She decided to fully open the door and found Tanya and Aimée chatting around the other side of the door.

"Hey, girl! Took you long enough. We thought about texting you but figured you'd try the door eventually."

"Well, that and the fact that no cell phones are allowed inside of this sacred place," Aimée quickly added.

Freya nodded her head in acknowledgment and then held up her hand before she closed the door once again to the room and plucked her phone out of her purse. She quickly walked over to the cash register and placed it behind the counter to prevent any curious customers from picking up more than just a book. She then walked back to the door and crossed the barrier between the charmed room and the physical realm. "I told you that she'd forget the phone rule. She was too busy hunting for us with a pregnancy brain."

"Gee, thanks for the vote of confidence, Aimée." Freya playfully squinted her eyes at her supernatural friends.

"I'm only speaking the truth, darling. When I was pregnant, it was as if all the smells in the world absolutely repulsed me. The only thing I wanted to do was sit near the toilet. Everything else was just a detail."

Freya placed a hand over her stomach as if to try and calm her little bundle from getting any ideas of rebellion. But it was also only two months along, so Freya felt like it was best to keep the news under wraps from the general public. Aimée and Tanya were obviously excluded from that list as they were now part of her family.

"In case you didn't know, Aimée has a thing for dramatics. We really brought you here because we wanted to ask you something, and this room was the best place. I offered that we just text you the question, but apparently that's not how these things are done."

Tanya sent a glance toward Aimée who suddenly found a book on changing the color of flower petals to be the most interesting thing in the world. Aimée looked upward when she felt two heavy gazes land upon her face and refused to move.

"Right, what Tanya and I would like to ask you, Freya, is if you will be the leader of our coven?" Aimée itched the inside of her arm in nervous anticipation. A habit that seemed to betray her composed and properly manicured facial features.

"Wait, so you both want to embrace the craft? And you both want me to be, like, the leader of our group?"

"Girl, it was a unanimous decision. We would have gone our entire lives living half-truths before you came here. Since you've come here, both of our powers have grown and not just from use. We think that our powers are stronger since the three of us have been living close together. You're levelheaded and obviously tough as nails when it comes to making hard choices. And to be honest, you had my vote after you turned Tom into a bird."

"Tanya, it was a rooster. We weren't exactly keen on the idea of having a rogue witch gallivanting around town, but you saved my precious Layla without a second thought. So either you're insanely brave or just insane, but I don't really care, as long it's geared toward looking out for my wonderful girl. You know, that day at the lake, you saved her life. She was technically dead, but you brought her soul back into her body. I could feel it the moment she left, and the moment she returned. You did that. So for some reason, you have the ability to commune between that distance like a seasoned witch. I want to learn how to be able to protect Layla half as well as you can."

When Aimée finished speaking, there were tears glistening in her eyes with the amount of sincerity spoken from her heart. She furiously dabbed at the corner of her eyes in order to avoid smudging her makeup. Aimée continued to stare at Freya with a look of pure determination on her face as she balled her pale fingers into fists at her side. "Please, Freya. Will you at least consider being the leader of this poorly trained coven?"

A smile full of surprised joy electrified Freya's face. She responded with certainty, "Thank you. I never wanted to be the leader of this coven. We could all just be equals."

Tanya pointed out. "Have you never watched an episode of *Sabrina the Teenage Witch* or *American Horror Story*? A strong coven needs a leader, and it just so happens that you brought Layla back from the other side and managed to save Axel all before your first Hallows Eve. If you're not a top witch, then I'm white and straight."

Aimée dramatically looked upward at the tall wooden ceiling and then turned her gaze toward the stained glass windows impressed with the stories of her ancestors. She raised a hand to the bridge of her nose and applied a subtle amount of pressure. "I envisioned this conversation much differently in my mind's eye. Freya, just agree to the title because it's already yours."

"Thank you. Yes, I will lead the coven. On another note, do either of you want to learn more spells about bonding with our familiars? I found a book about that last week, and it seemed very interesting."

Tanya and Aimée looked at each other for a minute, as if they were having a private conversation with each other that Freya wasn't invited to but somehow ended up accidentally attending.

"I told you that she already had a plan brewing in her cauldron."

"Ha ha, very funny, Aimée. You both know that I'm a horrible cook."

A few hours passed, and Freya stood in the middle of the bookstore with her phone in hand. Tanya and Aimée were headed to the town coffee shop for an afternoon pick-me-up, and Freya was heading home. "Freya, why can't you stay again?"

"I have to tell Axel that I'm a witch. I tried to tell him a month ago, but he just laughed it off, and we ended up getting distracted. No more secrets. We almost lost each other once because there was a lack of truth between us. I'm giving up on trying to tell him and will probably have to show him instead. If the powers don't get him, then having Cahira as a part-time house pet might prove another issue of conversation. I'll see you at Tanya's for dinner tomorrow.

Tanya turned her head sideways to express her confusion and asked, "Wait, you're planning to tell Axel about both secrets tonight? Also yes, we are making a properly seasoned dinner, so Aimée needs to bring a jug of milk."

Aimée scoffed in indignation in response to Tanya's blunt advice. She had never left Wishburn, so her exposure to food was rather limited. It was a fact that seemed to constantly gnaw at her when mentioned in any conversation. Reading about vast lands and different cuisines just didn't properly express the experience the same way as learning firsthand. A sour look crossed Aimée's face at the offhand comment but dissipated in less than a second as she gave the smallest shrug of acknowledgment.

"Maybe I'll bring a potato salad of some sort." Aimée sniffed in partial resignation.

Spicy food wasn't something she was accustomed to mainly because the spices of choice in Wishburn tended to be salt and pepper. It was mostly a direct result of the majority of the town descending from European settlers who had little knowledge or mastery of exceptional flavors.

"It's fine. I'll pick up some milk before Alysheigh and I start cooking. Every day it makes me a little more grateful that she was born and raised in New Orleans. The inability to tolerate spicy food is a total deal breaker."

Freya frowned in confusion at the conversation that had so easily become derailed. Apparently food was an extremely important pillar of both friendships and relationships. Freya thought to herself in casual reflection, *It only took several near-death experiences to gain an amazing circle of friends. No, to gain a family and a coven.* Freya felt like her facial features were getting the exercise of their life since she had walked into the town of Wishburn, for better or for worse. Freya walked over to the cash register counter and leaned against it in order to ease her aching feet.

"Well, I'm looking at it like a two-for-one deal. But I plan to read the room and just really go from there. I'm kind of banking on the fact that he is a massive fan of big cats. It's a leap of faith." Freya shrugged her shoulders for emphasis and then zipped her long coat upward and shook out her arms in an effort to free her shoulders from tension. "Another adventure begins. We lived through this one, so what else could possibly go wrong?"

Chapter 26

It was nearly midnight when Freya grabbed Axel's hand and instructed, "I want to show you something." She pecked him on his lips, and just as she was about to disappear from view, Freya entreated, "Follow me."

A sigh from the bedroom told Freya that Axel was only seconds away from following. Hopefully he wasn't going to panic when the dots finally connected. Apparently the first time Freya had tried to explain her new skill, it translated into a joke.

She walked faster and turned on the water from the kitchen sink. With a wave of her hand, the liquid swirled through the air and dispersed into individual crystals. They remained suspended in the air and created an enchanting environment. Well, as much as was possible in a rented log cabin in a technologically advanced kitchen.

Axel padded into the kitchen with bleary eyes and blond locks that stuck out in every direction. He rubbed his eyes and looked over to Freya with stifled curiosity. "What surprise do you have for us, Freya? Would you like me to make you something? I know that you were a huge fan of the triple cheese nachos from—"

His inquiry seemed to die in his throat once he took the time to properly look around the room. The solidified water remained in the air and looked amazing as the intricately shaped icicles reflected the gentle beams of light from the hallway. A noticeable dip in temperature helped to emphasize the reality of the situation and prove that the spectacle in the kitchen was, in fact, real.

"Axel, I wasn't kidding when we were talking in the tent. Before you say anything, I want you to know that you are safe and that I would never hurt you. I'm the same woman that you fell in love with, but now I really know who I am and where I came from. The magic actually managed to protect you when you were in a coma. I know it's a lot to absorb, and you can take as much time as you want to process this new information. But you have to know. Especially now that we are having a child together."

Freya felt her throat closing up as she continued to speak. Each sentence and individual word felt more painful than the last. Images of worst-case scenarios plagued her thoughts as she tried desperately to gauge Axel's reaction. She reached a hand up to her throat as she continued to choke out more of her increasingly panicked explanation. *The pregnancy hormones are really putting me into overdrive,* Freya thought to herself in partial realization, but it felt like her panic button had been activated, and there was no way she could rein it in. The sculptures of ice that were once so perfectly suspended began to drip as if the temperature in the room was steadily increasing.

Gray eyes seemed to look over the kitchen with a look of childlike wonderment, but Freya couldn't really interpret it through her heightened anxiety. Freya had always prided herself on her independence and self-reliance, but now she felt adrift at the thought of losing Axel for a second time. She wrapped her shaky arms closer into her body and waited for Axel to respond. He deserved the truth, and even if it ruined their marriage, it had to be said. At least that's what Freya kept trying to tell herself through a haze of panic.

"Hey, I'm not going anywhere." Axel walked over to Freya's shaking form with slow and measured steps. He pulled Freya into his large chest, and she instinctively wrapped her arms around his tapered waist. She took a few tempering breaths and allowed Axel's firm grasp to help keep her emotionally grounded. He continued to whisper sweet nothings into the room, and as the seconds ticked by, the icicles slowly regained their structural integrity. The moonlight from the window reflected off their surfaces, almost like miniature disco balls in the nearly dark room.

After a few minutes, Freya pulled away from Axel just enough to meet his gaze. She let out a small sniffle and asked, "So you'll stay?"

"Sweetheart, I was never going to leave." Axel bent down and captured her lips in a slow burning kiss. The air in the room crackled with electricity. Just as Freya was about to deepen the kiss, a drop of water landed onto her cheek and caused her to cast a confused glance to the ceiling. In her haste, she had forgotten all about the spell that had sparked their conversation.

With a flick of her hand, Freya simply moved all of the levitating ice into the sink. The sporadic puddles could wait until later.

Axel looked over at the sink as his eyebrow arched with satisfaction. It was a move that he had picked up from Freya early in their relationship. He turned to Freya as a casual smile graced his angelic face. "Freya, I just have one question."

"Anything."

"Are you the woman that has been visiting me in my dreams?"

"Who?"

About the Author

Camille Cabrera grew her love of reading into a blooming passion for writing. Ms. Cabrera enjoys reading everything, from short stories to even the occasional dictionary. Her love of creating strong female characters inspired this book. Her past titles include *Catalina's Tide*, a young adult novel set during the 1990s on Santa Catalina Island. She is the voice behind the international podcast *Creating with Camille* and editor in chief of *LAgendary Magazine*.

CPSIA information can be obtained
at www.ICGtesting.com
Printed in the USA
BVHW070955041021
618092BV00001B/104